En Plein Air

En Plein Air

Book Four of the Orla Paints Quartet

by

Mary Sharnick

www.penmorepress.com

ISBN-13: 978 1 950586-30-3(Paperback)
ISBN 978-1-950586-29-7(e-book)

BISAC Subject Headings:
FIC045000 / FICTION / Family Life
FICFIC050000 / FICTION / Crime
FIC107000 / FICTION / Italy

Editing: Lauren McElroy, Chris Wozney
Cover Illustration by Emilija Rakic

Address all correspondence to:

Penmore Press LLC
920 N Javelina Pl
Tucson AZ 85748

A Caveat and Note to Readers

Like *Orla's Canvas*, *Painting Mercy*, and *The Contessa's Easel*, which preceded this fourth and final book in the Orla Paints Quartet, *En Plein Air* is, from start to finish, a novel. While its protagonist and other characters develop and act within historical realities, at no time does the book purport to be a historical record. The plot has been influenced by the actual human trafficking activities of Naples' notorious Camorra, as well as by the attacks on New York City's World Trade Center on 9/11/2001; however, the story and its characters are products of my own imagination. Any resemblance to historical figures is coincidental.

Readers seeking non-fiction accounts about the above may wish to access the texts, articles, and videos I consulted, listed below:

The Ancient Shore: Dispatches from Naples, Shirley Hazzard and Francis Steegmuller, University of Chicago Press, 2008

The Serpent Coiled in Naples, Marius Kociejowski, Armchair Traveller, 2002

The Godmother: Murder, Vengeance, and the Bloody Struggle of Mafia Women, Barbie Latza Nadeau, Penguin Books, 2022

Roadmap to Hell: Sex, Drugs and Guns on the Mafia Coast, Barbie Latza Nadeau, Oneworld Publications, 2018

Gomorrah: A Personal Journey into the Violent International Empire of Naples' Organized Crime System, Roberto Saviano, Picador, 2006.

My Italians: True Stories of Crime and Courage, Roberto Saviano, Penguin Books, 2010

"Meet an Italian Nun Who's Been Helping Sex Trafficking Victims for 20 Years," Valeria Fraschetti, WGBH and PRX program and newsletter *The World*, July 21, 2015, https://theworld.org/stories/2015-07-21/meet-italian-nun-whos-been-helping-sex-trafficking-victims-20-years

"The Nun Rescuing Sex-Trafficked Women," Mathew Bannister, BBC program *Outlook*, November 22, 2017, https://www.bbc.co.uk/sounds/play/w3csvqq5

"I Was Responsible for Those People: The Manager of Windows on the World Survived 9/11, while 79 of His Employees Died. He's Still Searching for Permission to Move On," Tim Alberta, *The Atlantic*, September 10, 2021, https://www.theatlantic.com/ideas/archive/2021/09/glenn-vogt-september-11/620030/

9/11, a documentary by Gédéon & Jules Naudet, https://www.youtube.com/watch?v=QnOOspGYHzo

unMASKing HOPE, a film by Eric Christiansen, aired January 25, 2023, https://www.pbs.org/video/unmasking-hope-ukgevz/

www.911digitalarchive.org

To learn about and support the healing work of Sister Rita Giaretta and other sisters in the Ursuline Order, visit Casa Rut Caserta on Facebook and purchase handcrafted goods from New Hope Store, Caserta, Italy coopnewhope@gmail.com

To hear the duet, Bériot's *Grand Duo Concertante No. 1 for Two Violins,* which Aurora and Dieter performed at the concert in Fiesole, access https://m.youtube.com and search for Kin Fung Leung

Dedication

To My Family,
Whether by Blood or Friendship,
with Gratitude and Love

PART ONE

In times of dread, artists must never choose to remain silent.

— Toni Morrison

You see? In the fairy tales one does as one wants, and in reality one does what one can.

— Elena Ferrante

One

Frigento, Italy, August 16, 2001

If you can reach fifty without a catastrophe, you've won. You've got away with it.
— Shirley Hazzard

"I'm hot," I sigh, and fling the cotton sheet and coverlet off me.

We are still in bed, though the sun has already risen on Wednesday, August 16th, the Feast of San Rocco, a day of celebration in Frigento, the charming hill town we're visiting some sixty miles northeast of Naples. Last night my husband Tino (the diminutive of "Celestino") Bacci and our twins drove south from Fiesole, our home overlooking Florence. And yesterday morning I hired a car to get me here from Naples. I was conducting research there for my next exhibit, in Assisi. The exhibit will underscore the atrocity of human trafficking, part of a wider initiative led by a consortium of religious sisters, lay women, and Franciscan friars. It will open March 8th, 2002, International Women's Day. I've been gone from home two weeks. During that time, our twins, Luisa Allegra (Isa) and Lucca Francesco (Lu), attended the local music camp sponsored by their grandmother Aurora Bacci, Tino's mother and one of Italy's most beloved classical violinists, now retired. That freed Tino to wrap things up at work and at home in anticipation of our imminent family adventure, a one-year stay in New York City. All four of us are excited to live in the Big Apple for a while, each for different reasons. A bit later I'll clue you in about what inspired us to make this temporary move.

For those of you who are new to my story, and others who have not heard from me since my last installment in 1989, Tino Bacci and I met, fell for each other, and married in short order the year I traveled to Fiesole to host an exhibit highlighting the 45th anniversary of the town's liberation from Nazi occupation. Tino was then, and remains, director of the Emergency Department at Florence's Santa Maria Nuova Hospital. He also founded the AIDS hospice set on the late Contessa Beatrice d'Annunzio's estate, now operated by one of his former interns. Once my grandfather Castleberry's mistress, as many will no doubt remember, the late Contessa d'Annunzio had offered her villa and grounds for my exhibit. She was also Tino's godmother and our *yenta*. At the time of our marriage, she bequeathed her villa to us. So, born and bred Louisiana girl that I am and always will be, I have lived full time in Italy for the last twelve years, mostly painting portraits of families and politicians . My husband and children are native *Fiesolani*. Try as I might, I have not yet and perhaps never will speak the Italian language with the effortless fluency they each give voice to. They speak like songs. Even their English delights me, especially when Tino adds an extra syllable—"meat-a" and "sleeve-a," for instance—and emphasizes the "ed" in the past tense. "Close-ed," "stop-ed," "kiss-ed." Slays me every time. And therein lies the contrast between their native language and mine. Though its positive meaning is crystal clear, my "slays me every time" falls aurally short of their *"parlano come canzoni."*

At first, Tino and I were gun shy about bringing children into the world, given our individual circumstances. As some of you know, both of us learned our true paternity later than most people. I, at age eleven, after Mrs. Castleberry died and made me an heiress, when my mother, Minerva Gleason, and the long-absent Doctor Prout Castleberry told me he was my biological father. Tino, in 1989, when, because of one of my paintings, he ascertained he was the son of a German soldier who had carried on a love affair with his mother when she was just sixteen and a waitress at the Hotel Villa Aurora, a place the Nazi soldiers frequented. My God, Tino was already completely grown and had been practicing medicine for over a decade! Like his mother, Tino's birth father played the violin. Their musical talent brought them together even in the midst of war. And, as ridiculous and horrific as it sounds, they indeed made beautiful music together. My Tino was their best composition. His dad is still alive and living in Berlin, but thus far my husband has chosen not to meet—or, more likely, confront—him in person. Their only exchanges have been in writing. At some point, Tino has suggested to me many times, he must tell our children the truth of their blood. At present, they believe their grandfather was "lost" during the war. Complicit in that lie, I'm forced to admit that Tino and I have joined the seemingly endless list of parents who re-write personal history to protect their children.

But, at least in both our experiences, the truth eventually outs. We shall see.

At any rate, one autumn weekend in 1990, in Assisi (where we keep an apartment for long weekends), Tino and I threw caution and condoms to the wind and, voila, just like that, I became pregnant at age thirty-eight. Isa and Lu were born June 25th, 1991. Healthy and squalling, both, they made us forget our initial qualms. I hardly remember life without them. Their much older sister, Mercy (the Vietnamese girl I adopted in 1975 when she was six), is quite besotted with them. Mercy is married and works as a visual designer for Morgan Stanley in Manhattan now, and her birth mother, Thérèse, is a private duty nurse in the District of Columbia for a retiree from the U. S. Department of State. Thérèse's connections to the State Department were what eventually got her out of Vietnam to New Orleans, and led to her reunion with the child she had handed over to an American flight attendant not long before Saigon fell. If you've read my previous narratives, you'll know that I hated Thérèse when she showed up unannounced in 1989. But I eventually softened when I realized neither of us had "lost" Mercy. We instead had to learn to share her. Thankfully, we have. Our grown daughter puts up with both of us, very often reminding us of our failings and now and again acknowledging our love. Thérèse and I have become genuine friends. Soon after we settle in Manhattan, we expect to take the children south to the District on Amtrak and have Thérèse show them the sights. She's offered her apartment to us, as well.

"*Cara*,"—Tino puts his hand on my chest, then jerks it away, shaking his head—"you are a furnace, for sure. Always, as you Americans say, 'hot stuff.'"

"I hate menopause," I say, getting out of bed to stand. I stretch and peel off my short cotton pique nightgown. It is drenched. I drop it onto the marble floor.

"Hot stuff, I tell you." Tino turns his expression into a leer, gets out of bed, walks around the mahogany footboard, and plants a kiss on my forehead.

I look down at his navy undershorts and laugh. He grins.

"The children are still sleeping. So why don't you and I enjoy a cooling shower together? Maybe you will make a miracle, turn the water hot-a."

I sigh again.

"What? You are tire-ed of me?" He makes a forlorn face.

"Never," I answer. "Just hot." I shake my head so my hair, chin-length now and dyed chestnut, makes a slight breeze around my neck.

Tino takes my hand, we open the bedroom door, tiptoe to the bathroom, and, once inside, he turns the lock.

Neither of us knew what to expect in Frigento. We understood only that it was a small village of some 4,000 inhabitants, that it was 900 meters above sea level, and that no train or bus stopped there. I had accepted friend and fellow-NYU-alumna Amelia Pelosi's invitation to use her parents' little stone row-house near the elementary school only because I wanted a brief escape from the notice of those who follow my career, whether fans or detractors. My upcoming exhibit has been attracting a great deal of notice, not all of it positive, especially in Naples and Caserta. It is tentatively titled: *Bought,*

Sold, Rescued, or Murdered: The Trafficked Women of Castel Volturno. It is even more controversial than my *Portraits of AIDS* exhibit from 1989, no doubt because the mob known as "the Camorra" is involved. My best friend Tad Charbonneau—some of you will remember him as an immigration lawyer/historian—is drafting the language to accompany my paintings. Anyway, when Amelia told us that Frigento boasted gracious and welcoming citizens, Etruscan ruins, a Roman cistern, a cathedral, a bar named Roxy, and breathtaking views of the countryside from i Limiti, the spacious park and promenade at the top of the village, we were interested. But the message that sealed the deal was, "A person has to make an effort to get there." In short, as Amelia said, "The town is a good place to relax and become invisible for a little while. An Italian Brigadoon." So we've planned to stay a week before flying to JFK for our year in Manhattan. I'm calling our stay "the great escape," a chance for family time without interviews, press, or other career-related distractions.

"Mamma!" Lu shouts, "I have to go right now!" He bangs on the bathroom door.

I wrap a bath towel around me as Tino grabs his razor and pretends to shave. Opening the door, I try to kiss my son's forehead, but he darts past me to the toilet. Naked but for his Superman undershorts, he is as bronze as his father. His wavy hair, however, mimics mine. I will—must—paint him before puberty strikes.

"You are a fountain," Tino tells him in a booming voice, then turns to wink at me. Cooling shower or not, I already burn like a red sun. I have to get dressed.

Yesterday was Ferragosto, the Feast of the Assumption, a national holiday in Italy. The country's entire populace generally builds their vacations around the date. And in Frigento, Amelia had told us, one day later, the name day of San Rocco, the Frigentini go all out to celebrate the holy fellow who, legend has it, protects them from the plague and all other contagious diseases. Every year until this one, Amelia, her husband Hal Symonds, and her parents have returned to Frigento for this event. It is the way they reunite with their fellow *paesani*, many of whom, like themselves, emigrated to various places in America. Amelia's family chose Glen Cove, Long Island, a city popular among many former Frigentini. But Papa Rocco died the day after last Christmas—"Dropped down dead," Amelia said—just after unplugging the Christmas tree for the night. And her mother's Alzheimer's has worsened. Amelia, her brother Tommaso, and Hal have hired a full-time caretaker so Valentina can remain in her home. "Routine is all," Amelia told me when we spoke by phone last month. "We don't want to disrupt my mother's. So why don't you go in our stead? I promise, you'll love it."

Amelia and Hal both practice law, she as a sex-crimes prosecutor in Manhattan, he as a defense attorney in Glen Cove. They have no children. Amelia and I took several literature courses together in college, and we became friends as members of the fencing club. I kid you not, fencing was fun. It provided real workouts in a cool costume, had legit historicity, and served as a haven for students who sought some novelty away from the standard college sports. If I demonstrate any grace at all, it is partly because I became more aware of intentional movement in that club. At any rate, Amelia and I have followed one another's careers since we graduated, and she is our children's godmother. When she read about my upcoming exhibit in the NYU rag, she phoned and told me she planned to attend the opening. "Orla, your exhibit is right up my alley. Hal and I will plan a vacation around it. Tommaso has already promised he will see to Mom and, God-willing, her nurse will stay on."

Had it not been for Amelia, I might never have even had the idea for the exhibit. A couple of years ago, when I traveled to New York to judge the portfolios of several art professors seeking tenure at NYU, she and I got together for dinner at Becco. It was over *osso buco* that she told me about a Neapolitan-born woman named Filumena Curti who, since 1995, has headed the Camorra clan out of Curti, the town Filumena's late husband's ancestors had lived in since its founding. After her husband and his two brothers had been rendered "indisposed" (Amelia made air quotation marks when she said that), Filumena not only took charge of the clan, but also added human trafficking and prostitution to the menu of crooked activities long indulged in by those who work within "the System," as the Neapolitans and their provincial cronies call their organization of mobsters. Nefarious as they are, the male Camorristi had deemed prostitution off-limits. Not so Filumena. Often referred to as the "*piccola amata*," the short beloved one, a moniker of respect among the Camorristi and the very poor, who benefit from her routine food distributions and job offers (perfidious as those jobs tend to be), she trafficks young women from Albania, Romania, and Nigeria to Naples and environs for 2,000 American dollars per girl. Her "go-betweens" —no, let's be honest and call them what they are:

pimps. Her pimps lure girls from destitute families by promising them positions and better lives in Italy. The girls from Nigeria are especially abused, as their agreements with female procurers called "*mamans*" typically include juju, a bloody voodoo rite that assures the deaths of their family members if they do not cooperate with their keepers.

I had a slew of questions to ask Amelia that night. But the curtain was going up on *Kiss Me, Kate* at eight, so our conversation ended as soon as we cleaned our main-course plates. With no time for coffee or dessert, we hightailed it to the Martin Beck Theatre, arriving just as the last-call lights were blinking. But Amelia's account staked a seemingly permanent claim in my consciousness. It continues to disturb and haunt me. In fact, it compels me, and led me to my recent on-site research into the Camorra, Filumena Curti, and the Roman Catholic *Suore della Madonna* (Sisters of the Madonna) in Caserta, who defy her. Whoever visits Assisi come next March will be able to view and assess my rage. Will the exhibit change anything or help the victims? Who knows? Doubtful, at best. But it is the job of the artist to paint what she sees, no matter the reception or consequences. My brushes are ready. I am determined. And NYU has granted me a loft with plenty of light.

I know, I know, at age fifty I'm way too old to be shocked. You likely think that. Nonetheless, I *was* shocked that night in the theater district two years ago—and still am, even more so after my findings the past two weeks. You're probably thinking, Why the fuss, Orla? None of this is new. Trafficking and prostitution have been going on all over the world for millennia. Do you really need to call anyone's further attention to them?

You're naïve, maybe even nuts, if you think you can mitigate, let alone obliterate, these activities. Why are you so troubled?

Well, I guess it comes to this. I recently learned that Curti has a daughter herself. Just like I do times two. Probably like most of you do, too. Can she not see her own flesh, as I can Isa's and Mercy's, in the girls she abuses and destroys? Does she consider those outside her own wildly flourishing clan to be sub-human? Perhaps she prohibits herself from looking directly at her victims, deploying her deputies to do her dirty work instead. Or maybe she lacks a conscience at all? Is she a female Ebeneezer Scrooge, holed up in a barricaded hideout counting the money she makes but not assessing the cost her greed inflicts on her victims? I've got to find out and paint my findings as both record and condemnation.

"Hi, Mamma." Isa skips into the kitchen, where I'm brewing espresso for Tino and me and squeezing fresh oranges for the children's juice. Tino has gone to the *pasticceria* to pick up four *cornetti* for our breakfast. On my way downstairs, I saw that Lu was already dressed in blue Bermuda shorts, a red-and-white-striped linen shirt, and brown leather sandals. He didn't notice me as he hummed and assembled a wooden airplane.

"How do I look for the feast?" Isa asks, spinning around so that her two braids fly. She is our Pippi Longstocking.

I smile at her. "Wonderful."

She is wearing a white eyelet shirtwaist with ruffled sleeves and hem, red leather sandals, and red ribbons at the end of both braids, which she now twists herself. Her hair is copper, her eyes as blue as Tino's, and her sweet mouth a little heart when she is quiet. But silence is a rarity in our girl. She bursts. "Like a balloon," my mother-in-law says. "Pop. Pop. Pop."

Breakfast is a success. We like the intimacy of the Pelosi place. Small as it is, with one gathering room on the ground floor, its second level has five divided spaces, three of them bedrooms, one a sitting room with a small television, and a bathroom/laundry. While my family goes up to "brush and floss, brush and floss," as Isa singsongs, I restore the galley kitchen to its former order. I hear Tino's footsteps above and know that he is locating baseball caps for Lu and himself, wide-brimmed straw hats for Isa and me, sunglasses for everyone, and sunscreen for my Irish/French-American skin. The moment he comes downstairs, he mutters, "My wallet," and, two steps at a time, hurries upstairs again. "There will be a collection, no doubt," I hear him murmur, talking to himself.

Suffice it to say that the four of us are presentable and ready to leave the house as the cathedral bells chime ten o'clock. Once outdoors, I sense that, unlike my own body's bursts of heat, Frigento's actual temperature is surprisingly moderate for mid-August. Just 32 degrees Celsius, or 90 degrees Fahrenheit. Drinking plenty of water and seeking shade should allow for most everyone's basic comfort. Isa skips while her brother, Tino, and I walk up cobblestone streets to the cathedral, where the day's festivities are to begin with a Mass, followed by a procession through town. Later in the evening, Amelia told me, after large meals and afternoon naps at home, people gather in the main square to dance.

Entering the cathedral, I adjust a blush-colored chiffon shawl over my shoulders in the customary sign of respect, since my taupe linen dress is sleeveless. The pews are crowded and the majority of the Mass attendees are older women dressed in their best attire. Many of them hold colorful pleated fans. As soon as she sees our children walking ahead of us down the center aisle, a white-haired lady in a pink floral dress exits her mid-church pew so we can all sit together. "*Bella famiglia,*" she says, smiling at Isa and Lu and resuming her place on the aisle. She fingers crystal rosary beads as she speaks.

At ten-thirty, we rise for the processional and, as if on cue, the fanning women's repetitive wrist movements become as synchronous as the organ's strains and the choir's chorus. I am not sure if the women actually feel hot or if the fans are part and parcel of their summer attire. Whatever the truth, they and their fans grace the congregation with a practiced intensity. I imagine a kaleidoscope of butterflies fluttering over the altar.

The church is filled with flowers: white lilies, blue hydrangeas, red and yellow roses. The various fragrances intermingle so that the interior marble and stone and wood of the cathedral seem to be part and parcel of a fecund natural world. Three priests concelebrate the Mass. They are relatively young, none older than fifty, I would guess. One is tall and already balding. His shoes are shined black. Another smiles each time his meaty hands gesture for the congregation to sit or stand or kneel. The third is the homilist, his tone fervent and familiar. He carries a folded handkerchief with which he wipes his forehead periodically. An infant girl four rows down from us cries briefly, then is comforted by the pink pacifier her ponytailed father places in her mouth. When he takes her from her petite mother, who has been rocking the child side to side, he bounces her up and down, and she is content.

After Mass, the twins reluctantly stay with us in the slow-moving recessional line. Sustained applause greets all of us exiting the cathedral.

"Look!' Isa and Lu simultaneously point ahead.

Leading the faithful are the town's band members playing a recessional that paces the Mass-goers. Our steps are forward moving, slow, and deliberate. The all-male musicians are dressed in navy blue slacks and lighter blue shirts. The three priests, two altar boys, the mayor, and several *carabinieri* in full dress uniform, follow them. The clergymen and their acolytes, one carrying a shiny cross, the other swinging a censer, remain in their religious garb. The suited mayor wears his official red/white/green sash diagonally over his chest. Behind them are eight men carrying a heavy statue of San Rocco on a varnished wooden plinth: two men on each side, and two each in front and back. San Rocco is bedecked in gold, with long necklaces streaming from his neck. Coins are scattered beneath his feet. His halo glints in the sun. Townswomen devoted to him carry *mezzetti* on their heads. The heavy, round wooden containers are decorated with woven wheat, colored ribbons, and plastic flowers. Lights strung across the narrow roads, likely the same displayed at Christmas time, await darkness, when they will be illuminated for the dancers.

We have a marvelous time saluting strangers, watching hundreds of people filming the procession, and taking photos of our own. One of the women lets Isa carry her *mezzetto* for several hundred feet. "I am Clara," she tells us. Isa hands her straw hat to Tino and has to hold onto the *mezzetto* with both hands so it won't sway and fall. "It's really heavy," she says. But she is proud that she has held on. *"Brava, brava,"* several passing women say to her. Lu asks if he can run ahead to be with the band. We let him and, when we catch up with him, we find him discussing the best drums to buy with a percussionist named Vito. We stay with the procession until the children decide that they're hungry. But now not even the bar is open for business. It appears that everyone has officially begun their holiday. So we make our way back to the Pelosi house which Tino, God bless him, has made sure to stock with staples he brought from Fiesole in several coolers, shopping bags, and baskets.

"Shall we have some *pasta aglio e olio con acciuga*? he asks.

"Yes," we three answer.

"And I'll make a salad," I add.

The children go upstairs to play Monopoly, a favorite American gift from my parents last Fourth of July, and Tino goes to our bedroom to change. I decide to stay in the shift I've worn all day, I see an apron on a wall hook; I take it and tie it around my waist. I can't help but smile at the one large duck that decorates its center. I set the kitchen table and drink two glasses of seltzer water in succession. Just as I pull some arugula from the vegetable drawer of the refrigerator, I hear several quick knocks on the door.

When I open it, a tiny woman gripping a walker looks up at me and smiles.

"*Buon pomeriggio*," she says. "I am Gemma. I live next door. Amelia wrote to me that you were coming."

"*Buon pomeriggio*, Gemma," I say. "Please come in."

Gemma grinds her walker on the stone crescent threshold. She is wearing a loose-fitting yellow house dress, support hose, and tan loafers. Her hair, dyed black, is artfully arranged, with curlicues across her forehead. Though wrinkled, her face is animated as she speaks.

"This has come for you," she says, and points to a package in the basket attached to the front of the walker.

"Oh?" I take the package and look at it. It is wrapped in brown-bag paper, the same we used to cover school books when I was a child. About two inches deep and eight inches long, with "Sra. Orla Castleberry" written in flowing script in black marker.

Gemma grinds her walker again. "At midday, I was sitting there to take some sun and waiting for the procession to pass." She points to the small, squat wall—think of it as a stone chaise lounge—that separates her home's entryway from the Pelosis'. "Perhaps I dozed, for I awakened with a jolt. The motorbike was very loud." She squints and frowns.

"Are you sure you would not like to come in?" I ask.

"No, no," she insists, putting her right hand to her forehead for a moment. "I am cooking." She shakes her head. "There was such a noise. It jerked me awake. I was startled and upset."

"I'm sorry," I say.

"And they laughed like it was some joke and gunned the engine." She catches a breath. "I had to cover my ears." She lets go of her walker and holds her hands on both sides of her head until she wobbles and grabs the walker again.

"Who laughed?" I ask. Tino joins me at the door. "Tino, this is Signora Gemma from next door. She has brought a package for me."

"*Buon pomeriggio, Signora,*" Tino says.

But Gemma is frazzled and does not speak to him, continuing her story instead. "The two *guaglioni*. The two *cafoni*. Terrible *cafoni*. In helmets and pointy black boots." She stands erect, even as she grips her walker.

Neither Tino nor I speak. We just wait until she is ready to go on.

She takes short breaths. "I see they leave the package at the door and I tell them the family Pelosi is not here. They are in America."

I hear her agitation. Tino is quiet, attentive.

"'It's not for the family, old woman,' the one who did not drive said. 'It's for the painter-bitch.'"

I cringe and Tino puts his hand on my shoulder.

I can't imagine who the rude delivery men could be. Over the years I've received some hate mail from people who oppose my points of view, especially regarding AIDS victims. But no one acting ugly has actually delivered it. And if the package contains a welcome gift from my friend Amelia, well, she'll be angry and embarrassed to hear about the bad manners of those who got it to me.

I frown and shake my head. Gemma's facial expressions mirror mine.

"'Your mother taught you better,' I said to him. 'The painter is a famous lady and a good one, the Pelosi family say,' I tell him." Gemma grinds the walker's legs onto the stones again. "Then he took off his helmet, laughed again, and spat on me."

"*Dio*," Tino muttered.

Her eyes were watery now. "He had a beard, if you could call it that. It looked like some black strings hanging from his chin. Ugly. Barely a grown man. An ill-mannered hoodlum."

"Oh, Signora Gemma, I am so sorry," I say, and place my hands over hers on the walker.

"Please," Tino says, "have some lunch with us."

Gemma gathers herself together and smiles. "Amelia has told me you are good people. Maybe tomorrow we will have coffee together. But now I go and make a little frittata and pray to San Rocco to keep me safe from the *cafoni*."

Tino steps outside and accompanies Gemma around the low wall to her doorway. "Stay well," he says. "We are very sorry you were disturbed."

I step out, too, package in hand, and speak across the divider wall. "Thank you," I say. "Thank you for taking care of this." I point at the package.

Inside, Tino fills a pot to boil water for the pasta. He pulls a colander from a cabinet and places it into the sink. I have yet to make the salad.

"I win!" Lu exclaims upstairs.

"Let's play sweep now," Isa says.

I slip my fingers under the taped paper at each end of the package, then slide the white cardboard box out, letting the wrapper fall onto one of the place settings on the kitchen table.

"I wonder who it's from? I'm a bit nervous to open it, given Gemma's description of the guys who got it here."

"I don't know," Tino says. He stands right behind me as I lift the cardboard cover.

The children hear me scream and come running.

A bloodied, dead rat has been flattened over the newspaper article in today's *Questo Giorno*, the Naples daily. Reddened by the rat's blood, the headline reads, "American Artist Takes on Human Trafficking in the Region." I fling the package onto the floor.

The children see it before Tino can hide it from them.

"Gross," says Isa, wrapping her arms around me and hiding her face in my chest.

"I want to look," Lu says. "Let me get a good look."

He picks up the box and holds it in his hands, staring, while Tino gets a plastic garbage bag from beneath the sink.

"Here," Tino says, and Lu drops the "gift" into the bag. Tino knots the bag tight and goes outside to place it in the metal trash can beside the low wall. I hope garbage pickup is tomorrow.

"Dead rat, ugly dead rat, rat a tat, rat a tat." Lu dances around the kitchen. "I wonder who killed it."

"Stop it!" Isa says. "Rats are disgusting."

I try to become the mother my grandmother Castleberry would expect me to be. "Somebody was trying to make a joke," I say. I modulate my voice, despite the warning bell clanging inside my skull. "But it's a very stupid joke. Someone acted stupidly here."

"I can't believe you said 'stupid,' Mamma," Isa says. "You never let me."

"Well, it was stupid," Tino agrees. "This is the right sort of thing to call stupid." He looks at me, his eyes a question.

"I'm fine," I say. "It's no use getting upset over something stupid. Sorry I screamed. I just wasn't expecting a dead rat. Yuck."

Lu laughs and turns himself into a rat. "Here I come, Isa," he threatens.

Isa shrieks a pretend shriek and runs up the stairs. He follows. "Rat a tat, rat a tat."

When they are out of sight, Tino raises his eyebrows, brushes his hands over my hair, and hugs me. The water is boiling a rollicking boil. I move away from him to open the box of spaghetti on the kitchen counter, then slip the long strands of pasta into the water. Several drops of the water leap from the pan, landing on my right arm. I flinch, then look up at my husband as I toss the empty spaghetti box onto the counter.

"Jesus, Tino, what have I done?" I whisper.

Tino pulls me close again. Then, keeping one hand around my waist and with the other selecting a long wooden spoon from a ceramic container next to the stove, he stirs the pasta. But all I see is a cauldron and a witch. The witch's name is Filumena. She slaughters children. I cannot stop the tears that wet my cheeks. Tino sees. He lets go of me for a moment, puts the spoon down on the counter, and lowers the heat so the water doesn't boil over. Then he pulls me close once more.

"They try to scare you," he says, his lips moving on the top of my head. "They think you will be too scare-ed to paint what they do."

For the first time in our life together, I realize without a shadow of a doubt that Tino's arms around me no longer guarantee protection. Not for me, not for our family. And it's all my fault.

I look up at him.

"I *am* scared. For me, for you, for our children."

Isa and Lu pound their feet on the floor and laugh upstairs. I raise my arms upward, then let them drop.

Tino shakes his head from side to side. "You are surprise-ed. You experience for the first time the way they act. They have shaken you."

A motorbike whizzes by and I flinch again.

"Yes," I say. "They've shaken me. Like a big wind that knocks me down and sends me spinning over cobblestones."

He puts both his hands on my shoulders and speaks like a school master. "But your art is as strong as they are. Your paintings will show the truth."

"But they found me. They're following me, us."

I wrest myself away from him, pick up the empty spaghetti box, and rip it into pieces so that it litters the counter. I am furious. I want to shred Filumena and her lackeys. Rip their rotten flesh. Drown them in the Bay of Naples. I slap the cardboard pieces off the counter and onto the floor, grab the handles of the cauldron without benefit of pot holders. Hands smarting from the heat, I fling the spaghetti into the colander in the sink. I am burning now. Orla on fire.

Tino turns me around to face him.

"That is better," he says. "Angry is better."

He moves to the sink and shakes the colander, then eases the spaghetti into the waiting bowl of garlic, oil, and anchovies.

"*A mangiare!*" he calls up to the twins, then bends down to pick up the cardboard pieces and throws them away.

Before the children make it down the stairs, Tino pulls out a chair and motions for me to sit. I do. He fills my plate.

"The salad," I say, and make to rise.

"Never mind," he says. "Wine is better now. We will have salad tomorrow."

I can't help but laugh.

He fills two glasses.

The children are ravenous and twirl their forks. I do not give Lu the evil eye when he slurps. It is Tino who raises his eyebrows instead. Then he raises his glass and intones, "Next week we all go to New York. We will have lots of fun and also work very hard. We will find many new things in Greenwich Village. Isa and Lu,"—he looks to the children—"Mamma and I expect that you will become fine students at the Academy of Saints Francis and Clare. I will join the faculty at NYU School of Medicine, and Mama will paint an important story in a high-up loft."

Isa swings her legs under the table. "I want to climb the Statue of Liberty," she says. "And see the Rockettes."

"Both good ideas," I say.

Lu wipes his mouth with his napkin, then looks to me and smiles. "Mama, I want you to paint a rat. A big rat with whiskers as wide as my arms." He pauses from eating to stretch his arms either side of him.

Isa scrunches her face and shakes her head no.

"I'll see what I can do," I say. "In the meantime, here's to New York." I raise my glass.

"Agree-ed," says Tino. "To New York."

Chapter Two
Two Weeks Earlier in Naples

Until today, I've been to Naples only three times. The first and briefest was when I was in college and drove down from summer art school in Florence with friends. We took a ferry to Capri and spent most of the day drinking on the beach. The second was to join Tino at a medical conference before the twins were born. He met my train at the *Stazione Centrale* and we connected with a large group of emergency-room physicians for dinner at Zi Teresa on the *lungomare*. The third was to visit the National Archaeological Museum of Naples with Amelia when her first cousin, Carmine Famiglietti, a professor on the law faculty at University of Naples Federico II, gave a talk about how Augustus, Rome's first emperor, impacted public life in Pompeii. Thanks to Amelia, Carmine is to be my contact and anchor for the two weeks I plan to spend in Naples, starting today.

"Orla!" He waves from the station platform, both arms high in the air, hands moving back and forth. *"Benvenuto a Napoli!"*

A porter rolls my suitcase and holds my wrapped easel to his chest. Carmine and I kiss each other on both cheeks, twice.

Carmine is the consummate Neapolitan—colorful, kinetic, vocal, dramatic, nimble, emotive, savvy, street-smart. He looks like a Southern Italian Kurt Vonnegut, with a mass of salt-and-pepper curls that match his significant eyebrows. His face appears always in the interrogative, eyebrows raised, cigarette ready to be snatched from his mouth so he can speak. "So, Orla, how do you find my *bella Napoli*? Not as decorous as Firenze, right? They are snobs there. Not you, of course. You are American."

He is shorter than I, wiry, and quick on his feet. He wears a parchment linen suit, the jacket Neapolitan style. No shoulder padding, rounded pockets, and sleeves short enough to let his white cuff-linked shirt sleeves show. He hasn't bothered with a tie, so gray chest hairs peek from his partly unbuttoned shirt. He is sockless, and his amber loafers seem to glide over the slippery floor as we walk through the station.

The station is crowded with locals, business men and women, and many tourists, the younger travelers wearing backpacks, sometimes with sleeping bags rolled and tied to them. The public address system blares, both muffled and loud, while passengers and greeters bump into each other as they hurry to trains and one another. Trash bins overflow with tossed cardboard coffee cups and Styrofoam takeaway containers spewing pungent remnants of fast food. I have my purse hung over my neck so it rests in front of me, pickpocket-proof, I hope. I'll be glad to get to my hotel.

I tip the porter. Carmine takes my rolling suitcase in hand, while I carry my easel (the Contessa's easel, as some of you will remember), bubble-wrapped and wound round with awning cloth. There is no graceful way to transport it. When I do, I always wonder if people think I'm carrying a bow and arrows or several long swords. In a way, I am.

Carmine walks at a brisk pace and I follow him to the car lane and his white Fiat. He wastes no time, getting me, with plenty of horn accompaniment, to Hotel Excelsior on Via Partenope, right across from the *lungomare* with a long view across the bay to Vesuvius. Once there, he opens the trunk, lifts my suitcase, and brings it to the curb. He had laid the easel diagonally across the back seat. When he passes it to me, I try to look graceful until a bellhop saves me the trouble.

"I will pick you up for dinner at eight-thirty. Then, Saturday, we will visit some of the spots where Filumena's victims ply their trade."

I take a deep breath. "Sounds good," I say. "Or, perhaps, ominous."

He gets into the driver's seat. "Oh, I forgot to tell you, I will have a surprise guest at dinner. She can help you."

My eyes light up. "I like a helpful surprise," I say. "And dinner's on me, of course."

"Don't worry," Carmine says. "We will eat in." He twirls his right hand three times, forefinger pointed upward. "*Ciao, ciao.*" He waves and is off, tires squealing.

I walk to the covered entrance of the Excelsior and up the several steps to the lobby.

"*Benvenuto*, Signora," the doorman says, and gestures to the reception desk at my left.

The concierge greets me. "Signora Castleberry, we are very happy you will be staying with us," He is tall and thin, clean-shaven with an admirable head of white hair, parted smartly on one side. His name tag reads "Antonio," and his hands move swiftly to enter my arrival into a computer and hand the porter a key. "Room 112," he tells him. Then, to me, "The best view."

He is correct. The Excelsior is the grande dame of *lungomare* hotels and Room 112 is worthy of the hotel's title. First off, it is large, as large as the Contessa's dining room in Fiesole. A king-sized bed holds center stage. Two night tables flank it. They offer two drawers each and ample lighting from twin bronze lamps with pleated parchment shades. The mahogany headboard is carved with putti and grape vines. To the left of the bed is a desk and straight-backed chair. The desktop is also well-lit by a green glass library lamp. Several feet from the other side of the bed are two pink-damasked club chairs separated by a round, glass-covered table. A vase of white hydrangeas graces the table, a card peeking from among the blooms: *Sra. Castleberry, we hope you enjoy your stay with us. With best regards, Carlo Semprini, Manager.*

A high chest of drawers nestles between one chair and the entrance hallway. A massive built-in armoire faces the bathroom, where the tub resembles a sarcophagus, so deep is it. A green marble counter and floors contrast starkly with an abundance of white towels and two robes, crested with the Excelsior logo and hanging on brass hooks over the bidet.

But, wow, the windows please me most. Both directly across from the bed and stretching from floor to ceiling, facing southeast, they offer an unparalleled view of the *lungomare* walkway, the bay, and Vesuvius over the coastline. A push of the matching buttons on the wall beside each window raises and lowers metal storm shutters so that complete darkness or full light are the occupant's choice. I will be able to sketch some prefatory cartoons for my anticipated paintings in excellent light. And tonight, after dousing all the room lamps, I'll raise the shutters so that dawn, the water, and Vesuvius will wake me.

A little stomach growl—oh, let's call it more of a street cat's snarl—reminds me that I'm hungry. Breakfast consisted only of two gulped *espressi.* I decide to venture across the street and try my luck at one of the restaurants on the pier just down the stone stairway to the left of Castel dell'Ovo. I grab the latest copy of *ARTnews* as my companion and walk down the winding staircase to the hotel lobby. Even though I'm in Naples, I'm reminded of *Gone with the Wind.*

Antonio nods at me as the bellhop opens the door. *"Buon pomeriggio, Signora,"* the bellhop says, tipping his lookalike military officer's hat. He is as turned out as an admiral. Italians do love their uniforms. Compared to him I am decidedly underdressed in my own summer day outfit—persimmon-colored linen shift, cinnamon leather espadrilles, plain gold wedding band, one vanilla ceramic bangle, twin gold hoop earrings that dangle just beneath my hair, a roomy straw satchel. And sunglasses that scream Jackie-O.

I have decided on La Scialuppa, with its terrace overlooking the marina. Church bells on Via Santa Lucia, a side street near the hotel, chime two as I make my way across one-way Via Partenope and the sidewalk that parallels the water. White taxis make for most of the traffic. Once across, I slip into a moving line of tourists on their way to the castle. We navigate around several folding tables of trinkets for sale. Along the cobbled walkway that leads to both stairway and castle, I encounter a mime dressed as a clown entertaining several gleeful children no older than six, two sinewy teenage lovers (he in a Speedo, she in a purple bikini leaving little to the imagination) atop the protective seawall, and two collared priests in animated discussion, their hands moving cat's-cradle style. Once down the stairs, I follow the pier until a white-jacketed waiter greets me with a practiced smile.

"*La signora* is dining alone today?" he asks.

"*Sì*," I answer, and he leads me to an iron cafe table from which I can see a half-dozen boats, four of them sailing vessels, the other two fishing trawlers.

"Water with gas, please," I say, and lift *ARTnews* from my straw satchel, which I place on the chair beside me. I scan the magazine until lunch arrives.

It is for the *baccalà* salad that I have come. It doesn't disappoint, all cold flakes of cod with cannellini beans, tart green olives, chopped celery, shallots, and cilantro dressed with olive oil that shimmers like golden threads. Two slices of crusty bread on the side. A taste of aquatic heaven. Try it sometime.

After I have literally cleaned the plate, the bread my sponge, I scan the terrace. I like being able to study a place through lenses too dark for others to see the movement of my eyes. Tino tells me I am a voyeur. He's right. Isn't every artist? It's how we take in images of the world.

At a square table on the terrace is a family of four—mother, father, and two teenaged sons. Their accents are Australian, and both boys are spitting images of the father: very long and lean and blond. Mother is petite, with dark brown hair piled on her head in a becoming knot. "Merry" pops into my mind watching them interact. They are playing some sort of word game. Every time someone offers a correct response to a question, the mother stops twirling long strands of pasta, puts down her fork, and claps her hands. Father is drinking a Peroni. He speaks with a radio voice.

An elderly nun in full black habit but for the white trim on her wimple sits with a much younger man wearing a plaid sports shirt, blue jeans, and tennis shoes. The man is deferential to her, asking if he may pour more Pellegrino into her water glass. They speak softly. Now and again, the nun reaches across the table to touch his cheek. I hope he is a nephew.

Just as the waiter appears to clear the plates and inquire if I'd like an espresso, three Italian women enter the terrace. They clearly are intimates, finishing each other's sentences and nudging each other playfully. They all look as if they've just come from the hairdresser's or a nail salon. Standing by my table, they smell like a bouquet of freesia. My eyes are level with their dancing hands. The tallest of them wears a garnet set in a thick gold band.

"*Un momento,*" the waiter says to them.

The garnet-ringed woman acknowledges him with a smile. He leaves with my dish and flatware and they chat until his return, when he leads them to a table directly behind me. They follow. All of a sudden, the garnet-ringed woman turns back.

"You're Orla Castleberry," she says. "I remember you."

I take off my sunglasses and look up at her. Her jet black hair is pulled tightly off her face and cinched into a ponytail set high on her head. She is a handsome woman.

"I photographed you for the piece in *Nostre Donne*," she says. "In March. You wore that terrific magenta sweater dress."

I stand and kiss her on both cheeks. "Yes, you are Lina. How nice to see you again. I'm sorry I didn't recognize you. Your hair was different. Short."

"It was," Lina says, and calls over to the other two women. "This is someone I photographed for the magazine. Orla Castleberry, the American painter I told you about."

"Yes, yes," the other women say. They are a duet of chirping.

I wave at them.

"Come," says Lina, "you must join us. We are here for the sweets only. Nothing healthy. Strictly sugar and fat, I promise. Please, join us." She looks to her friends, who wave me over.

The waiter brings my espresso.

"Here," Lina directs him.

I am commandeered into the fourth chair, next to Lina.

"Toni," Lina says—she obviously knows the waiter—"*sfogliatelle* and cannoli and rum baba, please, for the table."

"And coffee," Toni says.

"*Grazie*," Lina replies.

I look across the table to the women. "Do you both work with Lina?"

They laugh. Cackle, really. "No, we just bask in her reflected glory," the short-haired one says.

Lina rolls her eyes.

It turns out the three were roommates in college, all having attended the same university where Carmine Famiglietti lectures. Every August they reunite for a long weekend to start off their individual vacations. This is their twenty-first year post-commencement.

"We are just coming from the spa morning," Lina says. "Can you tell?" She holds out her red-lacquered nails. "Now we will indulge."

"I am Assunta," the woman with the shortest hair and the widest smile says. "A sociologist in Padova." She offers me her hand. Her nails are palest pink. She wears a platinum wedding band.

"Pleased to meet you," I answer.

"And I, Gioia." The woman blows a kiss. She wears no nail polish or jewelry, but her square red eyeglass frames demand notice. "I am an obstetrician-gynecologist here in Naples."

Lina chimes in. "We call ourselves the triumvirate. But today we become a quartet."

"I'm honored," I say. "By the way, my husband likes the photos you chose, Lina. He says you captured my spirit so I do not look like a statue."

"Well, then, good on him."

I know right then that Lina learned English from a Brit.

Toni arrives with the tray of sweets. Another waiter follows with coffee and four translucent shot glasses of *meloncello*.

"Cheers," I say. "To the triumvirate."

I end up staying with them for two hours. I learn that Gioia treats knocked-up teenagers—"generally with an STD or two," she tells me—in a local clinic and pregnancy safe house run by the Brigittine sisters. "The sisters run a good shop," she says. "No overt judgment on their part. When I prescribe birth control pills for the teenagers, I record, 'for the regulation of menses' in my notes. The nuns who transcribe the orders have never questioned me." She takes off her glasses, wipes them with her napkin, puts them back on, and says, "They're realists, I have to say. No doubt about it."

Assunta chimes in, "Meanwhile, during the academic year, I study migrant domestic and care workers all over Campania." She runs her fingers through her feathered hair. "These people are what stand between intact family units and the large old-age homes that proliferate in North America." She shakes her head from side to side and stretches her neck in a circular motion. "I do not intend to insult Americans, you understand, Orla. Nonetheless, I'm not in the least objective about what my research has unearthed." She moves her neck in a circle again. "Without these workers, the elderly infirm would be abandoned and housed in institutions away from family. Warehouses. *Che schifo!*"

I nod and pretty much agree, knowing that social status and wealth mainly determine the fate of the elderly (and every other age group) everywhere. The Contessa, for example, frail as she became, was able to remain in her villa until she died. Tad's Parkinson's-afflicted mom back in St. Suplice is the beneficiary of her husband's and son's largesse with a full-time, live-in nurse. But my daughter Mercy's birth-mother had to scramble for an apartment and a job after Saigon fell. Some of the AIDS patients in our facility in Fiesole have absolutely nowhere else to go. And there is no shortage of street people in Italy's larger cities. Assunta makes a valid point.

Lina sighs and shrugs her shoulders. "My sisters here labor for noble causes. I merely photograph both good and bad, beautiful and ugly." We all nod. "Luckily for me," she says, "several images have paid my bills and then some."

"True," Assunta agrees. "You are the money-bags of our coterie."

"Do tell," I urge her on. I pick up a *sfogliatella*.

"I got one of a Comorra drug-dealer brandishing a gun while he lounged by a makeshift above-ground pool outside a Vele apartment building in Scampia. The international press picked it up to underscore the flagrant audacity and financial success of Campania's particular syndicate." She pauses and pulls her pony tail tighter. "That photo bought me a car and allows me to rent a two-bedroom apartment in Posillipo."

"Ah, the life of an artiste," says Gioia with a laugh.

I take a bite of *sfogliatella*. It is still warm from the oven.

"Who knows, Orla? Maybe a photo from your shoot will eventually propel me to millionaire status," Lina comments, laughing. "Let's see what kind of response your exhibition receives next March. That will decide the tale."

I open my eyes wide. "Let's just hope the exhibition forces a politician or two to crack down on the traffickers."

"A pipe dream," Gioia says, and purses her lips. "They're in bed with them." She breaks one of the cannoli in half and takes a bite. "It's the nuns," she says, sugar coating her lips, "only the nuns have the balls to confront them. Get yourself in touch with Sister Parisi, Sister Ilaria Parisi, in Caserta. Steel and silk, she is, that one. Everyone knows of her. She houses girls who leave their pimps. When she first started going right into the streets to rescue girls, she and her fellow sisters and volunteers rode bicycles. When they bought a Fiat, the thugs stole it. But she kept on. The Camorristi leave her alone now. You see her in a van now and again on the Via Domitiana around Castel Volturno."

"Why don't they bother her anymore, Gioia?" I ask.

Gioia purses her lips. "They fear divine retribution, maybe, or their grandmothers' wrath if word ever got back to them that their grandsons had harmed a nun. Or they respect God's virgins."

"Hmm," I murmur.

"Gioia takes a deep breath and sighs. "There is a stereotype about Italian men, that to them women are either virgins or whores. There is no in-between. Except for mothers. Well, sometimes that sterotype is true."

"I'm very interested in Sister Ilaria, Gioia," I say. "In fact, I read about her in the issue after the one where I was featured. You likely know the one I mean, the one in which Lina photographed her in Caserta along with three lay women in Assisi who help the rescued girls." I take another bite of the *sfogliatella*. "By the way, they'll each be speaking at the colloquium in Assisi come March. I've written the nun since then, and hope to see her operation while I'm here."

"I hope you have the chance," Gioia says. "She's fearless. If you do see her, send her my regards. I treat some of her residents now and again. The really young ones."

Bells chime four-thirty and I stand up. "I must go," I say

Lina places a wad of lire on the table.

"Let me help," I say, and reach into my satchel.

"Not today, my friend," Lina says, smiling.

Toni must smell the money, for he arrives in the instant.

"*Grazie.*" He bows as if to a full house, pockets the cash, and disappears.

"Thanks. I've enjoyed meeting you all. Expect invitations for the exhibit. I'll get your addresses from Lina."

"No need," says Gioia, and she and Assunta reach into their purses and hand me their cards.

"You'll all be my guests in Assisi come March. Then it will be my treat."

"It's a deal," Assunta says. "Is that how you say it?"

"Exactly," I say, and put my sunglasses back on. I kiss Lina on both cheeks and wave to the others as I make my way back to the Excelsior to nap, shower, and get ready for whatever the night promises.

Chapter Three
Dinner

"I should have walked," I say, as Carmine pulls into his inner-courtyard parking space off Via Chiatamone, in the Santa Lucia neighborhood. We are just blocks away from the Excelsior.

He waves his right hand above his head. "Is better like this. Too many thieves on scooters. Cousin Amelia, never mind your husband, would not be pleased with me should you come to any harm."

"Well, thank you," I say. "I don't want to be any trouble to you. I'm already imposing on your generosity."

Carmine raises both hands, as if in supplication. "It is my great pleasure to spend time with an artist such as you."

Full transparency, dear readers: I never can differentiate a genuine compliment from sheer bullshit when it comes to my art. Maybe I'll know Carmine's actual point of view before our two-week intensive is done. I wonder if he even looked at the portfolio of past work I sent him. At any rate, he has been most available and kind thus far. We'll see how we fare together for the rest of my stay.

Carmine has already gotten out of the car and comes over to my side to take the substantial shopping bag of wines and antipasti I ordered from Salumeria Ruocco as soon as I learned we'd be dining at his apartment. It's a quick walk from the car and up three flights of stone steps to the varnished wooden door of his flat. Once inside, I'm mesmerized. A pool table covered with six neat stacks of law tomes separates the kitchen/dining area from the lounge/terrace area of the apartment. To the right is a tiny half-bath painted a flat aubergine with white trim and brass fixtures. A free-standing stairway to the left rises to a loft bedroom with one wall of translucent glass (separating the sleeping area from a full bath, I suppose). Although the entire space save the half-bath is painted a soft parchment, it is enlivened with bold contemporary paintings, a carved ebony chess set on a mosaic-topped iron table, a red leather couch for five or six, two steel-and-black leather accent chairs, a round glass dining table centered on what looks like a truncated Roman column, with six transparent Nunley armchairs around it, and a kitchen that shines with stainless steel and turquoise tile backsplashes. *Architectural Digest*-worthy in every way. I wonder if he hired a decorator.

"How lovely," I say, as Carmine brings the shopping bag into the kitchen, where he lifts its contents out and onto the veined turquoise and white marble counter. He takes the cured meats from their butcher wrappers and places them on a ceramic tray decorated with vines. "*Grazie*, Orla," he says. He points to the label on the shopping bag. "This is a good store."

Then he lifts and puts aside a linen dishtowel to reveal several types of hard and soft cheeses on a square cutting board.

"May I help?" I ask.

"*Sì,*" he says, pointing to open shelving above the sink, where I see a stack of small plates.

I take three of the plates in hand and wait for his next direction.

"Shall we go onto the terrace?" he suggests. Letting the readied appetizers stay on the kitchen counter, he moves from the domestic area of the apartment, past the pool table, to closed floor-to-ceiling slatted shutters. He pulls the shutters apart.

"Better with the natural light," he says.

"I couldn't agree more."

Before us, below, are the bay, the boats, the hum of traffic and voices and live music at nearly dusk. The balcony holds a long narrow iron table with four matching chairs, two placed at either end and the other two facing outward for the view. The table boasts a quartet of thick eucalyptus-scented candles of varying heights. The vines and blooms from two potted pink hibiscus plants have been trained along the balcony's elaborate iron railing. Carmine flips a switch on the outside wall and tiny white lights outline the balcony's roofline. I almost forget the humid heat.

"Who will be joining us?" I ask, my tone a bit of a tease as we walk back to the kitchen for the antipasti. I've been curious all day.

"Ah," he answers, "her name is Flavia Esposito. She is the assistant prosecutor of your bad girl Filumena, whom the authorities apprehended in June." He takes a green olive from the antipasti plate and pops it into his mouth. "The chief prosecutor, Vincenzo Caruso, is on holiday in Sardinia, or I would have invited him, too."

"I didn't realize Filumena was in jail." I don't know if I'm glad the cops got her or disappointed I won't be painting her while she's still on the lam. There's something about the thrill of a chase that motivates. And maybe she's not as powerful as she and others thought if the police caught her. Frankly, I hope she'll be on the loose again come time for my exhibit. Oops. Mind pause. Mind re-start. And there it is, the cat leaping out of the bag. My ego superseding right thinking, as is frequently the case.

Carmine must read my disappointment, for he smiles and pats me on the shoulder. "In jail or out, dear Orla, she is still in charge. No one dares cross the woman who ordered the murders of fifty-three rivals in 2000 alone."

"Seriously?" I say.

"Dead seriously." He laughs at his little joke. "Her swift brutality toward her enemies left no doubt that her capacity for revenge was equal to or greater than that of any man who preceded her in the organization. Her execution of vengeance was superb." He laughs again. Punster.

"What did they do to infuriate her?"

Carmine takes one of the two cigarettes peeking from his breast pocket and lights it with a lighter from a metal ashtray on the kitchen counter. He offers me the other. I shake my head no.

"A batch of drugs had arrived from Turkey. Filumena's people knew it was too strong and would kill its buyers. Her rivals, the Puzzo clan, went ahead and sold it anyway. Over a thousand people died. The general public protested. And Filumena saw to it that the Puzzo clan would never defy her decisions again."

"What did she do?" I ask.

He takes a drag on his cigarette and smiles. "She sent twenty-five units of her hit men to each of the Puzzo hangouts. At exactly eleven p.m., when the gang members were full of food and wine, relaxing, playing cards—you see, this is how detailed her plan was—they machine-gunned the Puzzo operatives, then set fire to their cars and motorcycles. The sirens of fire engines sounded all over Naples. I was told that the dead could only be identified by their shoes. Their faces had been shot through."

I shudder.

"She made quite an impact, then, showed everyone who was really the boss," I say.

Carmine exhales a trail of smoke and continues. "The Puzzos were stupid, if you ask me."

I watch him take another drag on the cigarette.

"How so?"

He exhales again. "I ask you, Orla, what kind of drug dealer wants buyers dead? Only the living guarantee sales." He crushes the half-smoked cigarette into the ashtray. "Filumena understood that. She is all about the business, that one."

"It seems so," I say.

We carry the food out onto the terrace. Carmine motions for me to sit, then joins me. We both face the water. It promises to be a languid night. Humid, even heavy, but with a slight breeze from the bay.

"Flavia and I reconnected several years ago on a soccer field where her husband Leo and I play in an old man's league."

I smile.

"During her first year of law school, she was one of my best students. She knows the deep background about this '*piccola amata*,' as I am sure you already know Filumena is called."

I nod.

Carmine cuts a slice of provolone from the serving platter and eats. "*Buono*," he says. He motions for me to join him.

"In a bit," I say.

He finishes chewing and swallows. "As you wish." He takes a monogrammed handkerchief from one of his pants pockets and wipes his brow. "Perhaps you do not know, Flavia and Vincenzo are lucky to be alive. Filumena tried to kill them when she believed they were close to capturing her in 1999. She had their office bombed. But they were not there at the time."

"My God," I say.

"Leo wants Flavia to quit her job and teach the law with me. He worries for her safety. In addition, they must consider their school-age daughter Elvira, and Leo's mother Norina, who lives with the three of them over the pharmacy Leo owns in Colli Aminei. But Flavia has her own mind. She says the Camorristi just wanted to scare Vincenzo and her into discontinuing their search for Filumena's colleagues. 'They wouldn't have missed if they actually wanted to kill us,' I've heard her say. Leo calls her a hard head, *una testa dura*. She's been at her job fifteen years."

"Really." I shudder to think how on edge Tino and I would be if I were she. Always looking over our shoulders. Suspicious of all but our nearest and dearest.

The doorbell rings.

Carmine stands up and walks inside to open it, calling back, "They were at a conference in Milan. And so you can meet Flavia now. Because she and Vincenzo eluded the bomb."

I stand and walk inside, as well. Carmine greets Flavia. If I hadn't learned what he just told me, I would have pegged her for a twenty-something grad student. Her face shines with an enviable complexion and she giggles as she and Carmine exchange the customary kisses on both cheeks. Short and compact, with tight black curls circling her head, she is still dressed for work in a beige linen suit, her lanyard's laminated identification card reading "Flavia Esposito, *Procuratore Assistente*." She wears no jewelry but for a wide gold wedding band, gold stud earrings, and a red-leather-banded supersized watch.

"Signora Castleberry," she says, "how happy I am to meet you, and glad to know we share a common enemy as well as a friendship with the professor." She nods Carmine's way. He returns her comment with a broad smile. Her delivery is polished and clear.

I walk around the pool table and reach out my hand. She takes it. Her grip is firm, her nails unvarnished and filed straight across.

"*Molto piacere*," I say, "and thank you very much for taking the time for me. You and Carmine are most generous."

"You are most welcome," she replies. "But I really came because I learned that Carmine was to cook." She giggles again.

Carmine revolves his right hand in the air three times, a gesture I am realizing is a signature one. "Your flattery is appreciated, Flavia. Now go, you two, onto the terrace and converse about criminals while I attempt to live up to your culinary expectations."

He points us toward the open shutters.

"You must call me Orla," I say as we walk.

"Of course," Flavia says. She removes her lanyard and jacket and drapes them on the couch, revealing a fitted sleeveless white blouse, erect carriage, and exercised biceps. While her brown pumps and easy-care hairstyle both speak of practicality, she moves with the graceful confidence and efficiency characteristic of a working gymnast or dancer. When she crosses her bare legs once we're seated, I see from her toned calves that she must be a workout aficionado. Leisure is likely a foreign state to her.

The smell of garlic browning in olive oil wafts our way from the kitchen as Carmine joins us with a tray of Aperol spritzes, cocktail napkins, and a bowl of mixed nuts.

I make a toast. "To Carmine and Flavia."

"And to Orla," Carmine counters.

"Delicious," Flavia says, taking a long sip of her drink. Then, she sits up straight and, without any preamble, proceeds in a clipped delivery. "Orla, I have reviewed the portfolio of your work to date that you sent Carmine. He delivered the package to me last week. I see that your major exhibits consist of social commentary. The Civil Rights movement in the United States, the war in Vietnam, the AIDS crisis, and, if Carmine is correct, your intended next exhibit, human trafficking in Campania."

Carmine raises his bushy eyebrows and looks to me, I guess for my response to Flavia's change of affect.

"Right," I say. I feel the need to uncross my legs and straighten my shoulders. I'm glad not to be on the witness stand. "When I first learned of Filumena Curti from Carmine's cousin Amelia, I was horrified that Curti, a woman herself, and a mother of a daughter, had initiated the trafficking of other women—girls, really. Does that sound naïve to you?"

I watch Flavia's face. Carmine scratches his head, pulls the second cigarette from his pocket, and leaves us for the kitchen.

Flavia sips her drink, then looks directly at me. "In my world, yes," she says. "Frankly, very naïve."

I feel uncomfortable, the way I always do when I'm about to learn something new and disturbing.

Flavia grabs a handful of nuts. She eats one at a time and speaks between bites. "You see, Orla, we in law enforcement have found that when a woman is called to lead her local Camorra gang because her husband or father or brothers are dead or in prison, the criminal activities run more smoothly and efficiently. The woman takes charge, depends on those who carry out her wishes, and disposes of those who contradict or betray her. She delegates with clarity and precision and brooks no opposition."

"Really?" I say, then remember myself. "Carmine was telling me about Filumena's murderous efficiency earlier."

"Yes. You must also study the history of Assunta "Pupetta" Maresca, for example. She, too was a woman in charge. Her story will confirm my point of view. I will see to it that you receive the resources."

"Thank you. I'm eager to do so." I wish I had brought a notebook with me.

"And in Filumena's case, she saw trafficking as a way to expand her group's influence and make more money than her male relatives ever had. Plus, the conditions were right." Flavia's glass is nearly empty.

"How so?" I ask. I take a sip of my drink.

"During the last two decades, many Nigerian immigrants came to this area, especially Caserta, the men to work in the tomato fields, their women as domestic workers. But when toxic waste dumped by the Camorra ruined many Campanian fields, leading much of the province to be dubbed the 'land of fires,' the men needed to find other means of employment. The Camorra worked an agreement with them. The Africans pay the System a fee, traffick the girls, and house a number of them in the Coppola apartments in Caserta's Castel Volturno. This has been very lucrative for Filumena."

She continues, as if a university lecturer. I am her rapt and ignorant student.

"Built without regard to best practices and flouting local building laws, the apartments used to be popular among vacationing Italians and U. S. Naval families. The brothers Coppola, the builders, had intended their site to become Castel Volturno's own Miami Beach. Over the years, as the builders were discredited, the apartments lost their vacationing tenants. And after the 1980 Irpinian earthquake, people who lost their homes were transported and housed there. The whole area degenerated. Now it is squalid, with drug users throughout and with the trafficked girls selling themselves along the ancient and busy Via Domitiana."

I stand and move my chair closer to Flavia's. She leans toward me, too, more animated with every fact she reveals. "Carmine says he will take you there." She turns her head to face indoors. "Right, Carmine?"

Carmine doesn't answer. Perhaps he hasn't heard her. Perhaps he doesn't want to. I am both eager and leery.

"It's strictly business with Filumena. Morality plays no part in her decision-making and actions. And whenever we question her, she insists she is only a seamstress in Caserta. Like those few women bosses who preceded her, she works quietly behind the scenes, moving from one hideout to another, calling no attention to herself."

I am thoroughly intrigued and appalled.

Flavia continues. "Filumena runs her gang as if she is CFO of a multinational company, all the while keeping her little shop open. Her old seamstress, who must be in her eighties, is a mute who specializes in wedding gowns. The younger seamstress, in her fifties, is the woman's half-witted niece. Perfect cover, no?"

"I guess," I say.

Carmine returns from the kitchen with two more spritzes. I have yet to finish my first. He puts them on the table without a word. Flavia pauses a moment only to wink up at him. "Without Filumena, both those women would be outcasts left to fend for themselves, likely living on the street. When the police have attempted to question them, they simply nod and smile and go about their sewing." Flavia has emptied the dish of nuts and is on to the cheeses. No wonder she must exercise. "There is much money to be made in human trafficking, Orla, and there is a virtually endless supply of extremely poor girls in Nigeria, Albania, and Romania, among other places, who are routinely convinced by so-called friends and authorities that they can find legitimate jobs as hairdressers, nannies, shop girls, and the like, in and around Naples. Add to their availability the fact that there is no end of mob-affiliated pimps, *mamans* from Nigeria, and boat runners, and you have, under the exacting leadership of someone like Filumena Curti, a well-oiled machine that is, in truth, unstoppable. My job, at best, can only slow it down or minimize it now and again."

"I see," I say, and finish my first drink.

"*A mangiare,*" Carmine calls.

We both stand and gather the remnants of our appetizer plates and glasses and carry them into the kitchen.

"Come," Carmine says, and points to the dining area chairs.

We sit to a steaming bowl of linguini with fresh clams. He has uncorked a bottle of pinot grigio and poured its contents into freezer-chilled wine goblets for the three of us.

"Proceed," he directs us, as he fills our plates. "I will listen and eat."

I smile a toothy smile at him, then turn to Flavia. "How do you keep at your job, then," I ask, "if there is never an end to the criminality? Don't you ever despair?"

Flavia twirls strands of linguini with practiced ease. She opens her eyes wide. "I might ask you, Orla, why do you keep painting social commentary? Do not racism, war, and deathly diseases still exist despite your denouncing them on canvas?"

She twirls and eats another forkful of pasta.

I look right into her brown eyes. "I admit you have rendered me speechless, Flavia," I say.

Carmine laughs and pats his mouth with his napkin. "Now you understand what those she prosecutes face."

Flavia giggles. Her girlish laugh misaligns with her otherwise no-nonsense demeanor. "By the way, Carmine, you remain my favorite chef." She winks at him again, then continues, "Filumena and virtually everyone else, man or woman, who is a Camorristi, has been raised from birth within the System. And the System goes back centuries."

"I had no idea," I say.

For several minutes we eat our pasta in silence. My head feels full of weighty facts.

Carmine stands and takes our plates. "Now, some *branzino* and fried *zucca*."

"My favorites," Flavia says with the exuberance of a happy child. She resumes talking. "Remember, many in the System originate from small villages whose inhabitants have suffered generations of poverty and ignorance. The government has failed them again and again, no matter who is in power. But every once in a while, when a *nonno* dies, perhaps, the family learns that funeral expenses have been paid. Or a doctor appears with penicillin for a sick child. And, if the father of seven children has been shot by a rival of the local gang, a weekly bag of groceries is delivered to his family with no explanation. This is how the System gains loyal supporters."

"Okay," I say, "I follow you."

The *branzino* is flaky and redolent of lemon juice, and the *zucca* flowers are as crisp on the outside as they are soft inside.

"This is delicious, Carmine," I say.

"You see," says Flavia. "I tell the truth. Both about Carmine's cooking and the System."

Again we focus on our food. Carmine refills our plates without asking if we desire more.

When I eat the last bite of fish, I ask, "But what of the brutality?"

Flavia pats her mouth with her napkin and drinks some wine before she answers. "Orla, it is a mistake to think that the only brutality the people know is that of the Camorristi."

"Go on," I say, nodding in the affirmative to Carmine as he holds the bottle of wine at the ready.

"Often, brutality comprises the bulk of their life experiences. Hunger, joblessness, lack of education, endless pregnancies, little health care, primitive housing. If running drugs or beating up someone puts food on the table, gets a young tough a motorbike, or a girl with no dowry married to a local thug, life changes, seemingly for the better. And, as long as these folks remain loyal, they survive."

Carmine again collects our plates, goes into the kitchen, and calls out, "I make espresso now."

"Orla, you may find this difficult to believe, but when the *carabinieri* or the local police arrest one of the gang members, his neighbors protest. They fling furniture into the streets, torch a car or two. This is their way of showing their loyalty to the System and their disdain for the authorities you and I have been taught to respect, despite our often significant flaws."

I push my chair away from the table and fold my napkin into a triangle. "This is disturbing and fascinating," I say.

"I agree," says Flavia.

The phone on the kitchen wall rings.

"*Pronto*," we hear Carmine say into the phone, then he laughs so hard that he coughs. "*Sì, sì*, come now. I am making espresso. We will enjoy a nightcap."

I wonder who it is he's invited. But more to the point at the moment, I turn my attention to Flavia again and ask, "How may I become more knowledgeable?"

Carmine calls from the kitchen, "It is your husband on the phone, Flavia."

Flavia stands and says, "Come into my office next week, Orla. I will make all the Filumena Curti files available to you."

My eyes open wide. "Thank you, Flavia," I say.

Flavia and Carmine crisscross between kitchen and dining table, where Carmine joins me again. "Does she give you the information you need?" he asks.

I nod my head up and down. I'm pumped. "All, and then some, Carmine. Flavia has invited me to her office come Monday."

"Ah, then, she has decided you are worth her time."

I feel myself blushing, as if I'm a teenager who's been asked to homecoming by the high school quarterback.

"*Ciao, Caro,*" Flavia says and hangs up, then joins us at the table. "Leo is coming to fetch me." She sighs. "Since the bombing he will not let me out alone at night. He thinks they will target me again."

She might be discussing butter or postage stamps. As if her being a target has become quotidian.

Jesus. My interior monologue is cranking up. *The guy must be really frightened. I wonder if they argue about this. How could they not?* I'm eager to meet him.

"In the meantime..." Carmine says, drawing my attention into the room again. He stands and walks to the pool table. Twisting his head to look sideways at the spines of the books assembled there, he settles on two hardcover tomes. "Lest I fall short of dear Flavia's generosity, take these back to the hotel and study them, Orla. You must pretend you are my student."

"*Grazie*, Carmine. You're giving me quite a bit of homework."

He twirls his right hand in the air. "Mah, what else do you have to do alone in a hotel room?"

Both Flavia and I laugh.

"Well, reading will keep me out of trouble, I guess." I take the books from him and place them on the table, then sit. The black covered volume is titled *The History of Prostitution on the Boot*, by Ashton Clark Goldthorp, published by Oxford University Press.

"It is only out one year. Very good. His dissertation."

I nod. The faded purple volume is called *Regulations Concerning Prostitution in Major Italian Cities*, by the Institute for Legal Studies.

"The information is current to last year. If anything has changed, Flavia will know."

"Always giving me more work, Carmine. I am surprised you have not asked me to grade your exams." Flavia winks at him so often it appears her eyelids have their own exercise routine.

Carmine smiles and twirls his right hand again. "Good idea," he says. "I will book you now for next year's finals."

The doorbell rings.

"Ah, Leo." Carmine stands and walks to the door.

Just after he goes, I lean across the table to Flavia and speak *sotto voce*. "I must ask you, Flavia, are you ever afraid?"

She looks at me, then toward the door, then back at me. I hear the refrigerator hum, smell the espresso, and see the minute hand of the kitchen wall clock move from fourteen to fifteen minutes after eleven.

"Yes," she says, also in a whisper. "Every. Single. Day." She looks as if a funerary mask has been placed over her face. Then, in a voice I might associate with Filumena herself, "But I will never let them get the better of me."

She pounds the table once with both hands. "Never."

I shudder and stare.

"Leo!" Carmine bellows, while Flavia slips behind him and into the aubergine half-bathroom before her husband enters the apartment. She closes and locks the door.

"Come, come," Carmine says. "Meet the famous American painter."

I take a deep breath and, making myself smile, reach out my hand.

Chapter Four
Night Ride

"*Ciao, ciao,*" we chant as if a chorus, when Leo and Flavia drop me off at the Excelsior.

It is well after one in the morning, and we've all had our share of *limoncello*. I'm ready to sleep, but I'm glad I've had at least a brief time seeing Leo and Flavia together. He is as tall and lanky as she is short and square. His family came to Naples from Genoa after his father died in 1980 and his mother wanted to return to her birthplace. He inherited the pharmacy from his maternal uncle, now retired. As we enjoyed espresso, biscotti, and *limoncello* with Carmine, he and Flavia periodically held hands, mostly when talking about Elvira.

"She wants to be a ballerina," Leo said, and showed me a photo he keeps in his wallet. The image is of Elvira wearing a white tutu with silver glitter. Her face is her mother's. "I am glad," he continued. "We encourage her." He turned to Flavia and caressed her cheek. "It is much safer than what my wife does." Flavia kept silent and pressed her husband's hand. Then she removed it from her face and lowered it palm down onto the table, where she patted it several times. Leo sighed.

Now he and Flavia are smiling their farewells.

The night doorman approaches the car. He opens the door for me and, as I wave goodbye, Flavia leans across Leo and says, "Come at ten o'clock Monday morning. Via Grimaldi. You will have to go through a security check, so bring a photo ID and be prepared to give your phone numbers and addresses."

"I'll be ready," I say. "And thank you again. Both of you."

Once in the lobby, I see the remnants of a wedding reception being cleared from the ballroom. Several gowned and tuxedoed guests lounge or, more accurately, sprawl on the purple divans. I nod at the night desk clerk, who smiles briefly, and take the stairs to my room. The maid has lowered the mechanical shutters and lit a lamp on the near side of the bed. It is only moments before I complete my nightly toilette, settle in bed, and drift off.

A knock at my door wakes me. *My God, the clock reads ten-thirty.* I grab my robe from the bedpost and hurry to the door.

"For you, *Signora*," a porter says. He carries a long box of chocolates and a note.

"*Grazie*," I say, and rifle through my bag for a tip.

The note and the candy—truffles, to be precise—are from Carmine:

> *I will pick you up at nine o'clock this evening and take you to the Via Domitiana. It will not be a sweet journey. Please accept the chocolates as my way of telling you that your company, however, was a delicious treat. I am no longer doing only a favor for cousin Amelia. — Carmine.*

Hmmm. If I didn't know any better, I'd think he was coming onto me.

I have homework to do.

The day flies. I take the elevator to the rooftop pool and find some shade under an umbrella where I can drink coffee, enjoy a *cornetto*, and read. I learn that prostitution is legal in Italy, and I take a long look at Goldthorp's history. It includes chapters about prostitution during the Middle Ages and Venice's famed "honest women," as its courtesans were called. All this is intriguing. That said, the history does not consider the kind of human trafficking going on in nearby ports of entry right now. In fact, some of Goldthorp's entries come across as romanticized. I admit I do wonder if being an unattached woman who made her own money in bygone days did offer a way of life preferable to the nunnery, the drudgery of a peasant's life, or the gilded cage of a noble marriage and progeny whose social status was the highest priority. And never mind death by childbirth!

I've always felt cactus-prickly about the common, historically Church-held claim that prostitutes are a necessary evil required to fulfill men's predilections and assumed needs, while "good girls," i.e. girls from noble families, need to be virgins until their wedding nights. Gah. The hymen. Hi, men! What a crock. A crock of cocks.

No one up here on the hotel rooftop but me. Almost as peaceful as home. I decide to take a swim and get some sun before heading out for an early supper. I pick a pizza joint on a side street several blocks from the hotel where I can people watch while enjoying a salad, a pizza Margherita, and a Peroni. Back in my hotel room, Tino and I talk by phone, he assuring me that the twins went off with their *nonna* to her camp without a hitch and that the villa is eerie without us all. I miss him, though I do like sprawling alone in the big bed, especially during a hot flash.

Just after nine, while I wait beneath the hotel's canopy, Carmine arrives. He jumps from the car, its windows all the way down, kisses my hand, then leads me to the passenger side where he opens the door. Tonight he is dressed completely in black—short-sleeved shirt, slacks, and running shoes. I, on the other hand, am in the white version of my summer dress. I still wear my sunglasses, as it is not quite dark.

"Are you sure you want to do this?" he asks. "It is not the usual way I spend a Saturday evening with a lady."

I settle in, smile at him, and fasten my seatbelt. I wonder what lady or ladies he does spend his nights with.

"Of course I'm sure," I say. "How else will I know what to paint?"

"Okay, then, it is research."

"Exactly."

He takes a cigarette from his breast pocket and lights it, offering me a drag.

"No, thanks."

He takes several puffs, then snuffs the cigarette out in the ashtray. "Okay, then, let us go."

Castel Volturno is a *comune* in the province of Caserta in the region known as Campania, twenty-two miles northwest of Naples and twenty-two miles west of the town, also called Caserta, where the nuns has a shelter for the trafficked girls they save. The three areas—Naples, Castel Volturno, and the town of Caserta—form the triangle my intended exhibit will highlight. I've made sure to bring a notepad with me so I can jot down sketch ideas, should a multitude of them mix in my mind as we drive along the now-notorious road.

Via Domitiana, Carmine tells me as we enter the highway heading out of Naples, began as a major Roman road built in 95 AD to provide access to various ports in the empire. Only in the late twentieth century did it become affiliated with trafficked prostitutes.

"It is a very busy road," he says, his laugh not a joyful one, but not a cynical one, either. The entrance to the highway takes us over the port of Naples, its various colored shipping containers stacked like building blocks on both sides of the guardrails, and we soon find ourselves speeding along grassy suburban areas with occasional small shopping centers and factories scattered near the highway exits. Darkness is falling.

"Now we arrive," Carmine tells me. I sit up straighter and prepare to stare without blinking.

We are barely one half-hour from the Excelsior when we pull off the exit and follow the sign to Castel Volturno. I feel nervous, the way I might before having some dental work done or being called into my children's school at the request of the principal. I've taken my sunglasses off, but when we find ourselves in what looks like a traffic jam, the glaring of many brake lights compels me to put them back on. I stretch my neck out the passenger seat window.

"*Madonna mia,*" Carmine says, and twirls his right hand. "Is Saturday night. Very busy."

I pay close attention.

Two car lanes have formed. The left, the one we're in right now, consists of slow-moving vehicles in a stop-and-go traffic pattern. The right, with cars and motorbikes idling or with engines turned off, consists of vehicles whose occupants are buying services from the girls who stand, some at the curb, some further back near the brush.

"I drive around first," Carmine says, "so you can get an overview. Then we make a stop if you want."

I take a breath. "Go slow, please," I say.

"Mah," Carmine says, twirling his right hand, "what else can I do? It is impossible to speed."

I look to the girls. First I see a tall ebony teenager. She looks like she should be playing basketball at an American college. She is all leg. Barefoot. A shimmering pink thong barely covers her genitals. Her breasts are small, but emphasized by the push-up halter she wears. It is canary yellow. A silver Alfa Spider pulls up to her and stops. When she leans down to haggle with the client, her ass shines under a streetlight. She gets into the car. It inches its way into our lane.

Carmine continues behind it at a snail's pace.

A few hundred feet further along, just at the edge of the brush, three girls barely past puberty sit on a refrigerator turned on its side. The top freezer door is open. Leaves and branches protrude from it. Two of the girls are African, the third a light-skinned blonde with pigtails.

Two helmeted guys on a motorcycle call out to the two dark girls, "Both of you, back there, like last time." The men get off the motorcycle and go into the brush. The girls follow.

The white girl doesn't react, just picks at her nails, waiting.

We come to a curve in the road. I gasp.

"What?" Carmine says, then, seeing for himself, "*Dio*." A black girl, not as young as the three we just passed, but certainly not yet an adult woman, is on all fours, leashed to a telephone pole by a rope knotted around her waist. Should she try, she will not be able to stray more than three or four yards from the pole. She wears a fringed red chemise with spaghetti straps. A much older woman, her head wrapped in a multi-colored *gele*, sits on a metal lawn bench not far behind her, right where the sidewalk ends and the brush rises. The woman resembles a hippopotamus and drinks from a plastic cup. Her thick legs are spread and she stares at her mobile phone as she drinks. Her face is expressionless and leathery. Is she the girl's *maman*? The girl raises her torso so that her arms can circle a client's legs as she services him. He is wearing a fitted black suit and pointy shoes. A line of six other men wait their turn. They, too, are dressed for the office. Two have removed their ties and twirl them in the air like lassos. The men appear to be together. The girl spits and wipes her mouth with the back of her hand when the client (bastard!) zips his pants and turns away. Then she returns to her task, this time with a blue-suited fellow. He presses his hands on her head as she labors, while those behind him count out loud. "*Uno, due, tre....*"

"You want to leave?" Carmine asks. He looks to me, the road ahead, and to me again.

I want to puke. I am crying. Loud, snotty crying.

"No, I say," hiccupping, "keep on. I have to see. I want to speak with them, the girls."

Carmine grabs my arm.

"Ouch," I say.

He presses his fingers into my flesh. "Are you serious? You want to talk to them?"

My right foot is moving up and down as if it has a life of its own. I look right back at him and push his hand off me.

"Serious. Yes. I want to know them. At least one."

He takes a deep breath, then spits out the window and runs his fingers through his hair with one hand while tapping the steering wheel with the other. "And I am crazy for listening to you. *Pozzo*. I will live to regret listening to you."

We stop talking while he drives around the next rotary and signals to get into the right lane. Horns beep behind us. "*Vai, vai!*" a gruff voice hollers. Carmine inches the Fiat toward the right. Another beep from behind, and he makes it, thanks to whoever is driving the white Mercedes behind us.

"There," I say. "That one." I am pointing to the place under a streetlight where a broken stone Madonna and Child rests against a metal trash can overflowing with take-away cartons, empty beer bottles, and a pair of men's undershorts on top. Used condoms are scattered on the ground.

We pull over and Carmine turns off the engine. The girl comes toward us. She is wearing a little-girl eyelet dress, her hair in braids, as if she is going to a child's birthday party. Her platform heels have Tinkerbells attached to the toes. She wears a blue bow on top of her head.

She speaks without emotion. "You pay double for the both of you," she says to Carmine. One front tooth is missing, so she hisses when she talks.

I tell her, "We just want to talk to you, to find out how you got here."

She looks to her left and right, then back toward the brush. "For talk, four times as much," she says. "Fuck is quick. Talk is slow. Costs more." She folds her arms across her chest as I try to remember how many lire I'm carrying.

She scratches her nose. "Forty American dollars," she says. "Okay," I say. I open my satchel and show her the money.

"Mah, *Dio*," Carmine says, "what are you doing?"

The girl gets into the car, the back seat. She smells of sex and sweat. I feel faint.

"*Gesu*," says Carmine, turning to look back at her. "I will have to fumigate my car."

"Carmine!" I say, and contort my body so that I can look at right at her.

The girl remains stone-faced. How can she? Has all self-respect been beaten out of her?

"I am Orla," I say. "I work with the sisters who visit you, who want to help you." (I know, I know, it's a lie. But an almost-true lie.) I speak as if to my daughter. "What's your name?"

Carmine is quiet now, like a ghost hovering in the background.

The girl stares at me, then looks to Carmine.

He says nothing.

She looks at me again. She holds her hand out. I give her the money. She scrunches the bills and stuffs them into her bra.

"Adaoma," she says, then leans back on the upholstery. "I was Adaoma."

Was. Was Adaoma. She is no-name now.

Beads of sweat are dripping down my cheeks, under my breasts, along my spine. I study Adaoma's face. I need to remember her face. The jagged scar under her chin. The missing tooth. The hiss. The heavy-lidded eyes.

All of a sudden, Carmine leans over me. Adaoma tenses. Carmine opens the glove compartment and rifles around it until he finds an unopened pack of cigarettes and a small matchbox. He offers them to Adaoma. She grabs them both. Carmine still has several cigarettes in his breast pocket. He gives me one, then motions for Adaoma to light it. She lights his, as well. The three of us stay together, quiet and smoking, until most of the cigarettes are gone. We have created a cocoon of smoke and ignore the activity outside the car.

Carmine coughs. "Now what?" he asks.

I want to ask the girl many questions. How did she get here? Where and who and what did she leave? How she would describe a typical day in her life. But why would she tell me for forty bucks? Why at all? I need to see her again, perhaps several times.

I take my notepad and a pen from my bag, scribble my name and mobile number as well as the address for Casa di Dignità, Caserta. I rip the page out, and hand it to Adaoma. She takes the paper, squints at it, then asks, "What for?"

I look at her ruined face. Try to imagine her life as it is. Wonder if she will risk a chance or two with me.

"For if you want to talk with me, or if you want to escape this life. You can go to the sisters in Caserta."

"*Mamma mia,*" Carmine says. "Why you want to do this? You think you are Mother Teresa?"

I ignore him.

Adaoma takes the slip of paper, stares at it, then folds it into a folio. She takes off her right shoe, then shoves the folio in so that it rests under the ball of her foot. She gets out of the car and starts walking. She doesn't look back as we pull away.

Neither of us says a word all the way back to Naples. When he drops me off at the Excelsior, Carmine stays in the driver's seat, looks down at the steering wheel, and waits. I'm on my own.

"Thank you for taking me," I say, and let myself out of the car. I reach into my bag for some money. "Here. Let me take care of getting your car cleaned."

He pushes my hand away.

"Mah. Get out. Go now." His voice is gruff and he fingers his curly hair. I feel dismissed and, though I want to get out of the car right away, my legs feel heavy, as if they are sinking into quicksand. I sigh, grab the edge of the Fiat's roof with my right hand, and wrench myself out and upright.

Once I'm out of the car, Carmine leans across the passenger seat. Now his voice is moderate, soothing, even. "You are a good woman, Orla, I know. I can see that." He sneezes.

"God bless you," I say, and lean down to better hear him.

"Amelia is right. She told me this."

I look him straight in the eye. "But..." I say, and wonder if I will ever see him again.

He laughs, not unkindly, as I move to go. "*Aspett'*, wait," he says.

I pause.

He looks away from me toward the glittering *lungomare*, then back again. "I not want to see you for a few days. Too much. You are wilder than I expected. Rash."

I tap my foot on the pavement. Believe me, it's not the first time someone has called me "too" something or other.

"How so?" I ask.

He rotates his right hand as if it is a circular fan and speaks a screed of sentences, so fast does he talk that he sounds like a pitchman in a thirty-second television commercial.

"What if she calls you, eh? You will not be here in Napoli. You will be off to America doing whatever celebrity artists do. Living your nice life in a posh apartment. Going to parties with champagne. Then what? You think you can call me? You think that Carmine should pick her up and offer the black *putana* a home? Keep her? You have no idea what you are dealing with, Signora Orla. No idea whatsoever."

My face is flushing, my heart is beating fast, and my anger is rising from two competing epiphanies—the first that knows he is right about my ignorance, the second that asserts I must nonetheless act or be damned.

I force myself not to snap or cry. *Didn't you see her?* I want to shout. *Or the one roped like a mongrel, a fucking dog? Are you blind? This is flesh I'm talking about, not legal statutes or philosophies of life. Flesh done wrong, dammit. Spirits vanquished, Professor. Ivory tower bastard.*

Instead, I modulate my voice and speak slowly. "I'm sorry to have upset you. Very sorry. I won't impose on you further. I'll have your books sent back."

"*Gesu,*" he says. "I do not want that, Orla. We can be friends. I want us to be friends. *Dio,* we are already friends."

I don't say a word. Just stand and wait. He inhales. Again. "Friends, you see. Like you and my cousin Amelia. Not crusaders against an enemy that cannot be conquered. I am not Don Quixote or Saint Francis. Just Professore Famiglietti."

"I see." I twist each ankle around in circles, once, twice, three times. "I understand."

So that's it. Accommodation. I'll call it the Vesuvius Effect. The actual volcano and just as deadly metaphorical volcanoes loom always. Death and destruction are only a matter of time. So *carpe diem*, live and let live. Don't try to beat the System, just learn how to navigate around it. Then perhaps you will be lucky enough to die of old age outside the perimeter of its molten lava.

"Okay," I say. (Look at me, accommodating him too, already. What a hypocrite I am. But I can't hurt Amelia. And Carmine *has* opened some doors.) My arms and legs itch from the humidity. "Whenever you get in touch, I will be glad to see you. Again, thank you for going out of your way for me."

"Saturday. I will see you Saturday," he says. He is calm now. I have convinced him that I will not do anything wild, so he can be calm. "We will go to the beach so you can meet my lover. I think you will find her most interesting. She has a bungalow in Conca dei Marini. Pack a bag in case we spend the night. I will pick you up at ten o'clock. She expects us. And all of your questions." He crosses himself as if asking for protection or, possibly, absolution.

Lover. Huh. I'll get in touch with Amelia to see what beans she can spill. And of course purchase some goodies for the hostess. Glad I brought a swimsuit.

"What's your lover's name?"

Carmine's countenance relaxes, and he grins as he says her name. "Tiziana. Tiziana Paola Gargiulo." He blows me a kiss and twirls his hand in the air. I wave. Then he drives away, his car looking smaller and smaller until it disappears into what's left of the night.

Chapter Five
Files, Lists, and an Interview

I spend three days at the prosecutors' offices, arriving just after ten on Monday. The two *carabinieri* at the entrance are all business. The first one, a striking young man with piercing green eyes, has me prove my identity and stand before a computer screen to have my photo taken. Then he hands me a sticky nametag that reads *"Visitatore"* and points to my left breast. His counterpart, beads of sweat between his upper lip and prominent nose, scans my body with a wand lest I be packing heat. *"Bene,"* he says, and motions for me to sit on a wooden bench that looks like a discarded church pew. The first guard reaches for a wall phone and calls someone. At the sound of Flavia's voice over the wire, I know I am in.

The room she has reserved for me might as well be a prison cell. Eight by ten feet at the most, it contains a rectangular oak table, two metal chairs that do not make sitting comfortable, and a window facing the central office, its Venetian blinds down and closed. An air-conditioning unit above the door hums intermittently and dispatches infrequent bursts of air that can be categorized as moderately cool at best.

That said, Flavia has provided pure gold on the table. Not only all Filumena's records, but also—and certainly more helpful to an artist—every newspaper and magazine story about her, photos included. I am in business.

I read, take notes, and sketch. Most of the photos, even in the glossy magazines, are grainy. "We didn't even know about Filumena until after the bloodbath she orchestrated after the too-strong Turkish drugs," Flavia tells me. "Until then, she was a virtual ghost. Then we tried tracking her, first at the shop in Caserta, then at several supposed 'safe' houses and apartments here in Naples. But we didn't get her until the police stopped a car without a license plate. She happened to be a passenger, one with 400,000 American dollars on her. That's when she became interesting to us." Then, as Flavia walks out the door, she adds, "I've got work to do. You'll read all about it yourself."

This morning, Thursday, back at the hotel in my light-filled room, I find myself staring at the sketch I made from Filumena's mug shot. She looks straight at the camera, her expression one of apparent calm. Her lips are closed, neither pursed nor smirking. Her eyes are open, not wide with shock, surprise, or ire. Her hair, layered and short, has been styled and dyed the color of expensive dark chocolate, as I saw in the glossies, and her eyebrows are neat, expertly waxed and tweezed, no doubt about it. Her lipstick is vibrant enough to be noticed, but does not scream red. She is wearing a black knit turtleneck. When I get to the studio in Manhattan, my task will be to paint her in a manner that convinces she is revealing nothing. That she never reveals a thing. That she is poised and controlled. That the authorities who have taken her to the *questura* are no more than mosquitoes who alight and itch momentarily. That she is, dammit, serene. Certain. Fatal.

The phone rings its double ring three times by the time I move from desk and window to night table.

"Hold, please," a polished voice says. Then, "Signora Castleberry, this is Carmella Sorrentino from *Questo Giorno*."

"Yes."

"I understand you are in Naples preparing for an exhibit for International Women's Day in collaboration with some religious sisters, laywomen, and Franciscan friars in Assisi."

I sit on the bed and twirl my ankles round and round. My feet ache. I was at the desk too long. How does she know I'm here? Maybe Lina told her.

"Correct."

"I'd like to interview you, to learn about how your art figures in with the subject of the day. Human trafficking it is, right?"

"Right."

A kite rises from across the street outside my window.

"Are you available tomorrow?"

I look at my toes and see I'm overdue for a pedicure.

"Let me check my calendar," I say.

Of course I'm available. I've not yet even made a to-do list for tomorrow. I stand up and stretch six times before answering.

"I have some time at eleven o'clock tomorrow," I say.

"Good. Then I'll meet you at the hotel."

I sit on the bed again.

"Fine," I say. "Come up to the pool area where we can sit under an umbrella."

"*Ciao*," she says.

"*Ciao, ciao*," I answer, then lay the phone down and sigh. The interview means another few hours away from sketching. I can hear my late great friend, agent, and publicist Luke Segreti, say, "Darling, all publicity is good publicity. It's the cost of celebrity. And you—thanks in no small part to me, my friend—are a celebrity."

By God, I miss Luke. Damn AIDS. He's been gone eleven years. We honor his memory annually, with his longtime partner, Tad, at our hospice fundraiser in Fiesole. Thank goodness Tad's HIV has not yet developed into full-blown AIDS. Fingers crossed it won't. If Luke was right about publicity, then I'm lathered in goodness. *Questo Giorno* has a gigantic readership and Sorrentino writes a weekly column. Tino takes dailies not only from Florence, our home base, but also from Rome, Milan, and Naples. I started reading Sorrentino's columns several years ago when she wrote about the complicated relationship between Italy's abortion law and medical providers. (Sidebar: Abortion has been legal in Italy since 1978. The law stipulates the 90-day mark for elective abortions, but extends the 90-day limit for abortions deemed therapeutic. At the same time, almost 80% of gynecologists in Campania choose not to perform terminations.) I'll spare you more details other than to say that Sorrentino explains facts clearly and quotes people opining about both sides of an issue. Thus far, I have found her evenhanded. Let's see how she angles my point of view about trafficking in her own back yard, as it is. At any rate, I'll have to get prettied up in case she brings a photographer with her or takes a photo herself.

In the meantime, I decide to sketch the dog-girl, instantly appalled at how quickly my own words have dehumanized her. I've just wound the rope around her waist and attached it to the telephone pole several yards away. Next I intend to emphasize how her knees scrape on the cement sidewalk so that, after an evening's work, they are bloodied and pitted from small stones and grains of sand. I'm thinking I'll depict her in between clients, unable to decide whether to show her spitting or wiping an arm across her mouth, when I'm interrupted by three quick knocks at the door.

"Dammit," I say. I can't seem to work for one hour straight. I go to the door.

"Excuse me, *Signora*," a bell hop says. He hands me a small envelope. "The concierge says your phone line was in use, so he sends you the message, as it is time-sensitive."

"Thank you," I say, and find my wallet to tip him.

I take a long drink from the can of Coke Light on the round table between the club chairs, then sit and open the envelope.

> *Signora,*
>
> *I call on behalf of Sister Ilaria from Casa di Dignità. She is away this week, but advises that you are welcome tomorrow afternoon at 3 o'clock to meet two of our residents who will speak with you. Please phone the number below by 5 pm today only if you are unable to come. There is no need to respond otherwise.*
>
> > *Thank you,*
> > *Sister Norina*

My heart leaps. Good. I can meet at least two girls who got away. I need to order a large basket of provisions to send to Casa di Dignità ahead of my visit. I'll write a check to bring along with me, as well.

I empty the can. Tomorrow promises to be a busy day.

*****

Carmella Sorrentino wastes no time. She arrives five minutes after eleven dressed completely in white, shakes hands with me, sits down in the direct sunlight, and opens a steno pad. Black marker at the ready, she ignores the waiter who places the two *espressi* and *cornetti* on the table, and asks, "Why are you, an American, so interested in human trafficking here, in Naples?"

The photographer who accompanies her, a lanky, brown-bearded man dressed in a black tee-shirt and khaki slacks, says not a word, just motions with one hand for me to stand by the open umbrella, then sit with legs crossed looking out at the *lungomare*, and finally to fold my arms across my chest and not smile, shaking his head "no" when I do. "*Grazie*," he says, then nods to Sorrentino, and leaves. She waves him off and repeats her question.

Dear reader, as you are already well aware of my interest—obsession, really—with the Comorra's trafficking enterprise, I'll spare you a repetitive response. I'll tell you only that not once does this reporter soften or ask any questions about how art can function as social commentary and now and again effect societal change. I have to insert that idea into the interview myself while she sips her espresso.

No, Signora Sorrentino's focus is single-minded. "Do you not feel that, as an American, you are intruding, uninvited, into territory not yours? After all, there is plenty of human trafficking in your own country that you might consider."

Rather than being baited by her and going on about being married to an Italian and having given birth to two Italian children and having lived in Italy for the past twelve years, I smile. Then I carry on for some time, telling her that I hold "a less nationalistic or parochial attitude" toward trafficking. (Take that, Your Arrogance!)

"Trafficking is indeed a heinous world-wide activity," I say, using my best professional voice, "and I am glad to have been invited to join the Franciscan friars' and the Suore della Madonna's crusade against it. While our event next March in Assisi will indeed focus on this region, we are certainly calling to light, and protesting, sexual violence against *all* women *everywhere*. And, as you are clearly aware, our consortium will take place on International Women's Day, in March of 2002. *International* Women's Day. So my purview is hardly limited to Campania."

But the signora isn't buying my package. I can only imagine how her article will slant. She moves on to another question.

"Do you consider yourself an expert on the topic of human trafficking in the area?" she tries again.

"Hardly," I say. "But I have communicated with, learned from, and joined with those who are. And I hope my art will attract more attention to the problem and encourage more of the local populace to become activists helping the women who are so unjustifiably and brutally treated."

She scribbles on her pad, then caps her marker, and looks at me across the table. "You can expect the article next Thursday, the 16th, in my usual column." She takes one bite of her *cornetto*, pats her magenta lips with a napkin, stands, and grabs her bag to leave.

"Thanks for coming by," I say, and rise to walk her to the elevator.

Not even a "*prego.*"

I push the "Down" button.

"Oh," she says, before the ding that announces the elevator's arrival, "researching you, I found that your previous exhibits have received quite a bit of acrimonious press. How do you feel about that?"

I smile again. This answer is easy.

"Paintings I do exposing difficult topics, such as racial discrimination, the scourge of AIDS, the effects of a long-term Nazi occupation of one's village, and now this, are bound to upset the apple cart," I say. "I can't control audiences' responses to my work." I scrunch my shoulders and raise my arms with palms upward. "That's the price an artist pays for her vision. But other viewers understand the difference between depicting and endorsing. Not all reviews are acrimonious." I keep my voice easy, calm. Absolute confidence is my goal.

The elevator door opens, and Signora Sorrentino steps in, keeping it from closing with her right hand.

"Well, Signora Castleberry," she says, "it will be interesting to assess the cost of this exhibit after all is said and done and painted."

She is giving me the creeps. Does she know something I don't?

"It will," I agree. "Perhaps we will talk again after the consortium."

Only then does she show her teeth. They have a clear relationship with nicotine and coarsen her white attire.

"Bye, then." I wave her off. Can't be happier to see her go. God forgive me, I want the elevator to get stuck between floors.

"*Ciao,*" she says, and lets go the elevator door. As it slides to a close, we look straight into each other's eyes. Neither of us blinks.

Chapter Six
At Casa di Dignità

The concierge assures me that Luigi, the driver he has procured for me, will relish driving to and from Casa di Dignità in Caserta. "His *nonna* lives on Via Giordano, perpendicular to Corso Trieste, where the convent is. She will spoil him while you do whatever you must." He chuckles. "Then Luigi will drive you back as cloyed and contented as a nursing baby."

Jesus, I hope the guy won't fall asleep at the wheel after his carb glut. I have visions of the two of us flung from the car to thrash in the water between docked cruise ships, or crashing through the windshield and rough skimming from shipping container to shipping container in the Port of Naples. Crash, fly, drop, flop, repeat, repeat until, finally, both of us lie sprawled on a rusty container, rag-doll dead.

Back in my room, I try to forget the Sorrentino interview and consider instead how best to present myself to the sisters and, more importantly, to the two women I'm about to meet. How did Sister Ilaria pick them? Did they volunteer? Why have they agreed to speak with me? Do they have a message or messages they want me to translate onto canvas? Shall I barrage them with detailed questions or let the conversation wander where it may? I'll bring my sketch pad. Should I ask their permission before using it? Maybe I'll just try to read the room accurately and play the rest by ear.

After he stops the car parallel to the wide driveway of the apartment building where the sisters and their guests share two attached units, Luigi gives me his card. "Call me when you are ready. No rush."

"Enjoy time with your *nonna*," I say, and smile when he pats his stomach.

Once out of the car and onto the broad sidewalk, I look up and down the street. It's residential, with small shops and cafes on the ground floors of apartment buildings, the majority presently closed. Many windows are shuttered. Quiet as it is right now, the area appears to be a fine place to live. Even a bit trendy. What surprises me is the absence of foot traffic. Maybe the majority of folks have already left for their holidays. Only one shop selling small decorative pieces for households a few hundred feet from me is open, with a middle-aged Italian woman and two older gentlemen sitting on navy deck chairs outside. The woman wears a sleeveless checkered dress and fans herself. The men wear identical straw hats and smoke, one a cigarette, the other a cigar. No customers appear to need their assistance. Diagonally across the way from them, an outdoor bar with one long table set for its six customers hugs the cracked grey stucco wall of the adjacent restaurant. The group's laughter floats above their table. "*Beng Beng Beng*" by Femi Kuti is playing. My kids have been prancing to the song for the past couple of years after hearing it from a group of musicians in Fiesole just after it was released. I hope Isa and Lu are still unaware of its racy lyrics. I admit, one can enjoy a fine aerobics workout by replaying the piece four or five times. I feel like dancing now.

Other than these two places, the rest of the street resembles a ghost town. No voices stream from apartment terraces, trash bins show no evidence of recent detritus, and the usual medium-sized-city combination of strolling, biking, motorcycling, jogging, baby-carriage-pushing humans has disappeared. August, I guess. Any other reason would make me suspicious.

Having nothing else to distract me, I turn my attention to the cement drive leading to the apartment courtyard. Two stories above it a rectangular cloth flag with horizontal stripes in purple, navy, turquoise, green, yellow, orange, and red is affixed to the metal balcony railing. A vivid white cross is centered over the colors. Surrounding the flag are potted and hanging plants, their greenery softening the pinkish-beige brick of the building. To my left is a homemade painted plaque, with *"Casa di Dignità"* written in cursive. Three corners of the plaque are embellished with a curlicue in orange, while the top right corner boasts a yellow flower with two green leaves. A mimosa flower, the traditional flower of International Women's Day. That makes sense. Underneath the plaque, a mailbox with a keyhole and a nameplate reads *"Suore della Madonna."*

I draw in a startled breath when I see the open marble stairway leading upstairs. It feels familiar. There are metal railings either side of the steps, and two-inch decorative wood dadoes divide the bottom portions of the walls from the top. The lower level is painted lemon yellow, the upper a creamy beige. At the top of the stairway, the double doors do not close the convent to visitors. Rather, they are both fixed wide open, as if in invitation. And even before I climb the stairs, I see a tall, open armoire with empty coat hangers, several umbrellas, and a boot rack welcoming me. My consciousness immediately reverts to my and my daughter Mercy's high school, the Ursuline Academy in New Orleans, Louisiana, where the fragrances of the convent could be depended on—waxed floors, beeswax candles, eucalyptus wreaths, pine-scented soap. And if calm were a fragrance, as well, then calm wafted over all the other fragrances. That is the atmosphere I'm breathing in now as, step by sandaled step, I leave my lay person's quotidian reality and enter into an ethereal one that aspires to transcendence. I am drawn in, soothed, and hopeful.

About to knock on the open door as I reach the top step, I don't have to. A nun glides on soft-soled sandals to greet me. Perhaps the open door is counterbalanced by hidden cameras to protect the rescued women, and the sisters. After all, this place has its enemies. And, regardless of their vow of chastity, these sisters are not naïve. Flavia told me so during dinner at Carmine's. "The nuns are crusaders, warriors against the devils they know the pimps and *mamans* to be." I remember her downing a shot of *limoncello* and laughing sardonically. "They would cut off the traffickers' balls if it came to a knife fight."

I wonder now if the sisters carry protection in their pockets or shoulder bags when they venture out to Castel Volturno.

"*Buon pomeriggio*, Sister," I say.

The nun smiles and I am struck by her frank eyes. Though she is past mid-life, the skin on her face is smooth and her cheeks a healthy pink. "Welcome to Casa di Dignità. I am Sister

Norina." We shake hands. "Sister Ilaria has told me about you and sends her regrets. She is on retreat, but asks me to tell you she looks forward to the next conference call of your consortium group. She also gives you freedom to explore our home so you may paint us as we are."

Since I am already standing, I need only bow my head and dip my knees as we were taught to do when Mother Superior entered our classrooms. I know, I know, you probably think this kowtowing medieval and anachronistic. And perhaps it is. But, dear reader, let me tell you the comfort it brings me when Sister Norina, her habit a serviceable gray skirt, blue short-sleeved blouse, shoulder-length gray veil, and black leather sandals hugging her bare feet, lifts my chin and says, "Come, make yourself at ease here. Hadiza and Abeni are eager to meet you and share their stories. Sister Ilaria has already shared yours with them." She tilts her head and laughs a bit. "Our guests are Orla Castleberry experts now."

"I'm honored," I say. I wonder what Sister Ilaria has shown them.

As I follow Sister Norina's quick, silent tread along a corridor decorated with framed black and white photographs of mostly smiling dark young women and mixed-race babies, I breathe in the convent atmosphere, glad for at least a while to be away from the marvelous/overwhelming/begrimed/extravagant/invigorating energy that is Naples. But when Sister Norina turns right at the end of corridor and ushers me through glass-paned double doors into the community room where the sisters, their guests, and their several children gather for meals, play, projects, and prayer, I am shocked.

Only one person is in the room, with her back to us. She is tiny, bony and frail. She sits on a straight-backed chair with a plump checkered pillow underneath her so her hands can reach the Formica table top where they are busy at work. Her bare feet do not touch the floor. A box of assorted acrylic colors offers her considerable variety for transforming the school of white ceramic fish on top of the table into vivid sea creatures. She has selected purple and red for the one she is enlivening now. She doesn't appear to know we have entered the room

"Abeni is deaf," Sister Norina says, as she motions to me to walk around the table with her so the girl can see us. "Her *maman* regularly punched her ears while dragging her from her hiding places under a cot or in a cupboard to avoid going into the streets. She abused the child for a full year."

"Will she get hearing aids?" I ask.

The child jolts as she notices us. Sister Norina waves and smiles. I do the same. The girl does not return our greetings, but bows her head and continues painting instead.

"Yes," says the nun. "She has been with us only three weeks. The medical staff just this morning finished all her medical intake. She has a long road ahead to whatever healing can occur. All the recused girls come to us with STDs and other bodily abuses. Never mind the emotional and psychological battering they have endured."

I struggle to maintain a pleasant face. I want to un-see this child or weep instead. Abeni is malnourished and has burn marks on both arms. Puberty does not seem to have visited her yet. At the same time, her oval face looks old. Circles form demi-lunes under her eyes. The skin on her hands is wrinkled and dry. A half-drunk glass of milk rests by her left arm, and a plate of green grapes, almonds, and a sweet bun sits atop a white cloth napkin. A bite has been taken out of the bun.

The sister says. "Our job is to nourish Abeni's body and soul, to help her feel human and valued again. As I said, she has been with us only three weeks, brought here by the police who found her collapsed by the side of the road. When she was released from the emergency department, they drove her here. She slept for two days straight."

Dear God, she is only one of thousands. When we spoke in the spring, Sister Ilaria told me her community can house nineteen women and three children at a time. Twenty-two drops of rain in a monsoon. It will take an army to free the enslaved. How do these sisters avoid despair? How do they not abandon their efforts?

Sister Norina continues. "At this time, we can assure her only of a safe refuge, her own bed, access to a daily shower, fresh food, and the friendship of other women recovering from the same torture she has endured. Her trust in us, in anyone, for that matter, will take much longer to evince than her body's healing."

I nod, my eyes on the child who is smaller and obviously weighs less than my ten-year-old Isa. Withered, shrunken, stunted by a malice that proves the existence of Satan. Call me dramatic, a hysterical woman, if you wish, but if you could see her yourself, you would understand. My paintbrushes will compel you to see her. I will not need a photograph to instruct my brushes this time.

I am dying to know Abeni's story from the girl herself. Patience, I tell myself, gentleness and patience. Maybe over time she will tell me. Or perhaps she'll use her own painting to reveal herself, the way my Mercy did when she had just arrived in New Orleans from Vietnam in 1975.

Without words now, though, I try another tack and take my sketch pad from my shoulder bag. With a turquoise marker from the package of markers I carry, I write, "*Buon pomeriggio, Abeni!*" and draw a smiley face. She looks at her name and opens her lips, I hope in recognition. I sketch fast, drawing her hands painting the fish. Sister Norina watches. When I am done, I rip the page from my sketchbook and slide it across the table. Abeni looks at it, then at her hands, then across the table at me. A Mona Lisa smile. Something. I wave again. She turns her attention back to the fish.

Just then, another person enters the room.

"Ah," says Sister Norina, "here is Hadiza."

"Hello, Hadiza," I say. "I've been looking forward to meeting you."

The woman, for she is womanly rather than girlish, responds with a smile and a firm handshake across the table. She looks healthy, robust, even, and is dressed in a striking green and white *abaya* and a white blouse. Her hair is dyed blonde and she wears turquoise eye makeup and pale pink lipstick. Her nail color matches her lips. Her presence and manner do not suggest a difficult past. She might be any immigrant from the African continent who has created a successful life for herself in Italy.

Speaking in better than serviceable Italian, Hadiza tells Sister Norina that her little boy needed his diaper changed and is now down for a nap.

"He is two," she tells me. "You will meet him later."

Before I can respond, Sister Norina says, "I'll leave you to yourselves now. Enjoy your visit."

Hadiza pats Abeni on the shoulder. The girl flinches. Hadiza backs away, both her hands folding in a gesture of apology—to Abeni, I am guessing.

"I forget," she tells me, "—or shall I say I have forgotten?— how terrible another's touch can be." She sits on the chair next to Abeni and motions for me to take a seat across the table from her. "It took me several months here before I could bear any contact with another person's flesh." Hadiza rubs her right hand along her left arm.

"Were it not for Sister Ilaria standing right by me each time I visited the doctor, and even during childbirth, I don't know how I could have endured any more poking and groping and paining my body. Even though the one who delivered me of Abayomrunkoje was a doctor and a kind one. A woman."

Hadiza picks up the sweet bun and holds it out to Abeni. The girl grabs it and takes two quick bites. It appears they have a connection, fragile as it might be.

"His name is too long for the Italians," Hadiza laughs. "So we call him 'Aba.' But the proper name means 'God will not allow humiliation.' There will be no humiliation for my boy. I will insist." Hadiza punches the air with both hands like a boxer working out. Abeni watches.

"May I ask you some questions, Hadiza?" I say.

Hadiza nods. "Yes, yes. I want to tell you my story. It is the story of many others, as well. Sister Ilaria tells me you will paint it to the world. That is why I told her I want to meet you. I insisted."

Those are her words. *Insist. Insisted.* She will be calling the shots for herself and her boy now.

Abeni takes another bite of the sweet bun.

Hadiza has certainly reclaimed or, perhaps more accurately, gained confidence here. I wonder when she will be ready to move from this place. I'll be sure to ask her, but don't want to lose Abeni's attention at the same time. So I sketch the far wall to the left of me, the one with two long windows that are shuttered now against the afternoon heat.

"How did you come to be here?" I ask. "And when do you plan to leave?"

Hadiza sighs and cups her chin in her hands, elbows on the table top. "When I pretended to be sleeping and heard my *maman* instruct my pimp that he should take and sell my baby immediately after the birth, I knew I had to get away. That is what they do, sell or drown the babies."

I know right then, as soon as I get to the studio in New York, I will paint a mural of infants flailing in the Bay of Naples. But for now I'm sketching a shelf of stuffed animals, and Abeni stops her painting to watch my marker move. She follows my hands with her eyes as I curve an elephant's trunk upward. I pay her no mind and continue speaking with Hadiza.

"Did they make you work while you were pregnant?"

Hadiza sighs. "Yes. Some of the clients thought it was fun to beat my belly like a drum or make me lie down on it when they did me from behind."

I'm glad Abeni can't hear us. But, how stupid of me, she has been subjected to abuses akin to Hadiza's.

Hadiza puts her hands on her stomach and does not speak for as long as it takes Abeni to finish eating the sweet bun. Four bites more.

Then she lifts her head and I ask, "How did you get away?" Now I am sketching the bookcase in back of Abeni, who lowers herself off her chair, leaving her paintbrush and fish to come stand beside me, albeit at what she must consider a safe distance. I don't acknowledge her, just keep sketching.

"That evening," Hadiza continued, "I went out onto Via Domitiana as usual. I was big with child, some pig's child. An animal I will never know, have never known."

She shakes her head and looks straight at me. My eyes are question marks. "I never looked at the clients' faces. They did not deserve my acknowledgement. They were not human. Pigs and rutting rats. That is all they were. Bad-smelling, filthy pigs and rutting rats."

"But you were afraid for the baby. You wanted the baby? Even though one of the filthy pigs impregnated you?"

I can't believe my audacity. But Hadiza is unfazed. She sits upright and speaks as if in a hurry.

"You might wonder, why I did not want to rid myself of the child of such vermin."

I stop sketching a moment and scrunch my shoulders. "I admit I do wonder."

Hadiza folds her hands together, takes a breath, and continues, this time at a moderate pace. "It was not the baby's fault. It is never the baby's fault, I tell you." She speaks with confidence, certainty. "When I felt the child move in my belly, I felt like a human being, a woman, rather than a disgusting slut.

It was a good feeling, the only good feeling the whole while I prostituted."

"Jesus." I hear myself say the word and am at once embarrassed.

Hadiza laughs. "Jesus, yes. The sisters tell me Jesus wanted me to survive and be a mother to my little boy."

She is actually beaming now.

"You see, Signora Castleberry, I was sold. I was goods. I had no rights. I could make no decisions for myself about my own body. But when I knew I was carrying life, I was happy, believe it or not. My body, and only mine, was filled with life. The pig who impregnated me just spewed his sperm. He treated it like waste." She pursed her lips and made a spitting sound. "All around me were brutality and death. They try to defeat you, the *mamans* and the pimps and the clients. They hurt you at every turn. They knock life out of you and fill you with despair. But I, I, Hadiza, could grow life within me despite them."

Abeni is watching Hadiza. I hold my marker still. *You are a queen*, I want to say. *A veritable queen.*

Abeni takes the green marker from my case. She points to the sketch pad and I rip a page out for her. She takes it and returns to the other side of the table.

With her forefingers, Hadiza blots the tears under her eyes.

I try to make sense of her apologia. I wonder what Signora Sorrentino would write about it in her column. How it would sit with feminists. Pro-choice as a synonym for pro-life is an equation I'd not heard solved before Hadiza's computation. The man, or the pig, was as negligible to her as he is for women choosing to terminate their pregnancies. But Hadiza's choice was to protect the pregnancy and carry the infant to term. Her assertion. Her body. Her child's life.

Abeni is eating the green grapes. She lines them up on the table and takes them to her mouth one by one. She hums in a monotone as she chews. When there are none left, she moves on to the almonds, humming still. Hadiza and I are silent. The quiet feels right.

But the spell is soon broken when Sister Norina appears, holding Aba, who squeals when he sees his mother. Even Abeni smiles, and the baby claps his hands.

Aba goes to Hadiza's arms. She places him on the table and they play at pat-a-cake. He is a plump baby, with skin the color of chestnuts. His eyes are brown and his black hair is curly and frames his face, covering his ears.

"It is almost time to prepare dinner, Hadiza," Sister Norina says. She makes her way out of the room, but not before saying, "It has been a pleasure to meet you, Orla. I look forward to seeing you again one day, perhaps when your exhibit is ready for viewing."

"It will be my pleasure, Sister."

Hadiza nods to the nun and tells me, "I prepare the evening meal several days a week. Today is one of my days to do so."

I want to see these people again, to know them more, better.

"May I meet with you again sometime?" I ask.

Hadiza stands and, holding Aba at his waist, lets him stand also, and bounce on the table. Abeni watches and smiles when Aba looks at her.

"Yes, yes," says Hadiza. "Perhaps in Assisi."

I am standing now, as well. "Assisi? Will you be at the consortium?"

Now Hadiza takes Aba in her arms. He rests his head on her left shoulder.

"Probably. As soon as my work visa arrives—we hope by October—I will begin my new life in Assisi."

I'm thrilled to hear this.

"My family keeps an apartment there," I say. "We can see one another often. What will you do?"

Aba wants to be let down. Hadiza lowers him to the floor and he runs round and round the table. Abeni follows him, he looking behind at her, she grinning at him.

"I will be the reservations associate at a guesthouse operated by the same sisters who are here. Aba and I will have room and board, and he can attend a nursery school not too far from the basilica."

"How wonderful," I say. "I'm sure you will be missed here."

Now Aba is crawling under the table. Abeni follows suit.

"Maybe," Hadiza says. "But Sister Ilaria reminds us that her goal is to have us fully prepared to embrace as normal a life as possible after our stay here. She makes sure we learn the language, gain a skill and a work visa, and feel confident enough to make sensible decisions for ourselves."

I come around the table, leaving my sketch pad and markers for Abeni. Making sure not to step on Aba or inadvertently touch Abeni, I open my arms. Hadiza and I hug.

"I'm very grateful for your time and your sharing," I say.

"As am I for your helping us," Hadiza says. "I will walk you out."

Hadiza grabs and lifts Aba as he emerges from under the table. She holds him, and Abeni follows about a yard's length behind her. They lead me from the community room through the corridor of photographs, and to the top of the entry staircase.

"*Ciao e grazie,*" I say, and make my way down.

The three are waving when I turn to look up at them.

Chapter Seven

A Conversation with Amelia and a Trip to Conca dei Marini

I hear my friend Amelia crunching when she picks up the phone. "Salad," she says. "Sorry. I'm trying to get full on arugula and fruit. Doesn't work. I want pasta every day, and usually succumb to it by evening." It's just after six in the evening in Naples, while Amelia is lunching in Glen Cove.

I lie on the bed while we talk. "I know what you mean," I say. "I've never met a carbohydrate I didn't like."

When I tell her about my time with her cousin Carmine, she responds, "Wow, I don't know about any lover. And Carmine and I talk regularly, at least every couple of months." She pauses, then says, "Make sure you find out everything."

"Okay." I cross my legs and stare out the window where some clouds puff over Vesuvius. "I know nothing yet, except that we're going to some beach to see her. Carmine told me to bring enough clothing in case we stay the night."

"The beach?" Amelia says. "That's even more surprising than the lover. Carmine always says he is the only Italian who detests the beach." She pauses. "Although he has a reason I've never told you about. It's a family scandal that has caused Carmine tremendous sadness, not to mention an inability to commit to long-term relationships."

The clouds are moving left.

"What scandal? Can you say?"

The sound of running water is replaced by dishes clattering.

"Yes, if you promise not to bring it up with Carmine."

"Cross my heart."

I see all of Vesuvius now and sit up, cross-legged. The rose damask bedspread feels slippery-silky.

"I'm cleaning up here," Amelia says. "Bear with me. One of Hal's colleagues is coming by in a few minutes. You know how it is, centuries of alleged wisdom argue that a clean house is a fair judge of a woman's character."

I laugh. But I'm impatient to learn the Famiglietti family's secret. "Tell me while you clean."

Amelia sighs. "If Skip arrives while I'm telling you, I'll go upstairs and call you back."

"Right," I say.

"So, when Carmine was in his last year of law school, he became engaged to Elisabetta Capasso. She was studying opera. She sang at our *nonna*'s funeral in Frigento. She was diminutive in stature but grand in voice. They couldn't keep their hands off each other."

I stand and walk from the bed to one of the club chairs and back again. "And...."

"From what my father has told me, they quarreled over a wedding date."

I keep pacing.

"The same day they argued, they were to meet friends at Rocce Verdi beach, my father said. But Carmine got into a sulk and wouldn't go. Elisabetta went anyway. They parted angry."

"Oh, boy." I sit on the bed again, this time facing the club chair. "Then what?"

Amelia sighs. "Elisabetta dove off a cliff into one of the two saltwater ponds there. When she didn't emerge on the surface as one ordinarily does, two of her friends dove in after her."

"Jesus."

"They found her and dragged her up with them. But no amount of CPR brought her back. She was pronounced dead from drowning at Loreto Mare."

"How horrible!"

"For certain," Amelia says. "And of course Carmine blames himself."

I stand and pace again. "Of course."

Amelia continues, "I've never heard him mention a woman again, save for family members, colleagues, and social acquaintances."

I look at the bedside clock. "Well, thanks for telling me all this. My lips are sealed. And I'll call you back for sure after our visit is over."

The doorbell rings in Amelia's house.

"Oh, that's Skip," she says. "I've got to go."

"Understood. *Ciao* for now."

And so we are done.

What magic does this lover have that has made Carmine open to intimacy, if not commitment, again? I love solving mysteries. And we'll be far away from the Via Domitiana.

*****

The next morning, I take the winding stairway down into the Excelsior's main lobby.

Carmine greets me with a kiss on both cheeks. A grandfather clock outside the ballroom chimes ten.

"I am fortified enough to see you again, Orla."

Fortified. Jesus, I hope he's joking.

"I hope you're a little bit glad, as well." I smile a broad smile, the kind my husband calls "the American smile." Teeth showing, bottom lip a half-moon. A "Won't you be my friend?" working the room, utilitarian, democratic smile.

Carmine twirls his right hand into the air. "We shall see. Tiziana awaits our arrival. You are ready?"

I point to my bulging carryall. "Yes, ready and looking forward to meeting the woman who has your heart."

Carmine goes wide-eyed, raises his eyebrows, then turns and lifts a honey-colored leather overnight bag from the brocade settee across from the reservations desk. He looks back at me, his eyes merry now, glistening.

"My heart remains a question, Orla. My balls, most certainly."

"Carmine!"

I see Mario, the reservations clerk, smirk.

We walk outside.

"You cannot seriously be shocked by my directness, dear Orla. You, who forced me to share my car with a prostitute and gave her, a whore, your personal phone number."

"True," I say. "I just wasn't expecting it."

Carmine shrugs his shoulders. "Aha, you will get to know me better. Perhaps there are other things you will not be expecting, and not just from me."

"Well, then, this should prove an interesting two days."

"I hope so," he says.

I look around the portico's drive. "Speaking of cars, where's yours?"

Carmine motions for me to follow him across the street. "We go by boat. Tiziana always sends the boat."

"Nice."

"Yes, it saves me from the terrible weekend traffic all summer. It is very thoughtful of her."

Is she wealthy? A babe? A broad? How did they meet? Does he need to be fortified to spend time with her, too? I'm warning myself to go slow, to be a docile (I hate both the word and the characteristic) guest, to simply pay attention and learn the answers to my questions as they naturally reveal themselves.

We make our way along the *lungomare* sidewalk to the cobbled walkway to Castel dell'Ovo, and finally down to the pier.

"*Là*" says Carmine, pointing to a white motorboat with "*Gioia del Mare*" painted on its stern. The boat's skipper waves to Carmine as we approach.

"*Buon giorno*, Signora Castleberry, I am Gigi," he says, taking first my bag, then Carmine's, positing them underneath his skipper's seat. Then he offers his arm so that I remain steady for the two steps down onto the deck. He does the same for Carmine, who mutters, "I must be getting old to receive this attention." Gigi laughs but does not demur.

Gigi is a fairly common Neapolitan nickname for a man. I wonder idly whether his given name is Giovanni, Giancarlo, Virgili, or something else. We sit with our backs to the stern on cushioned leather while Gigi unmoors the boat from the pier, then stows the fenders and mooring lines. "Carmine, you know where the drinks are, should you and the signora wish any," he says.

Carmine points to a cooler stowed under the seat across from Gigi's. "May I get you something?" he says.

"Thanks, no." I answer.

"Now, we go," Gigi says.

For a few minutes Gigi takes his time navigating by and around a dozen or so other boats in the harbor. Once he does, he picks up speed so that I imagine myself a James Bond beauty escaping land-based civilization with two mysterious gentlemen for God knows where. Tino and I have been to the Amalfi Coast numerous times, mostly to Positano, but not once to Conca dei Marini. And never to someone's home, either. Always to a hotel or a yacht.

The day is luscious, luminous. Blue sky, cumulus clouds, wind that makes me forget the humid heat of Naples. My hair blows, Carmine holds onto his straw hat, and we fly, or so it seems, past monuments of rock, more than several international yachts, and many an outcropping of hotels, villas, and smaller dwellings before reaching Conca dei Marini. From time to time we are pelted with spray from boats boasting faster speeds than ours.

Carmine yells over them so I can hear him, "Gigi is on call for Tiziana all summer. She keeps him on retainer. So we can go to Ischia, if we wish, or Positano and Ravello. Tonight we will go to dine in Conca dei Marini."

"Lovely," I say, and grin into the spray. Again, I wonder at the mysterious Tiziana's means.

In just short of an hour, we arrive at a floating aluminum dock that juts out from a skyscraper-tall rock formation. The dock ends where a rectangular stone patio meets it. The patio accommodates two heavy wooden lounge chairs and an orange beach umbrella expansive enough to provide shade for both of them. The umbrella has been raised and is anchored to the patio by metal chains, as are the chairs. Does a body need chaining here, too? How windy does it get? Even now, the waves crash against rather than slap the dock. Gigi holds both of my arms tight when he lifts me from the boat. The dock rocks like a bewitched cradle and I totter as if I've had too much to drink.

Carmine manages better and runs ahead to call out to a man in red swim trunks and a short-sleeved striped shirt. "Malo!" he yells above the din of waves and wind and passing motorboats.

The man waves back. "*Benvenuto, professore!*" he calls, while he races down the stone steps as if they are a part of a practice session for an Olympic event.

It's a good thing I'm wearing dark glasses because my eyes open wide as tea cups when Malo greets me and takes my bag. A Quasimodo. That's what he is. It's not that he is hunchbacked, exactly. Rather, his left shoulder rises higher than his right so that when he walks he moves forward and back, forward and back, like a rocking horse. He's wearing sunglasses, too. When he takes them off to greet me I see that his face has been mutilated by flames or lye or some other burning substance. He has no eyebrows and the skin beneath each eye droops like two heavy bags. His cheeks are pulled tight to his ears, and matching scars on each side of his mouth tell of surgery that keeps his visage looking human, even if just barely. Malo wears a permanent mask of human tragedy. What happened to him? What does he do here?

I pretend normalcy and say, "*Buon giorno*," and "*Grazie, Malo*," as he motions for me to precede him up the steps. Panting and perspiring at the top of the stairway, I stop and see a miniature Eden before me. Lemon trees with their fruit ripe for the picking, clay urns of blue hydrangeas, rows of herbs—rosemary, basil, parsley, oregano—and a water element in the shape of a grinning frog. A round metal table, painted orange, with four chairs pillowed in a riot of florals. Several wooden lounges, and six live turtles sunning themselves just shy of the water that spills from a stone Medusa.

Malo directs us into the great room of a one-story gray stucco house, its trim turquoise.

"*Professore*, of course I have no need to show you the way," says Malo, and Carmine, removing his hat, heads off in the opposite direction from where Malo is motioning me.

"*Prego, Signora*," he says, and leads me to a tiny room painted the same turquoise as the house trim. A single brass bed is draped with a pristine linen coverlet and decorated with a variety of pillows, also covered in white linen. A chair upholstered in turquoise and white squares is tucked into a corner, with a tall reading lamp behind it. A bronzed armoire fills the wall opposite the bed. Sliding doors lead to a patio with a chair and table, painted orange. But it is the view of the sea beyond and below that beckons and makes me glad to be here. Naples feels far away. For an instant I have forgotten it.

"Donna Tiziana will arrive soon," Malo says. "In the meanwhile, make yourself comfortable. The bathroom is just outside the room to your left. Please ring the bell," he says, pointing to one on the night table beside the bed, "if you need me. I am at your service."

"*Grazie*, Malo."

He is as delightful as he is grotesque, his voice a cello as he attempts a smile.

No sooner is Malo gone and I am hanging my clothes in the armoire, than Carmine knocks on the open door to my room.

"My God, Carmine," I whisper, "what happened to him?"

Carmine speaks softly, too. "It is a sad story." I nod. "From what Tiziana has told me, Malo had been a long-time orderly at Ospedale Loreto Mare where the neighborhood boss's teenaged daughter was brought in for a burst appendix. The mother of the girl claimed Malo touched her daughter inappropriately when transferring her from the emergency stretcher to the gurney that was to take her to the operating theater. She said he caressed her daughter's breasts. The girl was just thirteen and already sedated."

"Did he? Were there witnesses?"

Carmine shifts his weight as he talks. "Who knows? Malo has sworn otherwise. Unfortunately, there were no witnesses. Only the drugged girl, her mother, and him."

I take my bathing suit from my bag, place it in a drawer in the armoire, and look back at Carmine. "So, it was a case of she says, he says. And she was the wife of one of the Camorristi."

Carmine nods his head. "Yes, her husband was Umberto Fiore. He managed money laundering in these parts. He is still alive, though in his nineties and somewhat demented, Tiziana has told me. The wife died several years ago."

I take two shifts from my carryall and hang them in the armoire. Again I face Carmine, who is standing in the middle of the doorway, now with his hands behind his back.

"And the daughter?'

Carmine smiles. "Her father saw to her financial security. She is married to the owner of shoe stores in Italy, Spain, and the United States. You may have heard of the brand, Scarpe Serie."

"Of course," I say. "Tino's mother wears them all the time."

Carmine ruffles his hair with his right hand as he speaks. "If memory serves, Signor and Signora Scarpe Serie spend the warmer months in Barcelona and the colder ones in Naples."

My flip-flops are the last to come out of my carryall. I place them beside the bed. Then I ask Carmine, "How did Malo end up here?"

Carmine folds his hands and holds them mid-waist. "Malo wanted to defend himself, so he pressed charges against the girl's brother, Attivo, who had been ordered to beat him up and ruin his face so no girl would ever want him. Tiziana defended Attivo. Of course, even before the trial, Malo was fired. Guilty or innocent, he could never work in a hospital again. He would terrify the patients."

I sit on the bed, pointing to the chair for Carmine. He sits, too.

"Then what?"

Carmine crosses his legs. "Malo looked forward to his day in court. He had never been cited for a disciplinary offence, and his superiors spoke on his behalf. That said, Tiziana's defense was that the brother's violence was justified to protect the honor of his incapacitated sister. The judge agreed, and Attivo was summarily acquitted. As Tiziana told it, the judge simply reprimanded the boy for his rash behavior, which Tiziana effectively argued was due to his youth—age sixteen at the time—and his love for his younger sister."

"Good grief," I say.

"But then," Carmine continues, "as soon as the trial was over, Tiziana hired Malo as her full-time man servant. 'Malo' is not his given name, but his self-chosen contraction of *mal occhio*, the evil eye that gazed on him."

A car pulls into the gravel drive at the side of the garden. Carmine looks toward the sound.

"So Tiziana is a legal Robin Hood?" I ask. "She earns her profits from the powerful and wealthy, then distributes some of her bounty, financial or otherwise, to those lacking influence and cash?"

Carmine stands. "Just so. A female Robin Hood. Come. Meet her and you will learn more."

We both leave my bedroom and walk to the great room. Tiziana comes in from the drive carrying two pink bags that read *"La Bella Donna."* Malo is close behind with several sacks of groceries.

"Carminuccio!" she cries, drops the bags and her car keys on the counter by the door, and pulls Carmine's face to hers. Carmine wraps his arms around her waist. I can't tell if their gestures are for show or for real.

Carmine gives her a noisy smooch, then lets go of her and says, "I have brought her to you, just as you asked. The acclaimed American artist who provokes with her brushes and zeal, as you do with your arguments and audacity."

Tiziana greets me with a quick, tight embrace. She is petite, buxom, and brunette. Even her high wedge sandals do not make her tall. A forty-ish Gina Lollobrigida lookalike. Her low-cut, cinched waist starfish-print dress accentuates her figure. And her cantaloupe-painted nails and toes remind one that is it high season on the Amalfi Coast.

"Yes, I have wanted to spend time with you since the moment Carmine said he would be introducing you to the dark side of Naples and its surrounds. I am part of it, Orla," she says while finding a paper towel to pat the back of her neck. "I told Carmine that he must bring you to me so I can initiate you into my portion of the story. Maybe you will paint that, too."

She is fanning herself now with the folded paper towel.

I waste no time. "Do you deal with the traffickers?" I ask.

Tiziana crumples the paper towel as she speaks. "Yes. I defend some of them who are careless enough to get arrested."

For a moment I am speechless. Amelia wasn't kidding when she said her cousin would help me.

"Really?"

"Really." She motions for me to sit at the table. "I argue that they will starve if they do not take jobs on the boats that carry the girls into Italian harbors. That their intention is not to traffick women and girls, but to make a living by working on a boat. I contend that they are mere pawns in a nefarious operation not their own."

My fingers are playing piano keys on the table top and I smile my American smile once more. "Do you get them off?"

She sits down across from me now, while Carmine goes to the refrigerator and retrieves a carton of grapefruit juice.

"They usually receive a fine or a suspended sentence. Then they go right back to work."

I stop my piano playing, fold my hands, and rest them on the table. "I certainly have a lot to learn from you."

Tiziana stands now, goes to a cabinet by the sink, and pulls out three glasses. "Juice?"

She is already pouring at the counter. Malo speaks not a word.

"While Carmine whiles away the afternoon reading one of his weekly Louis L'Amour novels up here, you and I can lounge down on the patio, and I can bore you into a stupor with my story," Tiziana says.

"I'm sure boredom will be the last state of mind your story will induce."

Tiziana puts our filled juice glasses on a tray she brings to the table. Carmine hands me one, then takes his in hand.

Malo has already emptied the grocery sacks and is plating an assortment of meats, cheeses, olives, peppers, and breads on a slate square. He goes to the refrigerator and takes out a bottle of white wine. He retrieves a red from a rack next to the refrigerator. In just a few moments, the table is set for four and Malo says, "Donna Tiziana, I will make the dinner reservation for nine and let Gigi know. Ristorante La Tonnarella is your preference?"

He addresses her as a great lady. Is he the only one? I'll have to take note.

"*Sì, grazie*, Malo," Tiziana says. "Enjoy the rest of the day. We will see you only as you wish during the weekend. Whether we will succeed without your care only time will tell."

Malo tries to smile again and bows. "I go to the beach now and later play cards with the old men. Some of them look worse than me."

I try not to react as Malo looks to me and shrugs his uneven shoulders.

"Take the car." Tiziana tosses him her keys.

"*Grazie mille, Donna* Tiziana," he says.

"*A mangiare!*" Carmine says. He pours the white wine. "While it is cold."

"To the weekend!" Tiziana toasts.

And so we begin.

Chapter Eight
Destinies or Choices?

"How did you two meet, anyway?"

Tiziana and I are sitting on the wooden lounge chairs, me sprayed all over with sunscreen for my fair skin, Tiziana oiled to a bronze. We drink seltzer water and air dry, each of us having taken a leap into the water. The sea feels like a wake-up call, brisk and resounding. For me the August oppression of crowded Naples has been replaced by a hyper-alertness to nature's singular power. The massive rocks rising from the sea, tides answerable to no human creature. Sun that warms until it burns. Air that refreshes unless it whips.

Just over two years ago at the annual bar association soiree in Naples." Tiziana's voice pulls me back to the present. "A fellow attorney, quite drunk, was stalking me during the cocktail hour. Despite my several blunt refusals of his attentions, he kept following me around the bar, to the patio, and so on."

"That must have been annoying."

"It was. Looking for an escape, I saw Flavia and several other women attorneys talking just outside the ladies' room. Carmine told me you have forged a working relationship with her, by the way."

I nod.

"I went over to them and made small talk for a bit. But the son of a bitch tailed me again as soon as I left the group. That's when I saw Carmine."

"Stop." I sit up straight on the lounge chair. "You know Flavia?"

Tiziana laughs like a bell tinkling. "Of course, Orla. She prosecutes those I defend. We see each other frequently in court."

"How do you get along?"

Tiziana laughs again. "We don't. We regard and respect one another as opponents in a gladiatorial contest. We each have our jobs to do. We do them and shake hands after most verdicts, like the *futballers* do after their matches. Sometimes Flavia is happy and leaves the courtroom with a bounce in her step when my clients go to prison. Other times, she is furious when they are acquitted. Then she closes her lips and strides out, not saying a word."

"Hmmm." I cross my legs and lean back in the chair again. "Sorry, I interrupted you. I will ask you more later."

Tiziana continues. "Well, back to the cocktail party. My stalker got himself another drink, then followed me to the bar table, where Carmine was sitting alone. I knew Carmine taught at the law school, but he didn't know me. I was never a student of his."

A motorboat with a dozen or so tourists passes by us. The children wave. We wave back.

"I walked right up to him and said, 'Please, pretend I'm your girlfriend.'"

I laugh, imagining the scene.

Tiziana lifts her hair off her neck and smiles. "'With pleasure,' Carmine said. He grabbed me around the waist, and kissed me full on the mouth."

"Then what?" I look to Tiziana, who appears to be reliving the moment, if her smile is any indication.

"The guy slunk away, muttering words I couldn't make out."

I finish my bottle of seltzer water. "And then?"

Tiziana lets go of her hair. "I invited Carmine to my apartment that night. We've been lovers ever since. Two of a kind."

I put the seltzer bottle in my bag so it won't blow away. "It sounds like a fairy tale, though not a traditional one."

Tiziana gets up from her lounge chair, walks to the edge of the patio, and dives in. I follow suit. She swims to the end of the dock and back several times, while I tread water and hope she'll answer the many questions I want to ask her. We stay in the water and I give it a go.

"How are you two of a kind?"

She dips her head into the water, then lifts it up and says, "Neither of us wants to marry or even live together. And certainly no children. We see each other most weekends and are content to spend a night or two in each other's apartments most weeks."

"I see. Do your families give you a hard time about your choices?"

She raises her shoulders above the water and treads. "I have only my father, failing now, and he has always understood my desire to ignore the typical expectations of women. My mother, God rest her soul, did not understand at all."

We start to paddle toward the dock.

"Let's dry off again before we go up," Tiziana says. "Ask your questions. Carmine tells me you are relentless. I like that. Just like me."

We take to the lounge chairs again.

"Okay, how did you come to be a lawyer for the Camorristi?"

Tiziana wraps a towel around her hair. "If it were not for the notorious money-launderer Umberto Fiore, I would not be an attorney at all."

Another boat of tourists is passing, this one blaring Frank Sinatra singing *"My Way."*

Tiziana becomes more animated, as if she has drunk three or four *espressi* one after the other.

"I grew up in Naples' Furcella neighborhood. The non-Neapolitans call it 'Forchella.' Go visit if you have not yet been there. My parents were the working poor, very protective of me. My mother's aunt was a nun, so they were able to send me to Catholic school free of charge. I didn't attend the government school where most of our neighbors' children went. My parents told me my father was a chauffeur and my mother was a midwife. It took me until my teenage years to realize that dad drove Umberto Fiore, and my mother was an abortionist."

"Jesus." I spray more sunscreen down my back.

"Fiore had a fleet of vehicles, one a town car, another pretending to be an appliance repair truck, and another an official-looking taxi cab. My father drove them all. One day in

June, 1980, he was driving the fake taxi and had dropped Don Umberto off at a dry cleaning establishment, no doubt a front of some sort. My father stayed outside with the meter running, as it were. Several minutes after Don Umberto had gone inside, my father told me that he watched three thugs from the rival Sforza faction get out of a car across the street and head toward the cleaners."

I nod and wait.

"He made a quick decision and ran them down. One of the men died. The other two sustained broken bones, but survived."

"My God. What happened to your father?"

Tiziana is standing now, her hands on her hips. "He pretended he had blacked out and his foot must have pressed the gas pedal. An ambulance was called. Don Umberto went to the hospital with him. The EMTs knew who he was and didn't dare prohibit him from entering the ambulance."

Tiziana throws her towel and seltzer bottles into her bag and puts on her sandals.

"My father became a hero in Don Umberto's eyes. He had saved his life. And before you knew it, he became a real chauffeur to Michele Giordano, the Archbishop of Naples."

I pack, too, and we take to the ninety-two steps, pausing now and again to converse.

"I was nineteen at the time and in nursing school. My mother's choice, not mine. Bed pans and vomit were not my ambitions. I wanted to make money, to make a life that promised pleasure instead of drudgery. I thought the legal profession could provide such a life. And, as you can see"—she waves her right arm, wand-like, from the sea up to her property —"it has."

We are halfway up the stairs.

"Don Umberto asked my father how he could reward him. My father told Don Umberto I wanted to go to law school."

At the top step, I see Carmine under a grove of lemon trees, reading.

"Don Umberto came to our apartment one night several nights after the 'accident.' He looked me over and rested his right hand on my head. 'My people and I look forward to your help after you have passed the bar.'"

We stand facing each other on the lawn, the house in back of us.

"Within a week, I received an acceptance letter to the law school at the University of Naples. I had not even filled out an application."

I shake my head.

"Carmine!" Tiziana calls out.

Carmine looks up from his book and waves.

"That's certainly influence," I say.

"And that is how I became the lawyer I am. I own this place and a terrace apartment in Naples. I do what I want. Even the mobsters obey me when I tell them how they must behave in the courtroom. How they must dress, when they must speak, and when they must be silent. I am like their nanny with a whip.

"I studied hard. I know the law well. And I perform in the courtroom as if it is a stage. I command attention and try to dazzle with my expertise. And it does not hurt that I always wear very high heels and crisp white blouses with v-necks when I stand before the judges, who are, for the most part, men." She pauses a moment, then says, "And I never smile."

Flavia must hate you, I think.

"One more question, Tiziana."

She nods.

"Why do the traffickers leave the nuns alone?"

She puts down her beach bag and folds her arms across her chest.

"It is like the Bible passage of the left and the right hands, Orla. The right hand is making the money, doing Filumena's bidding, running the business, the trafficking. The left hand is letting a few girls go to the nuns, honoring the Virgin Mary, if you will. I do the same. I represent the thugs, get paid good money for doing so, then lavish it on those the miscreants injure. Malo, for instance."

"Hmmm," I murmur. I can't think of any sensible thing to say.

Carmine gets up from his chair and comes toward us. Tiziana unfolds her arms, picks up her beach bag, and drapes its straw handle over her left shoulder.

"It costs the Camorristi nothing to do as they do," she continues. "There are always more girls, more families who have more children than they can feed. That is the reality, Orla. But there is only one Virgin Mary. All other women, those bastards believe, are born to be whores."

Carmine is nearing us. I speak softly. I don't want him to hear me.

"And Carmine," I say, what does he think of your associations?"

Tiziana's laugh tinkles again. "We do not discuss our work. It is our pact. When we are together we enjoy *il piacere di non fare niente*, the pleasure of doing nothing. We only enjoy. We are each other's refuge and escape."

I nod, not quite understanding, at least not yet.

"You had a good time?" Carmine asks.

"Yes," I say. "Tiziana has enlightened me."

She shrugs her shoulders.

"Has Orla made you tired?" he asks Tiziana.

Tiziana removes her sunglasses and looks first at me and then at him. "She has tried"—she laughs—"but not yet succeeded."

I laugh now, as well. "There's still tonight."

Carmine twirls his right hand into the air. "Mah," he mutters, and we all go in to ready ourselves for an evening of the pleasure of doing nothing.

*****

I'm dreaming, or maybe not. Phone ringing, a high-pitched vocal tone of alarm, door slamming, and tires on gravel. What's going on? I roll from my left side to lie flat in the middle of the bed. I stretch my arms upward and press my feet against the tucked-tight sheet. Listen. Listen hard. There is nothing but silence. The blackout curtains on the sliding doors are drawn, so the room is still dark. Until I sit up and look at the clock on the night table, I don't know that it's already eleven.

I yawn and stretch, then stand up. I guess it's true that recovery from a night of revelry takes longer when you're fifty. Several Negronis, a different wine with each of the three courses, and too many shots of *limoncello* after espresso with sambuca made for a velvety sleep.

En Plein Air

After the sun went down outside the La Tonnarella, strings of white lights lit the restaurant inside and out. At ten a three-piece combo set itself up by the dock and played traditional Italian music. Chairs scraped on the tile floor and emptied the tables of diners onto the sand off the deck. Strangers, families, and friends danced in circles, locking arms, clapping, singing along with the entertainers. Carmine waded into the water with a *nonna*, holding her upright as she swayed. It was already after midnight when I remember Gigi laughing as he helped me into the rowboat that took us to his motorboat and back to Tiziana's undulating dock. And, dear God, the steps again, up, it seemed, as high as the moon.

I open the curtains. The sun glares, so I avert my eyes. Off to my morning toilette in the bathroom, I'm distracted by a torn bit of paper taped on the wall next to the bedroom door.

> *"We will return as soon as possible.*
> *My housekeeper's husband has died. T."*

Good Lord, does it never end? Of course not. Don't be ridiculous. Yet, while who knows how many are right now reeling from the guy's demise, the hot water still rolls down my back and the rosemary-scented soap luxuriates. I shave my legs, towel myself in thick white comfort, rub lotion over my limbs, brush my teeth with mint paste. My night of intemperance gives way to clean contentment. Maybe it's just not my turn to suffer.

Finally, dressed in a linen shift and sandals, I phone Tino and the children. They are all with Nonna, about to get lunch and, of course, gelato. "Love you, love you, see you in Frigento!" I miss them. The touching most of all. But, then again, not right now. This new adventure has been stimulating—upsetting, yes, but exhilarating, also. Today is already Sunday.

In the kitchen I make an espresso, then another. I drink both standing up, as if I'm at a bar in town. Caffeine is a must. Huh, the double doors to the right of the coffee maker, doors which when closed I surmised led to a pantry or a laundry room, are open now, revealing a den. I walk in. White leather couch, large-screen television, fashion magazines on the glass coffee table, and a long marble-topped console table. Liquor bottles, a glass ice bucket with silver tongs, and a variety of glasses, stem and otherwise, fill the bottom shelf of the console, while its surface is covered with framed photographs. A black and white photo of Tiziana in a first communion dress and veil, posing between her parents. Another black and white one: Tiziana alone, this time blowing out ten candles on a birthday cake. A third photograph, the first of the group in color, shows her holding her law degree. Next to her, his hands behind his back, stands a man with slicked hair and a perfectly tailored pin-striped suit. Don Umberto? I follow the photos. Tiziana and Carmine sitting at a table, the background appearing to be a wedding venue. She is dressed in a yellow silk dress. Her cleavage would make a small-breasted woman envious. Carmine's curly hair contrasts with his fitted navy jacket and pressed pocket square. Magenta lipstick frames Tiziana's toothy smile. Carmine grins at her rather than at the camera. His left hand covers her right. I'm almost at the end of the console when I notice a framed map. The map looks like the letter Y. The legend on its left side reads *"Furchella,"* and a red dot, likely made with a Magic Marker, hovers over the street named *"Vico Scassacocchi."* I wonder if the dot locates Tiziana's childhood home. Finally, two more photographs draw me to them. One is of the house I'm in, a plaque to the right of the front door reading "*Gioia.*" The other is at the main door of an apartment building called "*Elegante.*" Tiziana stands in front of the door wearing a mink coat and holding a hand-printed sign. "*Sono arrivata,*" it reads. I admit I am moved.

I decide to make some sketches of the weekend. I'll paint them as miniatures and send them to Tiziana as a thank you. I'm on my way to my room to collect my sketchpad when I hear a car arrive. I hurry to the driveway.

Carmine gets out of the driver's side. Tiziana looks shaken. Her fists are clenched.

"What happened?"

"My housekeeper's husband was hit by a speeding motorcyclist right outside their apartment when he walked out to get the newspaper. When Giuseppina heard the commotion, she went outside. Carlo was already dead. Flung across the road. The cyclist did not stop. Giuseppina called here. She believes I will be able find the driver. The police came, and now her son has arrived."

We all sit at the kitchen table.

"Do you want a shot?" Carmine asks her.

"No," she says. Then, to me, "We will see if the police can find any willing witnesses or a motorcycle with some damage and blood."

"I'm so sorry, Tiziana. Why don't I have Gigi take me back to Naples?"

Tiziana smiles at me. "I like you, Orla. You are most kind, even though Carmine warned me you would be taxing."

I feign annoyance at him.

He shrugs his shoulders. "I cannot live full-time with a woman. I would have to fortify myself with too much liquor to do so."

Tiziana stands up. "And the same for me with a man." They laugh together, Tiziana's fists now open. Then, still looking at Carmine, she says, "But I hope you can spare two more days here so we can go to the funeral together. For Giuseppina."

Carmine stands, too, goes to the back of the chair and rubs her shoulders.

"Of course."

"Thank you."

She removes his hands and walks to the coffee maker. "Anyone else?"

Carmine and I shake our heads no.

"Orla, do not worry," she says, as she prepares the coffee, "Gigi will get you back to Naples by the time the sun is setting."

"No worries at all," I say. "Whatever works best for you, especially given the upsetting circumstances today."

She smiles, wistful for a short time. "Thank you. But, despite them, this afternoon we will keep to our plan. I cannot bring Carlo back to life. Gigi will escort us along the coast and we can enjoy a relaxing cruise. We will eat in Amalfi. You and I can shop a little before, if you like, while Carmine and Gigi critique us on the boat."

"Perfect."

"Gigi will be here at two."

"I will read about the cowboys for the next hour, then," Carmine says. He picks up the book near the side door and goes out to the shaded lemon grove.

"Excuse me, again, Orla. I want to phone someone who may be able to help Giuseppina and her family."

"Of course," I say, and head toward my bedroom. I'm not about to ask who that someone is.

Chapter Nine
Good-bye and Hello

"We will arrive in Frigento in one half hour," my Neapolitan driver Luigi says.

"I'll be glad to see my family."

He looks at me through the mirror and smiles.

These past two weeks have been nothing short of riveting. I've become friends with a prosecutor and a defense attorney, each the other's nemesis. Both women were introduced to me by the same man, the former's professor, the latter's lover. I've encountered crusading nuns, women they've rescued, and a child whose father, a filthy pig, will ever remain unknown. I've shared smokes with a hooker who thought only to be a hairdresser and has my phone number, unless she has discarded or lost it. I've driven through squalor and lived high on the hog. I've written thank you notes to each person who has made time for me, tried to re-frame a reporter's questions, and filled my sketchbook with first and lasting impressions. I am ready, eager to get to my New York studio and paint.

I read the note that Tiziana slipped into my pocket when she and Carmine waved good-bye to me from her dock in Conca dei Marini.

> *Dear Orla,*
>
> *It has been a pleasure to meet in the flesh the iconic painter I have read about, whose paintings I have seen only in the book of your collected works that the New Orleans Museum of Art published last year. I wish to commission a portrait of myself if you are willing to paint one. Not, mind you, the dreary type that hangs in too many legal studios and households with living or ancestral visages that nauseate. No, but one, Orla, that reveals the story I have told you. Price is irrelevant. I wish only to be seen as you envision me. And we will have the excuse to get together once more. Safe travels and happiness in New York City. Perhaps I will accept your invitation and see you next Spring in Manhattan.*
> *With affection and regard,*
> *Tiziana*

I tuck the note away and look outside. Luigi is driving us up and up, away from cities, highways, and traffic. We wind along a two-way road through farmland, past stucco homes, small shops and restaurants, a mechanic's garage, groves of chestnut trees, and long and higher vistas of mountains and sky. "Frigento," a tall sign announces to my right. My heart beats as steadily as a marcher's drum. I smile a mother's smile, then the smile my husband sees in bed each morning at waking. Anticipation delights. Fireworks, birthdays, ginger snaps, and full moons assemble in my mind. We reach the center of the town. "There they are, Luigi!" My children are playing in the park next to a church. I lower the window. "Tino!" I call out. He hears and turns toward the road. "She is here," he tells the children. "Mamma has arrive-ed."

Luigi slows the car to a stop. I leap out and run. Tino, Lu, Isa and I collide. People in the park applaud, surrounding us. They are smiling, too. I have never been here before. But make no mistake, dear reader, I feel as if at long last I've come home.

Part Two

"Skyscraper National Park"
— Kurt Vonnegut

"There are a few times in life when you leap up and the past that you'd been standing on falls away behind you, and the future you mean to land on is not yet in place, and for a moment you're suspended knowing nothing and no one, not even yourself."
— Ann Patchett

Chapter Ten
We Take Manhattan

"Are we the highest-up people in the world now?" asks Lu.

He is standing with his back to our table and looking at the panoramic view from Windows on the World. The iconic restaurant and its ancillary dining spaces, kitchens, storerooms, and break-out spaces take up floors 106 and 107 in the North Tower of the World Trade Center. I am a bit giddy with a combination of wonder and trepidation. Only in flight have I been as lifted as now. Looking out and beyond rather than down, I marvel at the architects' handiwork while smiling at our boy as he cranes his neck forward.

"Certainly some of the highest," answers Brody. He smiles back at Tino and me. He, Brody Bercik, the facility's food deliveries manager and my daughter Mercy's husband of almost two years, is our host and fellow diner. He is proud of his tower, his manner proprietary. This evening, he has shown us every nook and cranny of his domain and provided a memorable dinner, ending with baked Alaska topped with sparklers. It's Labor Day Sunday, just after eight, and we're sated with lobster bisque, grilled salmon, a mélange of fresh-dressed vegetables, hot scones, and Irish butter. We're waiting for night to fall over Manhattan and the city's lights to glitter beneath us. Tino holds Isa in his lap (How much longer will she flop into us, curving like a fetus?) and strokes her hair. She is sleepy from "so much New York," she tells him.

Brody's from Prague. He and Mercy met when she presented at a meeting about branding for Morgan Stanley almost three years ago. As Mercy told it, Brody was a welcome change from men she had dated previously. "So gentle, Mamma, the way Tino is when he touches his patients." I had smiled and felt relieved. "So different from me, too. Blonde hair to my black, optimistic to my skeptical. He sees only possibility, never loss." When he took her to meet his parents in Prague, I knew he was as smitten with her as she with him. Miloslova and Franto gifted her with a slender gold bracelet. Mercy had felt welcomed. Soon after the visit, they eloped. Just went to City Hall one October day and sealed the deal. "If we had planned a typical wedding," Mercy said by phone that very evening, "someone was bound to be disappointed and hurt. Where should we have had the wedding? In Fiesole with you, in Prague with Mamma and Pappa Bircek, in the District with my mother Thérèse, or even in New Orleans with my grandparents and Uncle Tad?"

"I know, you are right, of course," I said. I was nonetheless sad. Selfish, as usual. At any rate, they are happy and, even better, content. Brody often places his broad hand on the back of Mercy's head, and no matter how many times I've seen him do so, my beautiful wounded Mercy smiles.

We've been in New York ten days, and we have out-touristed many other visitors to the Big Apple. Tino has been here before, for several conferences and a friend's extravagant bachelor-party long weekend. And I've been a constant commuter since the age of eleven, when my paternal Tante Yvette jumpstarted my art career by garnering me a prize at the Metropolitan Museum of Art. She's gone to her eternal reward now, but her Upper West Side apartment served as my home away from home all the way through my teenage years and while I was a student at NYU. Isa and Lu have traveled some in the U. S.—to my parents' place near New Orleans, to Disney World, and to San Francisco, where Tino delivered a paper on the progress of AIDS research. They are mini-experts on Milan, Rome, Venice, and, of course, Florence, their native city. But in terms of buildings of soaring heights, nothing has prepared them for Manhattan.

Sure, Florence has its tower, and nearby San Gimignano has many. But nothing rises above the cathedral in Milan or the dome of the Vatican in Rome. Venice's wooden pilings cannot support buildings taller than six floors, and Florence's broad avenues contrast starkly with Manhattan streets as long as rivers between towering edifices of stone, steel, and glass.

Between the twenty-fourth of August and today, we've visited the Statue of Liberty and Ellis Island, the Empire State Building, the Bronx Zoo and Bronx Botanical Gardens, St. Patrick's Cathedral, Times Square, the Museum of Natural History (for the dinosaurs), and seen *Mamma Mia* on Broadway. Yesterday we took a Circle Line boat ride around the island. The children got their second taste of Chinese food — their first was in San Francisco — steamed dumplings and

General Tso's chicken in Chinatown. They're eager to gobble up hot pretzels and toasted chestnuts on the street when Fall properly arrives.

It's a good thing my year-long Chair in Societal Art comes with super nice digs and windows that block outside noise, because every night we arrive home both beat and over-stimulated. Tino tells me he is eager to go to work to relax! We'll likely take the kiddos to see our respective workplaces before school sports fill our Saturday morning calendar.

Home, by the way, is the Tav Nordqvist House on West 11th Street. It's a three-story townhouse willed to NYU by a fellow who evidently thought the university deserved it more than his son. As the NYU archivists tell the tale, in his will Norqvist left his son nothing but a written tirade of his alleged faults.

My little family certainly are the man's beneficiaries this academic year. We've got an updated open floor plan on the first floor—one long splay of a cook's kitchen, a dining table that can seat twenty, and designated areas of comfort for reading, viewing, listening, and dozing. The second floor houses two offices and two guest bedrooms either side of a full bath, while the top floor wows with a master suite/bath/tiny terrace and two other bedrooms perfect for Isa and Lu. They giggled upon seeing their shared bathroom, as it is wall-papered with giraffes munching on greenery from trees whose tops don't even appear, but are cut off at the room's formal green molding.

Tino and Isa have gotten up from the restaurant table and joined Lu and Brody at the windows overlooking Manhattan. Mercy and I are sitting next to one another, the only two left at the table. She didn't eat but a bit of her meal and excused herself twice between the salad and the dessert courses. She sips on seltzer water with lemon.

"Are you feeling okay?" I ask. "You hardly ate a thing."

She looks and me and smiles a no-teeth smile, then tilts her head.

"No and yes."

My face poses a question.

Mercy leans in to me and whispers in my ear. "I feel terrible, Mamma, but I am so happy. I'm pregnant."

I squeak with delight. "Does Thérèse know? Brody's folks? When is the baby due?"

Mercy wears a loose ikat smock that hides her entire torso. She has worn this type of dress for years as it "beats the heat," she's often said. But now, when she stands and pulls the dress fabric tight, I see that her belly has rounded. I stare at it, smile, then look up into her eyes. They glow.

"We phoned them today. They are ecstatic. We wanted to tell you all as close to 'at once' as we could. We called my mother this morning, as well. The baby is due February 15th."

"A valentine, or close to one, anyway."

"Yes," Mercy says.

I stand up now, too. It's been twelve years since Thérèse entered the picture, but I still cringe inwardly when Mercy refers to her as her mother. Again, I am a selfish bitch. The woman carried and birthed Mercy, for God's sake, then forced her onto a plane to ensure her survival. My maternity has been easy compared to hers. Jesus, half the time during Mercy's childhood I was annoyed that her activities interrupted my painting. I'm guilty of emotional neglect. A guilty artist. A "noted American artist," according to the *Encyclopedia*

Britannica and the New Orleans Museum of Art (NOMA). My ambition has cost my daughter. Probably has cost me, too. Isa and Lu have it better. My reputation established, a hands-on father, plenty of in-home help in Fiesole, Nonna living close by. Even when I am not with them, the past two weeks, for example, they feel as though I am available. I must atone for my neglect of Mercy. I must be present to her during her pregnancy, and involved in her child's life, even if that means taking time away from the studio. Can I do it, I wonder? Or will I fall short again?

"Shall we?" Mercy asks, holding a coffee spoon in her right hand.

I come to and nod, then take the spoon and clink it against my water glass. Everyone turns. Brody's face brightens and I can tell he knows I know. He hurries to stand by Mercy's side.

"Together," Mercy whispers to him. He grins and kisses her on the mouth.

"We're having a baby," they say.

Tino and the children come back to the table. Isa jumps up and down. "A baby is coming. A baby is coming." Tino walks round to Brody and Mercy. He shakes Brody's hand, pumping it several times. Then he lifts Mercy's chin, almost whispering, "I am so happy for you both."

The diners at the next table raise their wine glasses. Tino pulls me to him and we wrap our arms around the child who once was not my child and the man from Prague who loves her. Lu comes close to Mercy and looks at her stomach. She laughs, takes his hand, and holds it to her belly. He reddens and wrests his hand from hers.

"I hope it's a boy," he says. He appears to be speaking to himself. Brody and Mercy laugh. My boy reddens again. Isa spins and spins.

"I don't care either way. Just as long as I can hold it."

"This calls for champagne," Tino says, waving to a waiter.

A moment, I realize. This is a moment to revel in. Six people from four countries and three continents, an intentional if unlikely family. We are together in a place that acknowledges and celebrates the world, from its international staff to its global enterprises. Brody says the restaurant staff calls itself the "little UN." We are part of it. Together. In this moment. High up. Giddy with delight.

I sigh a lengthy sigh of gratitude. I am not worthy of this. I want to be worthy. The champagne arrives. Tino holds me close as the waiter pops the cork and fills our glasses. "To life!" Brody exclaims. Isa spins again. Lu comes closer to Mercy and lets her wrap her arm around his waist. Then, as if on the divine director's cue, the city below lights up. I am speechless with wonder. Amen.

*****

The next morning, Tino is getting ready to walk the children to school. I'm to pick them up.

Their shoes are so new they squeak across the kitchen floor. Lu decides he needs to carry the wallet Tino's mother gave him; it bulges from his back pants pocket. Isa sees no need for Nonna's woven shoulder bag gift, but ties her pigtails with red ribbons ("to set off the navy jumper and white blouse, Mamma"). Their backpacks filled with the required materials, wearing red wristbands that read "Welcome to the Saints Francis and Clare Family", they head out. I watch them go from the doorway. Our kiddos walk ahead of Tino as if to prove they know the way to their West 17th Street school.

They, especially Isa, want to be independent. There was no holding our hands during the various tours around Manhattan. Neither of them would allow it. They no longer need help with menus or buying subway tokens. Even the new school has not yet fazed them. At the welcome picnic last week, Isa was thrilled that the classroom building boasts a rooftop park with apple trees, a small herb garden, plentiful seating, swings, a sandbox, and two slides. Lu was amazed that their math teacher is a former Navy Seal. I hope the magic lasts, that any bullies are dealt with, and teachers care more about learning than walking in straight lines and shirts untucking at recess.

Tino winks back at me from the sidewalk. His briefcase, a leather one worn soft and scratched since his medical school days, bulges with files from his latest research and lecture notes for today. He wears a navy sport coat and carries his white monogramed lab coat. I hope he enjoys his visiting professorship. He has so much to offer. Mostly I pray his students learn from him not just the evolving treatments for AIDS, but also the difference between an AIDS case and a person afflicted with AIDS. Every single man I painted in my 1989 *Portraits of AIDS* exhibit has long since died.

It's wonderful that the newest drugs can keep the afflicted not only alive and functioning, but also ensure some quality of life. God bless Tino and others like him.

I walk to work, too, stopping first at a Small's Deli to pick up a corned beef sandwich on rye with plenty of grainy mustard, a

McIntosh apple, a small bag of Cape Cod potato chips, and a Diet Coke. I've been craving my college menu for several days now, and this lunch will go a long way to satisfying it. I'm dressed for college, too. Blue jeans, violet NYU windbreaker over a purple tee shirt, and tennis shoes. No socks. Sunglasses, wedding band, and a man's watch.

When Keys, the desk clerk, sees me, he struggles out of his battered captain's chair, comes around his desk, and gives me a big bear hug. He is a big man, his complexion a mix of the races and ethnicities that help compose Manhattan.

"I heard you were coming back," he says. He purr-growls like a satisfied lion.

"I'm so glad to see you again, Keys. When I visited last March you were out on medical leave, right?"

Keys points to his belly.

"Yup. A burst appendix and a whopper of an infection. But they fixed me up good. So I'm up to all my old bad habits."

He rubs his substantial belly.

"Eighteenth floor, Studio 189," he says, turning to the wooden key cabinet on the wall. "Best studio in the house, Dean Collier told me. For the best artist we got."

I take the key from him.

"Thanks, Keys."

I head toward the elevator.

"You be here all day?"

He takes a drink from one of the Gatorade bottles on his desk.

"Until three. Then I pick up my children at their school."

"Maybe I'll come up before you go. See what you got cooking this time."

The elevator door opens.

"As long as you keep it a secret." I wink at him.

He laughs, then coughs some.

"Keys keeps many secrets. You know that, Orla."

I wave and step into the elevator.

That he does. Even his real name, and Keys is not telling. NYU lore has it that a literature professor from London nicknamed him the first day he appeared to get his office key at the cabinet some two decades ago. The professor is alleged to have said, "If the Queen calls her piper Pipes, it is fitting and proper that we should call the man who manages the keys 'Keys.'" And there you have it.

When I emerge from the elevator, I'm awash with light. The top eighteenth floor is a sky-lit fantasy come true.

Earlier this morning, five-thirty or so, long before Tino and the kiddos awoke, I did my three miles on the treadmill in my office. While the daily habit certainly contributes to my physical health, it also settles my mind and piques my imagination. I knew that as soon as I entered my official studio, I would pin my Naples sketches to the wall and paint each one of them, day by day. I said their titles out loud in time to my strides on the treadmill. *"Dog Girl." "Baby Doll." "Hippo Maman." "One Saved." "Another Diminished." "Fatherless Child." "Crusading Sisters."* Then, the big one, a panorama called *"Business as Usual."* It's a landscape of cars lined up with mostly suited men stepping out of them. Their backs are to the viewer, waiting in lines of fours and sixes for young girls dressed gaudily in halter tops and short shorts. The girls are mostly black, with hair dyed hot pink and orange. One of the men grips the left arm of his pick so that she grimaces. Another follows two girls into the brush. They look barely older than my daughter. A third fellow holds a leather belt in his hand, waiting his turn. This is a still life of depravity. Factual. Orderly. The job I must complete by Thanksgiving, when Tad will fly in to write copy for the exhibit. Boy, do I miss him. Haven't seen him in person for two years.

Catching me off guard and interrupting the steady pulse of my treadmill walk, however, were two pictures that kept surfacing. The first was of the prosecution and the defense lawyers, Flavia and Tiziana. I kept seeing a match between them, more consequential than a tennis match, but less deadly than a duel. The painting will be a courtroom scene. Then, the portrait of herself that Tiziana requested. It was going to be big, a mural, really, to match her personality and her realized dream. When that one came to mind, I upped the speed on the treadmill and ended my hour panting. I could barely contain my desire to get to my new studio and start painting.

After a shower and tending to the children's breakfasts, I was ready for the first-day-of school sendoff. I'd even snuck a schmaltzy note into Tino's briefcase. You know, he saves them all. How lucky am I?

In less than an hour, my sketches are hung, four easels are set, three of the same size, one suitable for larger canvases. Even though it's only ten-thirty, I devour my deli delights, then set to work. *"Dog Girl"* is first. I weep as I paint, aching for her, hating the men she services and the System that manages trafficking like the multi-national enterprise it is. I strive for excellent execution, detailed and precise. I want viewers to see and gasp. Perhaps to turn away a moment, then to look back in disbelief and disgust. To stare. To understand the inhumanity. And then, do what? Support the sisters, I guess. Be generous to those few hundreds of women who consider futility an affront to their faith. The same with the prosecutors. Worldly saints they are, risking their lives like the nuns. My art is a meager protest by comparison. Then again, as I've already learned, the Camorristi consider protest an act of war. I must keep my family out of the line of fire. But be sure, dear reader, I'll relish painting the rat they sent me. Maybe Tiziana will give me an address to mail it to. To return the favor, so to speak. So there.

Chapter Eleven
Tad Phones

Dinner is uproarious. Lu and Isa cannot stop talking about their day. The 100-year-old nun in a wheelchair who led them parade-like to and from the cafeteria. "She waves a red flag with a print of our school on it," Isa reports. "Her name is Sister Aloise." The patio they're going to build in math class with the teacher everyone calls Seal from his Navy Seal days. "A real one," Lu insists. "For the wheelchair nun and another even older one we didn't meet yet." They stuck tiny stars onto a world map to denote the countries where they have lived, where their ancestors came from, where they would like to visit. "Miss Kippley said the starred places will become our humanities text," Lu tells us all this, having stopped eating for maybe thirty seconds to do so. "And lunch," Isa giggles. "It was grilled cheese sandwiches shaped like cows. "Afterwards we square-danced in the gymnasium."

Tino and I look across the table at each other. So far so good. "I will wait until another time to describe-a my day." He grins. "Maybe tomorrow night will be my turn to talk."

I can't help but laugh. He is the acclaimed AIDS guru from Florence, a top doc — except in his own home. Here he is Babbo or Daddy, depending on whether the children are speaking Italian or English. The mender of broken objects and voice of calm. Poached egg chef. Fixer of all ills.

The kiddos ignore us. They are trying to decide if they should avoid each other in class or stick together as usual. We don't intervene or interject. Who knows if there's a right way to be twins? Let them figure that one out. No one at the school has broached the topic. And, frankly, there doesn't seem to be a need to commit psychology right now.

There is no lollygagging in the process of going to bed. Both of them are exhausted. It's almost nine when Tino and I, alone at last, pour sambuco into our *espressi*, lounge on the loveseats either side of the coffee table, and take a breather. We don't speak. Only after the grandfather clock chimes the quarter hour does Tino come sit next to me. Arm around my shoulder, he says, "Tad phone-ed me today. It is not good news. His HIV has develop-ed into AIDS."

For a few minutes I remain still and silent. Only the voice in my head speaks. *It has finally happened,* it says. As we knew it would. As it must. The unfolding of consequences over time. Luke's infidelities back in 1989 New Orleans. I hear Luke's voice, telling me: "I was feeling old. I wanted novelty. Tad was happy as we were. Stable. Habitual. Domestic. But even he, younger than me by a decade, was sprouting gray hairs. So I found a boy. Several, actually." How I had hated Luke when he said those words. The man who had stolen my adolescent crush and dreamed of husband. The very same man who had orchestrated my artistic career and, to be honest, lucrative celebrity.

Tad's forgiveness and insistent love had been gorgeous and ghastly. "I will not abandon him. Foolish or not, I will never discard him." Luke's inevitable death occurred just after Tino and I married. Was his fatal fall off the cliff near our home in Fiesole accidental or not? We say it was, out loud. In silence, I am not so sure. Now Tad has inherited his beloved's doom.

I finally look Tino in the face.

"How? When?"

Tino stands up. "Another?" he asks, and reaches for my demitasse cup.

I nod.

"Me, too," he says, and walks to the kitchen.

I follow him. While the espresso machine hisses its steam, he tells me.

"He presented at a conference in Mexico City several weeks ago about the difficulties of unaccompanied migrant Mexican children and their adoption by United States citizens, even if the children have not actually been determined orphans." He pours the coffee into our cups. "He stay-ed in the city for several days and ate mostly at upscale places with the lawyerly and academic crowds. But, he told me, he also indulge-ed in a glut of street food before returning to New Orleans." Tino pours too much sambuco into my cup. "He took violently ill on the plane, diarrhea and vomiting, and was sent by ambulance to hospital immediately upon landing." I take a sip. My lips sting. "Salmonella it was, just the opportunistic infection to compromise his long-tested immune system. Despite his eight rather fortunate years on merciless AZT and four more on

Combivir." Tino murmurs the drugs' names again as if an afterthought.

I exhale a long breath, puffing my cheeks.

"Is he going to die?"

Tino sits down at the table.

"Not if I have anything to do with it. At least not from AIDS."

I smile at my husband, the man who after two decades of practice still considers every patient's death a personal failure. A tough stance to endure with those suffering from a disease that, without vigorous intervention, is a death sentence, a gruesome one.

The clock chimes ten. I go into the front foyer for my mobile. I keep it on the hall table in a square basket with keys, wallet, and sunglasses. My "don't forget" basket.

"I've got to call him. Is he in the hospital? Did you tell him to come to us right away?"

The news and the coffee are kicking in. I turn frantic, a moth ricocheting against a porch light. I pace from stove to refrigerator, from table to stove. Tino stops me and wraps his arms around my waist.

"A moment, please, *Cara*," he says, speaking to me as if I, too, am one of his patients. "Tad told me he would phone you tonight after he shares the news with his father. He was released from the hospital this morning and is seeing his parents tonight."

"Mamma, Babbo."

It's Isa walking down the stairs in her pajamas, crying. We go to her.

"Sister Aloise. She fell off the roof in her wheelchair and she died."

I pull her close and rub her head.

"You must have had a dream," Tino says. "No one is able to fall off the roof at your school." He speaks with certainty.

She pulls away from me and looks to her father. "For real?"

He takes her by the hand and walks her back up the stairs. Isa allows herself to be led. "You remember, don't you, that there is a very tall protective barrier all around the rooftop? It is very strong, very secure. I try-ed to push against it myself and it would not budge. Sister Aloise cannot fall off, nor will anyone else."

"Okay," she sniffles.

So much for an easy transition. I shrug and sigh, then take to the reading chair by the fireplace. Curling my legs under me, I wait for Tad to call. His poor father. He sure as hell doesn't need more bad news. Mrs. Charbonneau is almost completely hobbled with Parkinson's and in the last year has developed dementia besides. And although he has round-the-clock care for his wife in their home, Mr. Charbonneau spends the better part of each day with her. Tad commutes from the city to St. Suplice at least three times a week to spell his father—takes him out for supper and a stroll or over to the cottage on the Chartres River he and Luke bought together as a getaway from New Orleans. It will take all of Mr. Charbonneau's considerable fortitude not to despair when Tad tells him his news.

Tino returns. "She fell right to sleep after putting on the school wristband and saying a Hail Mary for Sister Aloise's safety." He sits on the chair the other side of the fireplace. "I appreciate that she is a sensitive child, Orla. But I hope not too sensitive. Life will be so much more difficult if...." My phone rings.

"Tad!"

My heart thumps.

"Orla, hello. Hello."

I love to hear his voice. He skips a prelude and starts right in.

"Helluva trouble, as I assumeTino has told you."

"Certainly is." I uncurl my legs and sit up straight in the chair. "Where are you?"

"At the cottage with a glass of scotch, straight up."

I find myself laughing, an appropriate response or not.

"Cheers. Is your father with you?"

"No, I just brought him back to their place. My mother no longer recognizes me."

"Jesus, Tad, I'm sorry." I am pacing now.

"She thinks I'm my father."

Tino takes to the kitchen and empties the dishwasher.

"And your father?"

"She thinks he's *her* father."

I stop at the fireplace and run my hand along the oak mantle. It isn't dusty.

"At least she won't have to know anything. That's some sort of blessing, right?"

"Yes, definitely." I look up at the ceiling and see a spider web in the brass chandelier. "What have you decided to do?"

Tad laughs now, a genuine chuckle. Not a hint of the sardonic. "You are suggesting that I remain in full charge of my future, Orla?"

I go back to the reading chair. "Certainly. Of course." I pause. "You have to be."

My voice slips to a quiver. It mustn't, I tell myself. I mustn't let it.

"Funny, that's what Tino told me. He said I could stay in New Orleans, where my care is better-than-average. Or, alternately, I might come to New York. He suggests he can connect me to a coterie of experts who will offer me more pharmaceutical options than my doctors down here. Perhaps even include me in a clinical trial or two."

I sit up straight again.

"Always a lawyer. Your life nothing but trials."

"Ha ha."

I wave at Tino.

"Then come, come right away!"

Tino nods, then hangs the dishtowel on the oven handle.

"I worry about my parents."

I slip my sandals off and on, off and on.

"Of course."

Tad clears his throat several times. "But Dad tells me to go ahead. In fact, he is adamant that I take Tino up on his offer. I told Tino I would let him know by Friday."

I stand up and walk to the kitchen. Tino is putting the leftover salmon and rice into a container.

"Tino's right here. You can tell him now."

Tad laughs again. Then there is, at least for me, an uncomfortable silence.

"You know I love you, Orla."

I sigh, and tears moisten my eyes. "Always have, dearest friend. And I, you."

"Yes," he says. "Certainly. I am sure of that."

I hand the phone to Tad, grab a wad of tissues near the refrigerator, and blow my nose, then head to the half-bath off the foyer where I stifle a sob. I cannot imagine not hearing Tad's voice.

Soon after, Tino finds me and hands back my phone. He and Tad have signed off.

"He will arrive Sunday morning if he can secure a flight."

I throw my arms around Tino.

"Thank you."

He kisses me hard on the lips. "Come to bed with me."

I don't feel like making love right now. But Tino has told me many times, "When death hovers at my work, I want to defy it, to kill it. You, you and the children, bring me back to life. You make me forget death for a little while."

I sigh again, think of several women acquaintances who say they've become invisible and undesirable to their men who used to covet them. Tino still lights up when he sees me, menopause and its annoyances be damned. And, besides, how can I refuse him? Seriously, how? I walk around turning off the lights. Then I go to meet him at the stairs.

Chapter Twelve
Sunday at Home

Thursday and Friday I paint as if my days are numbered. Three of the Via Domitiana paintings are done. As a reward to myself before leaving the studio Friday, I sketch out Tiziana's portrait on a twenty-four by thirty-six parchment. I feel electric as I imagine her emerging in vivid colors—yellows and purples, perhaps—from a background of gritty gray Furchella. She'll be sexy and strong, gams to stare at, eyes ablaze, red carpet glam. I'm eager to paint her, but won't until the conference work is completed. Just before Mercy's baby arrives shall be my goal.

The kids are damp when I meet them, having just run races around the gymnasium. Uniforms stuffed into their backpacks, wearing shorts and tee-shirts with the school logo on the back, they guzzle water when we arrive home.

"May we have Chinese tonight?" asks Isa.

"Good idea," Lu concurs.

Easy, I think, and leave Tino a message asking for his ETA. Seven o'clock it is, then. And The Dragon will deliver.

Saturday, I cancel the Merry Maids. I need to move, and doing the cleaning myself gives me an excuse. You would think I was preparing for the Second Coming.

Tino says to the children, "Let's go to South Street Seaport and let Mamma be."

To be honest, I'm glad they've left me alone. I scrub the guest bathroom, mop the kitchen floor. Iron just-washed dishtowels. Plump pillows on the sofas and chairs. By the time my family returns, the house looks impeccable. The larger guest room smells like eucalyptus, with new sheets on the bed and hospital corners snug.

After five o'clock Mass at the church affiliated with the kiddos' school, we pick up grinders at Carlo's Best Grinders, watch *Gladiator,* and go to bed early.

Come morning, I lay out bagels, muffins, butter, cream cheese, and jellies, brew a large pot of American coffee, then bake an apple pie, and make a Sunday sauce. Either the coffee or the sauce brings Tino downstairs. The children join us after much clumping around upstairs. The simmering sauce smells of garlic and fresh basil. Isa wants to prepare tonight's salad. "Caesar," she decides, "like that emperor who got stabbed to death."

"How long do you think Tad will stay?" I ask Tino.

Lu is putting the cold items back into the refrigerator while Isa loads the dishwasher. Then they scramble upstairs, Lu carrying the Monopoly box with him.

Tino is typing a lecture on his computer by the fireplace. He doesn't look up.

"If you maintain the five-star quality you have so expertly achieve-ed yesterday and today, I doubt he will ever want to leave. I know I would not."

I put my hands on my hips and feign annoyance. He looks at me and smiles.

"I'm going to shower and make myself presentable," I say. "And, by the way, why have the children gone back upstairs?"

"They are hiding from you. I told them they should."

Again, Tino keeps his eyes on the computer keyboard, fingers tapping. But his grin betrays him. "Lu told me he was afraid you would make him change from his jeans and rugby shirt into a shirt and tie. Isa said he should. I understand she plans to let her Uncle Tad know she is not a little girl anymore."

"Well, I'm just going to get rid of the flour under my fingernails and the tomato sauce on my shirt. I'll make quick work of my toilette. Tad should be here by one or so."

Tino waves me off.

I shower in water as hot as I can take, relishing the resulting steam, not making quick work of my toilette at all.

How will Tad look, I wonder? And how will Lu and Isa respond if he's changed drastically? They know he has an infectious disease called AIDS. They know that their father has become expert at treating patients who suffer from it. That's why the friend they consider their uncle is coming to New York. But they don't yet know the whole of Tad's story. They never even met Luke. He'd already been dead two years before they were born.

"All in its own time," Tino reminds me. "Just as you and I discover-ed our pasts, they will know when they need to know and when they can understand more than the bare facts."

The doorbell rings just as I'm putting on lipstick. I'm wearing camel slacks, a collared mustard shirt, and the softest leather loafers I own. A spritz of perfume. Gold hoop earrings, diamond tenth-anniversary wedding band. The usual ceramic bangle. I fluff my hair and hurry down the stairs.

The children are hugging Tad. He stoops to nuzzle the tops of their heads. Tino has taken his weekender bag and put it under the foyer table out of the way. A shopping bag, too.

When the kiddos let go, Tad points to the shopping bag. "Go ahead," he says to Lu, and Lu lifts from it a wrapped box of Godiva chocolates, a crusty baguette, and a box of macaroons. "My favorite!"

Tad reaches into the right pocket of his navy blazer and pulls out a small square box for Isa.

"May I open it?" She looks up at him.

"Please do." He puts his hands behind his back.

It is a thin silver bangle with a small heart attached.

"Ooh, thank you, Uncle Tad."

She slips it on her left wrist. Tad winks at her.

I watch with pleasure. It's as if nothing has changed. But, surely, Tad has. Never overweight, always lanky, he is now just too thin. His skin appears stretched across his face. And he sports more gray hair than brown. That's not illness, I remind myself. He's fifty-one, for God's sake.

"Orla." He opens his arms wide.

I wrap my arms around him, feel his ribs against my chest. I blink three times to hold back tears. I feel the children's eyes.

"He was my very first friend," I told them before they went out yesterday. "And my very best friend, as well."

"Even a better friend than Daddy?" Isa had asked.

"A different kind of friend. We shared our childhoods. Daddy's my one true love. And you two are the results of that love."

That was too much for Lu. "You sound like it's Valentine's Day, Mamma."

Isa giggled. "Sometimes, I see you and Daddy kiss," she whispered.

"Good." I smiled. "Happily married people kiss a lot. Maybe someday you'll do that, too."

And then they'd scampered towards the door where their father waited for them.

Tino clears his throat. "We are all happy to see you, Tad. Come, I will show you your room and bath." He picks up Tad's weekender bag and motions him toward the stairs.

They're gone for more than half an hour. I know Tino is as much doctor now as he is friend.

"Why are they taking so long?" Isa asks.

We are setting the table for five.

"Daddy's examining Uncle Tad. He needs to know how to proceed tomorrow at the hospital."

"Oh."

The two of them stay quiet on the floor near the coffee table. Lu studies the sports section of the *Times* while Isa returns to her copy of *The Lion, the Witch, and the Wardrobe*.

It's almost four when I put water on the burner to boil. My phone rings.

"Mamma," Mercy says, "are you home?"

"Yes, and Uncle Tad's here, as well. Where are you?"

She chuckles, "Just around the corner. May we come by?"

I open the pantry door and take out not one, but two pounds of spaghetti.

"Of course. Stay for dinner. It'll be ready in fifteen minutes or so."

She relays the message to Brody. "Alright, we'll be right over."

I set two more places at the table. Even before the water boils, they knock and walk in. Brody is carrying a bottle of champagne. Tino and Tad return. Handshakes and hugs all around once more.

Tino sees the bottle and gets some flutes from a cabinet. I ease the pasta into the boiling water.

"Are you having twins?" I ask.

"No, Mamma," Mercy says, laughing.

"But we are having a house," says Brody. "We just bought one in Fort Lee, New Jersey. With the in-law apartment for when my parents and Thérèse visit."

"Wonderful!" I say.

"We will be able to move in before the holidays, so the nursery will be ready before our baby arrives," Brody continues.

Mercy beams while Tino pops the cork. He even pours a bit of the bubbly for Isa and Lu.

"Congratulations! *Auguri!*"

We sit at table for well over an hour, from pasta to roast chicken, Isa's Caesar salad and Tad's baguette, plenty of wine, macaroons, apple pie a la mode, and too much espresso. And planning, lots of planning. What color will the nursery be? Have you selected any names for the child? How long is maternity leave? We would like to provide you with a housecleaning service for the first two months after baby is born. And so on....

Tad puts his hand over mine. He takes in the rectangular table. Tino at one end, me at the other. He to the left of me, then Isa and Lu. On the other side, Mercy and Brody, and the little one we will soon come to know. "Thank you, Orla. Tino. Everyone." He wipes his mouth with the cloth napkin Isa had folded just so. "This feels like old times. Remember, Orla, at the big house in New Orleans, before the troubles?"

"Yes." I nod. "It feels like that."

Tino raises his half-full wine glass. Brody, as well. Mercy's eyes tear, and Lu and Isa are silent. I wonder what each of them is thinking.

I know what Tad means. People who care about each other at the table. Sharing themselves without pretense. Enjoying the food and drink. Thankful is how I feel. Hopeful, too. As if nothing can possibly go wrong.

Chapter Thirteen
Oh, What a Beautiful Morning!

That's what I'm humming when I step outside. The sky is clear blue, the air crisp and dry. Manhattan feels clean. I slip into the moving mass of others walking to work. We are a motley crew, each of us solitary and aware, moving at a pace determined by some unspoken, intuitive agreement. I am comfortable in a cotton tee shirt, my usual NYU windbreaker, jeans, and paint-splattered sneakers. I'd rather go to the beach than the studio today. Maybe when I pick up the children we'll walk down to the seaport and enjoy the breeze.

As he did yesterday, Tad will join Tino today at Langone. Tino has set him up with a colleague who may prescribe the newest cocktail of AIDS drugs. In the meanwhile, Tino asks that I help Tad gain some weight back, and also make sure not to keep the both of us up too late every evening talking. Perhaps take a walk around the block each night after supper, then go to bed before ten.

We're happy that Mercy and Brody will have a place large enough to settle in well before the baby arrives. Thérèse plans to spend at least a month tending to her daughter and grandchild. Brody says his parents would like to spend July and August with them. And I'm hoping Mercy will allow me to spoil the child some. I'm going to ask her if I might paint a mural of whatever theme she chooses for the nursery.

Keys greets me with the news that he needs cataract surgery, but is going to put it off until his retirement, come next January. "As long as you can see the keys," I tease. Today I'm going to paint the scenes from Casa di Dignità. But first I need more coffee. I should have put some from home into a thermos. Oh, well, another chance to enjoy the pleasant weather if I take a trip to the deli. I might as well pick up a tuna on rye with lettuce and tomato for lunch. No chips, though. I'll save myself for ice cream with the children after school. Because my satchel is extra full and bulky today, I'll get rid of it upstairs first, then travel light. I've promised rolls of felt and thick ribbons to the parents' organization at the school. Evidently the stay-at-home moms or dads are in charge of seasonal décor throughout the building. When the kiddos handed me a wish list of "needed items" last night, I decided to divest myself of some fabric I picked up the other day to use for holiday décor myself. I should have sent the stuff with them this morning. But, whatever the reason, I'm clocking slower than usual today. Not quite on my game. Perhaps it is a combination of factors—our move here, new locations and schedules for the four of us, news of the baby coming, and then, of course, Tad. Not to mention my two weeks in Naples with the kicker in Frigento. A large coffee, it must be, then. Black with lots of sugar.

My studio is bathed in gorgeous brightness. I plunk the carryall on my desk, then reach in to take only my wallet and phone with me. My sunglasses are already on my head. If I'm being honest, I purposely walked right past the deli only so I could venture out again. It's a playing hooky kind of day. But I need to be fully focused by nine-thirty, and it's already eight-thirty-five.

"Leaving so soon?" Keys asks.

I laugh and hand him my key. "I want to be outside again. May I get you anything at the deli?"

"I'm all set, Orla." He points to a half-eaten bagel. "You coming right back?"

I check my pockets to be sure I have my mobile and wallet.

"Yes, sir. I've got a lot of pictures to paint. See you in a few."

It's less than a two-minute walk. I'm sixth in line. The small television on the shelf behind and above the meats and cheeses display case features *The Today Show*. Katie Couric and Matt Lauer are bantering about something I don't pay attention to, then break for a commercial. The TV is always on here, a sort of steady white noise that offsets the live chatter. When I first came to Manhattan from tiny St. Suplice in 1969, I fell in love with the syncopated racket of people placing orders, the cash register's dings, accented voices from around the world, variations of, "no mustard," "lots of mayo," "thanks," and "have a good day" filling my ears. Today the deli's double doors are open, no air-conditioning needed, so car, bus, and truck traffic join the metropolitan cacophony.

A humming sound superimposes itself over the usual mix. It seems distant at first, then comes closer and closer, causing a vibration. The four hanging lights over the deli counter sway and the chatter stops. The ground traffic sounds become indistinct, negligible. Something overpowers it—the hum, a steady humming, getting closer and closer, then resounding, loud and louder. Several of us step outside and look up. A thundering jet it is flying low, too low, oh, so low. We can read the name on the plane. American. Our necks stretch to follow the plane. Our eyes move in synchrony. I am thinking, the plane shouldn't be this low, this close. I must be imagining. Suddenly, something happens that makes no sense. There are new, big, undeniable sounds. A boom, a crash, a severing all at once. Orange flames, then big black spheres of roiling wreckage followed by cumulous clouds of thick gray smoke rising upward and outward both. Debris smashing. Hunks of metal and glass. Papers flying, then floating, floating down like mutilated petals. A smell—electric, plastic, acrid, stinging—makes us cover our noses and mouths. We stand and stare.

"Jesus!" Mo, the manager, shouts to no one and everyone. I look in to him. "They say a plane just crashed into the North Tower of World Trade." He points to the television and raises the volume.

Brody's building. Dear God. I make the sign of the cross and go back inside, pay attention now to Katie and Matt as they watch a tape of what just happened. They talk to a viewer who has called in. A woman. The three of them assume it was an accident. The North Tower, they say. So it's true. I grab my phone, call Mercy. He's got to get out of there. I've got to make her leave her building, the South Tower, too. Both of them. The baby. No answer. No answer. I leave a message. "It's Mamma, Mercy. I see what just happened. Leave, please leave your building and come to the house. We'll wait for Brody there. Call him and tell him you'll be there. Call me when you get out. Please."

My chest is pounding. I call the Saints Francis and Clare school. The line is busy. Obviously. I'll try again in a few minutes. Business has stopped in the deli. Several people leave, one woman in green surgical garb running south toward the Towers, screaming, "Billy!" A second person, frail and using a cane, looks both ways, then crosses the street and climbs the steps to the front door of a townhouse. A beanpole of a man in a fitted suit and wearing full make up turns away from the counter, says "Shit," and hails a cab headed north. The rest of us stand there and stare at the TV. It has become our oracle. The call-in woman is still on the phone. The co-hosts are awaiting updates. The plane hit at 8:46, they say. We watch the tape re-play, re-play, re-play. The hosts touch their ear pieces from time to time. I wonder who is feeding them news and whether the news is correct or just speculation. Then we hear it again, the same sounds as before. Slow motion now. It can't be, but it is. *Lord have mercy.* I look at the time on my watch: 9:03. Another hit! The South Tower, the TV announces.

"Mercy!" I scream. Everyone stares. "My daughter. She's there. She's pregnant."

"Jesus Christ," Mo says.

I try her phone again. Not even a ring tone. All I hear are sirens. Cabs pull up over the curbs on both sides of the street. Fire trucks, ambulances, police cars speed through. Pedestrians stare, cover their mouths with their hands. Some weep. Others hurry away, turning from the catastrophe, heading north as fast as they can.

"America is under attack," a newscaster announces.

Get a grip. Get a grip, I tell myself.

They'll know to get out. They'll get out. And the twins. I'll go to them now. Don't bother phoning again. I'll just go.

My phone rings.

"Mercy?"

"Good," Tino says. "You answer-ed."

"Do you think they'll get out of there? Can they get out of there?" I don't care about anything else but my children.

"I think they are getting out right now, *Cara*." He is speaking the way he does to a frantic patient. "You remember, Mercy told us her office practices evacuation once a month. By the roof or by the stairs, they will know what to do."

I'm standing on the sidewalk now blocking one ear, listening with the other. The air is filling with damp, gritty mist.

"I'm going to get Isa and Lu and bring them home."

"Good. Yes. Do that."

"Will you come home, too?"

"No. None of us can leave. We must wait for the casualties in the ER."

"And Tad?"

"I will send him back. You and he will manage. *Cara*, I know you can manage."

"Tino, what if Mercy...?" I'm sobbing.

"You must not think about that, *Cara*. You are strong. Go get our children."

"Yes."

I walk fast. I want to be a robot, to not feel anything. But all I imagine are Mercy and Brody twisting and turning inside two balls of black fire. Mercy covering her belly with her hands. Brody reaching out his arms, but they fall off, charred. My eyes drip stinging tears. It is unpleasant to breathe. The sun is gone.

It looks like dusk, but not a pretty dusk. No pink anywhere. Instead, gauzy gray. It is raining soot. I get closer to the school. A barefoot woman covered in gray-white soot walks past me. She looks like a walking mummy. She carries a briefcase in one hand, her heels in another. Her suit fits her perfectly. I nod at her. She nods back. I think of Ascot, of Audrey Hepburn, and the rain in Spain. Both of us so correct. Holding onto propriety in the midst of chaos. Jesus, I've lost it. Two men, both sweating profusely, drag a third man between them. All three wear business suits, sooty, as well. One man's glasses are cracked. The other man has bitten his lip and it bleeds. The man in the middle is open-mouthed and his eyes are closed tight. His chest heaves. The sirens do not stop.

As I near the school, I see several people leaving with their children. The first, a woman, puts three children of assorted sizes, a boy and two girls, into a cab that appears to have been waiting. The second, who looks to be a grandfather, takes a small girl by the hand and hurries her across the street from the school. He covers her nose and mouth with his free hand. When I reach the entrance, I try and gather myself. Be a confident mother. But I can't even open the door. It's locked. I ring the bell on the brick wall to the right of it. The principal, Dr. Desjarlais, lets me in and locks the door again. She looks at me as if I'm deranged. I might as well be. She touches my right shoulder.

"Mrs. Bacci, the children are safe. They are all in the gymnasium having a 'surprise' game day. We've told them that there has been a plane crash and that helpers are tending to the wounded. That's it."

I fail to hold back my tears.

"My older daughter and her husband work in the Towers, he in the North, she in the South. She doesn't answer her phone. She's pregnant."

I'm shaking. I don't have to be controlled here. Someone else is in charge.

"Come," Dr. Desjarlais says, and leads me to her office. She sends her secretary to the door when the bell rings again. "Use my restroom while I go get Isa and Lu."

I fling cold water on my face. My sunglasses slip off my head. Their lenses shatter when they hit the tile floor. I pick up the shards and fling them and the frames into the trash.

"Mamma!" Isa is happy to see me. Then she says, "You're crying."

"Yes," I say. "I'm feeling bad for the people in the accident."

Lu comes close. "Did you see it, the crash?" he asks. "Is Daddy helping?"

"Yes. He called. He's helping in the ER, just like at home."

Dr. Desjarlais intervenes. "You may go home early today," she tells them, just as Mr. Delaney, the father of Isa's friend Poppie, follows the secretary in. "I'll let you know our school plans for tomorrow in an email."

"Thanks, Dr. Dejarlais," we say. Like a Greek chorus in a play. Would this were a play.

"I'm glad you were able to get here, Mr. Delaney. Have a seat while I get Poppie."

"Rough day," Mr. Delaney says to me.

"Can't remember rougher." It's the God's honest truth.

Dr. Desjarlais leads us out. She squeezes my shoulder. "I'll be praying."

I nod. "Thank you."

Chapter Fourteen
Arrivals and Departures

Leaving school, at first the children are excited to be getting out early. It's just about ten o'clock.

"It smells bad." Isa says. "Like a fire that's not a cookout." She hands me her book bag and covers her nose and mouth with both hands.

"And it's too dark for morning," Lu says. He looks skyward.

They both go silent when they see the distorted faces and diminished conditions of many other pedestrians, most notably those walking north. Mummies all. Some wordless, others crying, one gentleman calling to Jesus out loud.

"Come on," I say in my most authoritative voice. "Let's get home."

They still think I'm reliable. I've got to let them think that.

All of a sudden, Lu stops walking and asks, "Did Mercy and Brody get out when the fire alarm went off?"

I stop a moment and pray for strength. Isa removes her hands from her face and clasps them together like she does during Mass.

"I'm sure they did what they were supposed to. They'll let us know they're fine as soon as they can. I left a message for Mercy to get in touch and to meet us at the house. So let's keep going."

We pass an electronics store. Several televisions have been turned on facing the street. Each one replays the planes crashing, one, then two. A throng of people stand and watch. There is no chatter. Though we pause, I don't let us remain.

"Come on now, Uncle Tad will be coming back, too. That's what Daddy told me. And I want to be there when Mercy and Brody call."

Am I wrong to say that? Should I prepare them for the worst even if I can't prepare myself? Just the fact of the twins' physical presence makes me want to believe in a happy ending.

"I hope they walked down the stairs," Isa says, "even though it's a long way. Daddy told me never to get into an elevator when there's a fire.

"Daddy's right, and I'm sure they took the stairs."

I see the house. A cab stops in front of it. Tad gets out.

Lu runs ahead. It's a good thing Tad's here. I've forgotten my house key in the studio. Keys must wonder what's become of me.

Tad waves to us, goes up the steps with Lu and unlocks the door. He reverses his steps to walk toward Isa and me.

"May I go ahead?" asks Isa, right after Tad ruffles her hair.

I let go her hand. "Sure."

She runs toward the house.

As soon as her back is to me, I fall into Tad's arms.

"I can't reach them. Either of them. Brody might have gone to the roof. A helicopter could reach him there. And Mercy and the baby...."

Tad lifts my chin and looks down at me. "Come inside and I'll fill you in on what has transpired in the last hour or so."

"Oh, no, Tad. There's more?"

The children are already upstairs.

"Wait," I say to Tad, raising my arm like a traffic cop. I holler up the stairs. "What are you two doing up there?"

"We're going to play Monopoly, Mamma."

I walk toward the television. I raise my voice again. "Good idea!" Then I turn on the TV. Tad comes right after me and lowers the volume. By the time he tells me about the attack on the Pentagon and the crash of a fourth plane into a field in Shanksville, Pennsylvania, I am sure the end of the world is near. Who are the hijackers? Helluva bunch of planners. I dial Mercy's number again. Nothing.

Tad raises the volume on the TV. We both sit and stare at the screen. A voice tells us we are watching the North Tower crumble and fall, the South Tower having done so some minutes earlier. The scene switches to street after street near what used to be the financial capital of the world. People are crying, covering their eyes. Police cars and ambulances are on fire. The FDNY chaplain, a "Father Mychal Judge," the announcer says, "is being carried out of the rubble dead." Replaying earlier horrors, the TV shows people waving out open windows, calling for help, then some of them jumping. In one case, three people hold hands during their free fall. Imagine jumping as the preferred option. I run to the bathroom to stifle the screams I want to release. I take big deep breaths and phone Tino.

"Where are you?" he asks.

"Home with the children and Tad."

"Good. Very good."

"Are you overrun with victims?"

He does not answer right away.

"No," he says. "We are realizing there aren't many. People either got out and ran or could not get out at all."

"How can we know what happened to them?"

"I am going to get in touch with St. Vincent's Hospital. It is close to the site. Perhaps they are there. If not, I will call all the other hospitals."

"Alright. Thank you."

I lower the toilet seat lid and sit on it.

"*Cara.*"

"Yes. I know, I must keep the house calm, stick to the children's routine as much as possible, and keep them from the television. That and wait. Wait and pray."

Tino clears his throat. "I have a feeling I will be home earlier than we all thought possible. It has been almost two hours and we still have no patients."

"Okay. Bye."

"*Ciao.*"

Tad is tidying up the living area, plumping pillows and re-folding two afghans that have slid from wing chairs to floor. I mimic him, only in the kitchen. By eleven o'clock, downstairs looks as if a cleaning crew has done a fine job.

I sit at the kitchen table, where Tad joins me.

"If the twins weren't here, I would start drinking." He gets up and gets the espresso machine going. "Not that we need any more stimulation."

He says it so deadpan that I laugh.

"Waiting is hard. Hoping, harder. Second-guessing, hardest of all," I say.

I phone my mother in St. Suplice and Amelia in Glen Cove.

"I've got to keep it short," I tell both of them, "in case Mercy calls." I'm crying when I hang up each time.

Lu comes downstairs.

"May we have lunch?"

"Of course," I say. "I'll make some peanut butter and banana sandwiches. How does that sound?"

"Delicious."

He half-skips to the stairs.

When the sandwiches are ready, I call up the stairs, "Isa, lunch!"

I press Tad to have a sandwich, too. He does. After they've eaten, he suggests teaching the kiddos how to play poker.

"Okay," Isa says, "but I don't have any money yet this week. My allowance doesn't come until Friday."

"Then we shall pretend," Tad suggests. "How about we play upstairs on the mezzanine? Arrange our own casino. Your mother can find a spot to take the calls from Mercy and Brody and your father."

They are agreeable. He is kind. In the kitchen, I am fidgety and irrational. Over-caffeinated, besides. I stick a soup spoon into the peanut butter jar and grab a glob of "chunky with no salt added" to jam into my mouth. The thick stickiness keeps me from crying aloud. The only other thing I think to do is pray with the crystal rosary beads Tante Yvette had wrapped around her hands in her coffin a decade ago. I stole them from her right before the morticians closed the lid. I keep them in the black velvet case with the turquoise ring Tino gave me as an engagement gift. I walk through the "casino" up to our bedroom to find them. I lie down on the bed, stare at the ceiling fan above me, then begin. *"I believe..., Our Father..., Hail Mary...* times three.... *Glory be....* Then I begin five decades of Hail Marys, each followed by a Glory Be. I am on the second round, the third decade, when the doorbell rings. Persistent knocking follows. Then another ring.

I leap from the bed and take the stairs two at a time, nearly losing my balance but for the railing post's support. I open the door. A policewoman holds Mercy by the arm. "Oh," I breathe, "oh, thank you, thank God." Mercy does not respond. She is covered in dust. The second mummy of the day. The dust of destruction, I think. Jesus, the dust of humanity. People pulverized. *You are dust and unto dust you shall return.* I hate what the voice in my head tells me. Mercy's eyes are rings of red, her body nearly limp. Her pocketbook strap hangs around her neck so that the bag rests on her baby bump, accentuating it. Oh, the baby! She is led, seemingly unaware of both of us leading her, to the couch, where we lay her down like a child herself. She looks up at us, alive. "Mamma," she says, and closes her eyes. I kneel beside her while the policewoman talks.

"We found her sitting on a curb five blocks north of Ground Zero. She kept repeating, 'I'm waiting for my husband. He works at Windows on the World. He is Czech. We always meet here.' I guess she meant the restaurant behind her. Czech Mates, I think it's called. She showed me she is expecting."

The policewoman has a medical mask around her neck. Her hair is in a bun that has come loose. Her black wingtips are covered in what looks like dried paste. There are crusted blood flecks on both her arms. Her nameplate reads "Distasio."

"I asked her if she wanted to get checked out at a hospital or if there was a safe place she could wait for her husband. She said her mother had told her to come home."

Officer Distasio pauses.

I nod.

"She said this address."

"Yes, she is pregnant. I am her mother. Her husband Brody would have been at Windows on the World this morning. He's the food deliveries manager."

"Ma'am," Distasio whispers now and points toward the door. I get up and follow her. She continues, "I sincerely hope he made it out. The plane hit around the 92nd-93rd floors. Anybody above them was stranded, unable to get to exit areas. People were breaking windows, jumping. And helicopters couldn't get to the roof for the fire and smoke." She shakes her head, telling me, making me believe, he didn't stand a chance.

"So you think he's gone."

Distasio shrugs her shoulders. "Let's just say I would become a believer of miracles if he's alive."

Fatherless children. Mercy and her baby, both. Jesus. So much suffering in store for them.

"Yes. Miracles."

Worried as I am that we'll never see Brody again, I can't help myself. I throw my arms around this cop who has delivered my daughter.

She pats my back. "I gotta go," she says. "We got another survivor in the squad car. He wants to get a train to New Haven out of Grand Central. I don't even know if the trains are running anymore. President Bush has stopped all air travel in and out of the country. Maybe the trains are frozen, too."

"God bless you. Stay safe."

I open the door to let her out. She waves back at me when she slides into the squad car.

I shut and lock the door. When I turn to go back to Mercy, I see Tad with his arms around Lu and Isa, who are on each side of him. They are standing like a triptych, their eyes riveted on the chalky creature prone on the couch before them.

Chapter Fifteen
Living Step by Step

I speak intentionally now, my voice the calm that counteracts the shrieking in my brain. "Isa, please go upstairs and get some washcloths and four bath towels and bring them into Daddy's and my bedroom. I want to get your sister clean and comfortable."

Isa does as she's told.

"Lu, go under the kitchen sink and take the box of trash bags up there. I'll need them, to put Mercy's soiled clothes in them."

"Yes, Mamma."

They are soldiers obeying commands. Afraid to counter me. Aware we are contending with a deadly force of some kind. My poor innocents. So many innocents.

I take my phone from the back pocket of my jeans and hand it to Tad.

"Could you please let Thérèse know that Mercy's here? You might try her mobile and land lines, both. She's in my contacts notebook in the drawer under the wall phone in the kitchen."

Tad takes the phone, goes into the kitchen, retrieves the notebook, and returns to sit by the fireplace.

"Then Tino. Would you let Tino know, too?"

Mercy moans.

"Come on, Mercy. You're safe now. I'll help you clean up. Make you and the baby clean and comfortable while we wait for Brody."

Tad's eyes meet mine. We both know I'm a liar.

I help my daughter sit up, then stand. Tad is leaving a message for Thérèse. "She is safe and whole. Orla is bathing her now. We will have her phone you as soon as she can. We have no word from Brody as yet."

Mercy and I walk upstairs, one slow step at a time, each one an effort for her. Isa and Lu stand at the top of the stairs, waiting.

I try for a homely tone. "How about you both set the table for all of us? Then maybe read or do something else quiet. No television. Let's keep the house peaceful for your sister and the baby."

They nod and are solemn, hands at their sides, eyes deep saucers. A duet now. I am glad they have one another. Isa's left eyelid twitches. Lu shifts his right foot up and down, up and down on the hardwood floor.

Once in our bedroom, I close the door and help Mercy remove her bag, her shoes, and all her clothes. The ashy detritus has infiltrated her clothes and covers her skin. She stands, mannequin-like, while I turn on the water in the shower. I strip to my bra and panties and take her by the hand. I grab two facecloths, test the water, then step in and pull her after me. The showerhead is round and as large as a dinner plate. At first I let the water run over her like rain. It makes rivulets between the pasty mess and her almond skin. I hand her a wet washcloth and a bar of soap, but she shakes her head no and points to me. This is the daughter who came to me at six from Vietnam, her first war. She already knew how to bathe herself and would only tolerate my presence from outside the bathroom when she used the tub. Now she is the newborn I never knew. The infant who needs me to remove the physical reminders of her present battle. I wash her with the gentleness that Isa and Lu have taught me. Twice over before her skin is devoid of soot and grime. I shampoo her hair, then lather conditioner over it. She smells like roses now. We switch places so the water rains on me now. I wash myself and she touches my face. When we step out, I wrap her in bath towels, one around her shoulders, the other on her head like a heavy veil. I dry myself quickly, run a comb once through my hair, throw my wet underwear into the hamper, put on a robe. Then I go into the bedroom and stuff all her clothes into garbage bags. Her once-red shoes, as well. I open her purse and let its contents fall onto the carpet. Wallet, sunglasses, make-up bag, mirror, Lifesavers, comb, tissues, phone. She bends, picks up the phone, and dials. I hear no sound at all.

"The phone is dead, Mamma." She pauses, lets the phone fall to the floor, and fingers her wedding band with her right hand. "Dead. Just like Brody, Mamma."

We hold onto each other and weep.

*****

Mary Sharnick

From the Sunday *New York Times*, October 14, 2001:

Brody Oswald Bercik (March 20, 1967-September 11, 2001), born in Prague, Czech Republic (formerly Czechoslovakia), Food Deliveries Manager at Windows on the World, perished in the attack on the North Tower of the World Trade Center. Mr. Bercik is the husband of Mercy Castleberry Bercik and first-born son of Franto and Miloslova Bercik of Prague. Mr. Bercik also leaves a brother, Martin Bercik, of Paris, France. Mrs. Bercik, employed by Morgan Stanley, survived the attack and is expecting the couple's first child in February. (Photo courtesy of the family)

The Dead
2,606 victims from the World Trade Center, including 79 employees from Windows on the World and 100 (approximate) diners
125 victims from the Pentagon
343 victims from the Fire Department of New York
71 victims from Law Enforcement
246 victims from four hijacked flights:
American Airlines Flight 11
United Airlines Flight 175
American Airlines Flight 77
United Airlines Flight 93

*****

167

We didn't fully accept Brody's death until we read the obituary. It was one of hundreds printed Sunday in the *Times*. With only twenty-one people rescued alive from the rubble during the first day of rescue efforts and no whole bodies to bury otherwise, printed hard copy was the only public physical evidence of the victims' lives. Amid the teams of volunteers, firefighters, police, and detection dogs working non-stop at Ground Zero, NYC sanitation trucks became a caravan of rubble and scattered remains. Sanitation workers drove truck after truck filled with the detritus of the attack to a landfill known as "Fresh Kills" on Staten Island. Over time, I hope those sifting through the wreckage will discover items that identify particular individuals. A wallet, perhaps, a key chain, or an engraved wedding band. A charm bracelet with grandchildren's names, pendants with picture lockets, a Star of David, a class ring. Something, one thing a family might recover and claim. Proof of their lost one's life and death, both.

I wish I could forget Mercy's call to Franto and Miloslova. Their wailing was an undulating keening of deepest sorrow. I wish I could forget walking with Mercy and Thérèse (she arrived by train from Washington on September 14th) into the Brooklyn apartment for the first time after Brody was gone. Mercy ran to the soiled clothes hamper, dug through it as a dog digs for bones, then pulled out his running shirt and shorts, pressing them both to her face. I wish Isa and Lu could un-remember what they saw and heard—Mercy looking like a mummy from a horror film, Officer Distasio's blood-flecked arms, my quivering voice as I read the email from Saints Francis and Clare that three of their schoolmates had lost a mother, a father, a grandfather. I wish that Tino and his colleagues did not feel helpless to help. No patients arrived by ambulance. No bodies filled the ER. Nothing but smashed, broken, burnt, pulverized, incinerated, suffocated remains mocked them. Their white coats remained pristine, their expertise was not required. I hated that Tad had to spend his diminished energy on us instead of on himself. I raged that all over the City makeshift monuments of desperation rose, each one filled with handmade posters and papers:

Please phone this number if you see

this man

this woman

my son

my wife

Always accompanied by a photograph. Sometimes with the relative standing close to the appeal, arms extended outward, pleading.

And the air. It was bad, poisoned. *Mal aria.* Tino brought us masks from the hospital. On September 13th, when Saints Francis and Clare opened again because it had power, the four of us walked to school as if preparing for a surgical procedure. Sara Michaud, Grade 8, had lost her mother, a pastry chef whom Brody would certainly have known. Sara was absent, and her classmates wrote her notes of condolence that Dr. Desjarlais would deliver that evening. Teddy Deeley, Grade 2, came in wearing a FDNY fire helmet. Its rim rested on his nose. Teddy's grandfather, a firefighter, had died of a heart attack after leaving the command center in the South Tower. Dr. Desjarlais would visit his family, too. Edgar Escolastico, Grade 4, was driven door to door by Tim Cahill, the partner of his late father, Officer Pablo Escolastico, NYPD. The boy had wanted to come to school. Officer Cahill held Edgar's hand all the way into his classroom. He came to the classroom again to pick Edgar up at three. Officer Escolastico had been crushed by a scorching metal beam from the North Tower. Dr. Desjarlais was asked to read at his funeral.

Father Carlo Brecca celebrated Mass in the gymnasium. Social workers visited every classroom and remained available for two weeks after. Classes resumed. "We owe our children security," Dr. Desjarlais had emailed all the families the night of the attacks. "As delusional as that may seem today, they must be confident in our ability to provide it. So we will do what we are charged to do. We will keep to routines the children know and trust. They will know they are safe and cared for at Saints Francis and Clare."

Only one teacher, Mrs. Chen, stayed out. Her sister had managed the cleaning staff in the Towers and had reported to work as usual the day of the attacks. A Sister Julia took her place. The rooftop garden was declared off limits until the air cleared. On the way to lunch, Sister Aloise hoisted two banners, the American Flag in her right hand, the school banner in her left.

She wasn't the only one. As soon as the afternoon of the attacks, Old Glories sprouted like flowers all over New York. A massive one was hung over the George Washington Bridge. Others of all sizes appeared in windows of shops, restaurants, apartments, police and fire precincts, schools, gas stations, Broadway marquees. People bearing gifts of food and bottled water showed up for cops and firefighters. NYU students set up shop in Washington Square to distribute the same for students who had been displaced from their dormitories. Places of worship unlocked their doors to those who needed a place to rest and pray if they wished. Chefs lit stoves and cooked on the sidewalks to feed exhausted rescue crews. The President came. The City welcomed him. People with little or nothing in common before the attacks spoke with one another as if old friends, commiserated intimately, and asserted themselves as New Yorkers who would never accept defeat.

I wanted our children to witness this, to become part of this surge of strength, determination, and resilience. On the way home from school, we were able to find and buy some bunting. Tad held the ladder while I tacked it over the front door. Isa made a "Thank You to the Helpers" sign and taped it to one of the living room windows facing outward. Lu said, "Who is going to punish the people who did this?"

Whenever the children were doing something else, I listened to the news. Who, indeed? What I did know was that these horrible days were NYC Mayor Rudolph Giuliani's finest hours. He held his City together like the rest of us were trying to do with our own families. Didn't miss a firefighter's or police officer's funeral. Walked fatherless brides down the aisle to their grooms. Showed up. Praised the indomitable citizens of the City that Never Sleeps. Believed in his people and they in him.

Only the baby is keeping Mercy alive. So Thérèse tells me. We speak every evening. They will come for dinner Sunday. "I make her walk with me in the park across the street every day. She eats only for the child. Thank God for that. She wonders what she will do. Move into the new house or not. Stay with Morgan Stanley or not. I tell her there is time. Plenty of time. I am going to quit my job. I will stay with her." This is the first time I am not jealous of Thérèse. I am grateful that she is freeing me from a terrible burden. I feel ashamed and guilty that I feel that, too. You who already know my maternal deficits have no doubt surmised that sacrificial love is not my strong suit. This zebra doesn't change her stripes.

I haven't touched a paintbrush or been to the studio in a month. "It's time," Tino tells me when we get out of bed this morning. He's right. But somewhere lurking beneath the gung-ho, Type A, "gotta, wanna get things done" Orla temperament, there is a demonic voice that taunts. "What's the point?" it asks. "Look at what's happened. First human trafficking, now enemy attacks, death, destruction, hatred. Your kid's husband smashed and burned to smithereens. Your grandchild without a father. Who gives a fuck what or if you paint? Do you, even?"

Usually, a hot shower and a nod to the Divine helps when I lack motivation or feel listless. Even so, naked and clean and toweled this morning, I ask myself and you, dear readers, can art still inspire and console? Does my art matter? What if it's simply ego translated to canvas or paper?

Tino packs me a lunch, sets out my painting uniform on our bed, informs me that we'll be ordering in tonight, and reminds me that I have contracted with the consortium to deliver a product by end of January in the New Year. "You are obligated," he says. And, in addition (here is the *sine qua non*, the damned truth, and the kick in the pants I need), you owe it to our children."

I want to smack him.

Lu and Isa are already out the door when he tries to kiss me good-bye. I turn away.

"I'm angry at you."

He smiles his biggest smile. "Good. I hope-ed to anger you. Now go to the studio and use your brushes like whips."

I grab him around his waist, bite his neck, then push him out the door.

"Get out of here, *Dottore*."

I see he is relieved when he looks back at me now.

"I go, I go."

Chapter Sixteen
Taking Back Control

Keys is snoring when I arrive. I slam the door to rouse him.

He grunts, opens his eyes. "Orla! I was wondering if you were ever coming back." He stands, comes around his desk, and opens his arms.

"How's your daughter? Dean Collier told me what happened. I'm so sorry. Young guy like that. So many others, too. What a world."

I take off my sunglasses and look him in the eye.

"Mercy is coping as best as she can. Carrying her husband's child is saving her from complete despair."

"God bless her," Keys says. He pauses, then goes to the cabinet for my key."

"Thanks," I say, taking it from his hand when he comes back . He sneezes and blows his nose. "Glad to have you back, Orla."

"I'm glad to be back." At least I think I am.

The studio is just as I left it. Recent rains have even cleared the skylights of the unimaginable dust that must have covered and caked on them. My consortium sketches are still tacked to the left wall, and several paintings are completed and unharmed. On the opposite side of the studio, one easel holds my sketch for the Tiziana and Flavia courtroom duel, the other, my cartoon of the big, brazen portrait of Tiziana. Since 9/11, two other future works haunt me—one of Mercy as she arrived at our place, the other my intended next gift to her, a portrait of her Brody, herself, and her pregnancy.

My former schedule worthless now, I rip its page from my notebook, crumble the paper, and toss it into the trash pail. I sit down and compose a new one:

1) November 21, 2001: All International Women's Day consortium works completed (Take photos and mail to Tad in St. Suplice)
2) December 1, 2001: Tiziana and Flavia courtroom duel
3) December 20, 2001: Portrait of Brody, Mercy, and Mercy's pregnancy
4) January 2-February 28: Portrait of Tiziana
5) January 31, 2002: Tad's final text for International Women's Day consortium works
6) March 1-March 15, 2002: In Italy for International Women's Day festivities
7) March 16, 2002: Arrive back in NYC.
8) March 17-June 29: Develop next project.
9) June 30, 2002: Leave NYC for St. Suplice with family.
10) July 10, 2002: Return to Fiesole with family.

I rifle through my carryall and see what Tino has packed me. Yum. A salami and mozzarella sandwich on a Portuguese roll, with plenty of spicy mustard. One of the brownies Lu and Isa baked. A Bosch pear. And a note. "*Ti amo.*"

I pace the floor while munching on the pear, working myself into the fury I need to paint the absolute affront to womanhood that trafficking represents. I call up the night on Via Domitiana, the sights of childhoods ruined, the stink in Carmine Famiglietti's car, the enormous obscene, emotionless *maman*. It is two forty-five when the alarm clock on my desk rings, and I haven't once let go of my brush. I have forgotten to eat lunch, to pee, even to think. It's time to pick up my children, but I don't want to leave the studio. God bless me, God help me. I'm me again. Orla. The girl who's always been meant to paint.

Chapter Seventeen
Seasons Greetings

It's nine o'clock in the morning on December 21st and I'm sitting alone in the first pew of Our Lady's Chapel of St. Patrick's Cathedral. My late Tante Yvette used to take me here for Mass whenever I visited her from St. Suplice. I'm here to pause, breathe a sigh of relief, and offer thanks. I've stuck to my schedule, done what I was contracted to do, and have Mercy's gift ready for Christmas Day. Our Long Island attorney friends Amelia and Hal are coming to dinner tonight. We have been wanting to reciprocate their many kindnesses to Mercy when she first moved to New York. Tino and I have cleared our calendars so we can attend the twins' Christmas Concert tomorrow morning at their school. For the first time since September 11th, I feel a sense of ease, maybe even peace. I close my eyes and listen to myself breathe. Nice and slow. Even. Relaxed.

It's strange how I've experienced time since the first plane struck the North Tower. From that moment on, until Tino nudged, or shamed me, back to work, time felt the way it does when one awakes from ether. It unrolls like an aisle-wide wedding runner, scatters white flakes like the innards of a shaken snow globe, streams like cirrus clouds above one's head. If it could speak, it would do so in slow motion, its syllables elongated and round. I thought of myself as a person in outer space, suited up for a foreign atmosphere, floating inside a rocket ship that only barely promised survival. I went through the motions of competent mother, attentive wife, caring friend. My true self, the Orla who seizes the day, who interprets lived experiences with her brushes, who now and then pontificates, falls short, means well, and sometimes shines, that Orla felt dormant. I was aware and doing and, at the same time, not. Suspended. That's what I was. Waiting for another calamity. Wondering who and what and where the next target will be. And then.... Then, like most, even those who suffered and still suffer the worst of that day, I, we, eventually got on with living. Whether sadly, grudgingly, guiltily, anxiously, gladly, wholeheartedly, or a conglomeration of "-ly"s, we put one foot in front of the other to face another day.

Tad and Mercy did this, too.

Tad and his new allotment of life-saving drugs flew back to New Orleans November 1st, but not before making Halloween a night to remember. Where he ordered the decorations or the food he would not tell, but the children and I came home to jack-o'-lanterns lit in all the front windows and orange paper bags stuffed with candy and popcorn treats. A half hour after Tino arrived, a four-course dinner was delivered to the door, complete with soft plastic spiders to place atop a ghost-shaped cake. Tad was looking healthier than he had when he arrived. And other than several unpleasant but bearable side effects from his new cocktail of medicines ("Trust me, Orla, our friendship has stood much. It does not need description or explanation of these annoyances. Intimacy has its limits," he said, and Tino chuckled), he had gained weight and kept his wry sense of humor. Tino had arranged for Tad's New Orleans docs to report his status weekly to the Langone group and, if all proceeded positively, Tad would not return to New York until the end of February, one week before he and I leave for Assisi and the consortium.

And Mercy. My daughter is now heavy with child. She is beautiful, sorrowful, and hopeful at the same time.

At Thanksgiving, the first American one Isa and Lu have enjoyed, she sat between the two of them. They have become solicitous of her, hugging her and rubbing her belly. That she lets them astounds me. She lets them feel the baby kick. Lu never fails to jump when her stomach moves. And I am grateful to Thérèse. After the turkey and its accompaniments, but before the pumpkin pie, Mercy clinked her coffee spoon against her water glass and said, "I've decided." We were all ears. "I'm going to move into the house that Brody and I bought." We applauded. "My mother has decided to stay." Thérèse nodded. "And she will be the nanny after I return to work." Isa clapped her hands. "The baby will have two grandmas near her, then."

We had been anxious to know what Mercy would do, but hadn't pushed or pressured her. I had told Tino that, whatever she decided, I wanted to give her everything my will states is hers, but now, right away. Bless him he understood my reasoning without me even having to explain it.

"I will make espresso," he said, while I excused myself to go upstairs and write the check. When I came back down, Isa was putting dessert plates on the table. I handed an envelope to Mercy.

"Mamma," she said, when she read the card I had written soon after Brody's passing. The check lay upside down on her dessert plate.

> *Dearest Mercy,*
> *Whatever you decide going forward, I want you and your child to enjoy financial security. Please accept this gift earlier than I anticipated giving it to you.*
> *Your loving Mamma*

Thérèse's eyes teared up as if she had read my mind. Lu and Isa applauded at Mercy's thank you.

"How much did you get?" Isa asked.

We tried not to laugh.

"Generally, one does not ask," Tino said, returning to his seat and opening his arms to our daughter.

Isa didn't cry at her censure, thank goodness, but instead let her father enfold her in his arms.

"May we have our pie now?" Lu asked.

"Certainly," I replied, and stood up to get the whipped cream from the refrigerator.

"One more thing," Mercy spoke again, stopping me mid-stride. "Our baby is a girl, and her name will be Phoenix Brooklyn Bercik. She will rise from Brody's ashes and learn where she was conceived in love."

For a moment, all of us went silent. Then emotion flooded the room. It was hearing the names "Brody" and "Phoenix," that turned Thérèse and me into puddles.

"Why are you crying?" Isa asked.

Tino rubbed our daughter's head. "Because we are a family," he answered. "Because we each have try-ed to help one another and we are sad and happy at the same time."

"Oh," Isa said. But she looked to me with a deer-in-the-headlights expression.

"I'll serve the pie," Lu said, and went to the kitchen counter.

I saw our boy rub his eyes before he rummaged through the utensils drawer for a pie server.

A tinkling bell startles me. I open my eyes. A priest and two altar servers process from the vestry to the altar. I am no longer alone. The chapel is almost full now. We Mass-goers are here in New York, alive and, if not yet thriving, striving to do so. Together we rise. "The Lord be with you," the priest says. "And also with you," we say in unison.

Chapter Eighteen
A Call for Help

We were supposed to have visited Amelia and Hal Symonds for an early autumn picnic in Glen Cove two weeks after our arrival in Manhattan. Finally, tonight, December 21st, they are joining us at our place for a lasagna dinner. Amelia and I speak by phone at least once a week, but it's been well over a year since we've met in person. They were very nice to Mercy when she first settled in Brooklyn. And Brody enjoyed their spacious back yard where he often barbecued with Hal.

Over supper our kiddos tell them about our Frigento adventures, including, of course, the incident of the rat. Amelia and Hal shout in disgust, as if they're hearing the story for the first time. Isa and Lu revel in their reaction. Then Amelia and Hal shower the kiddos with presents, the hands-down favorite a pass to Ice Magic, a Glen Cove skating rink, for the months of January and February.

"This way, you can skate and come visit us right after," Amelia tells them. "Bring your parents, too."

We don't finish dinner until well after ten, when I insist the children go to bed so they'll be "in voice" for tomorrow's concert and the last day of school before Christmas. Then our husbands decide cigars are in order, so they put on their coats and take to the sidewalk. Amelia and I cozy up close to the fire and she fills me in on a troubling case of an infant girl with numerous bone fractures and no irrefutable evidence thus far as to who her abuser is. "We don't know," she says. "It might be one or both parents, or the nanny. I've got to get the hospital to keep the baby there under watch until we can make an arrest. The child is just three months old."

I jostle in my chair. "There is no end to cruelty, is there?"

"Nope," Amelia says. "Never an end."

The fellows come back inside just before midnight. We've downed several more *espressi* with sambuco, along with other after-dinner drinks and sweets. Amelia and Hal leave at one. It's almost two in the morning when Tino and I finish cleaning up and go to bed. It's been a lovely night.

When my mobile rings, I think it's part of my dream where I'm on a roller-coaster with Tad when we are children. Then I jump up, wondering if Mercy has gone into an early labor. Tino doesn't wake, just rolls over and faces the wall. When I answer, the caller tells me she is Signora Clarissa Rotunno, a social worker at Pineta Grande Hospital in Castel Volturno, Italy, calling in regards to patient Adaoma Chukwu. It is just after ten in the morning there.

"Is Adaoma alive?" I ask.

My heart is pounding as I recall the Nigerian girl with the hiss, wonder what trauma has brought her to the hospital. She had kept my phone number after all.

"Yes," Signora Rotunno says, "but she was left for dead in the street. I will let her speak with you in a moment. She insisted I phone you. She says she wants to go to the sisters in Caserta and that you work with them."

We talk, I filling in the social worker about my one meeting with Adaoma and my connection with Casa di Dignità, she letting me know that several days ago Adaoma came out of surgery that repaired a perforated bowel and a slashed left breast. "She also has contusions on her face and neck."

I imagine how Adaoma must look and hope she can recover well once at Casa di Dignità.

"I have already phoned the sisters and they are willing to take her," Signora Rotunno says. "Someone must find a car to bring her to Caserta and pay the cost, as well."

Jesus, I say to myself, *can't you drive her yourself? What if her maman gets to her first? Makes her go back? Puts her on the streets again no matter her condition?*

I take a breath. Several, actually. "I'll take care of the car and the ride. No worries."

"Good," Signora Rotunno says.

"I will call back as soon as I arrange for a driver."

"Here is Adaoma," she says.

I leave the bedroom and walk into the hall.

A husky voice says, "Hello?"

"Adaoma?" I say.

"I am afraid the *maman* will come and take me back like she did with another girl before," she says.

"Don't worry," I tell her. "I am sending someone to take you to the sisters."

She keeps talking, her hiss and battered mouth making her words difficult to understand. "The client hurt me too much this time, so I pushed him away. We were in the usual place, in the brush off the road. When I yelled and shoved him, he got very angry and punched my face. Then he pulled a knife strapped to his ankle, slashed my breast, and turned me over. He found a branch and pushed it up my ass. He dragged me into the street. I was screaming and bleeding all over. I passed out when I heard the sirens."

I shake as she tells me. Then, I say, "Adaoma, I am going to call Signora Rotunno back as soon as I get a driver. I have her number. I will call back as soon as I can."

"Please hurry," she says.

I am pacing.

Tiziana picks up on the second ring.

"Thank God," I say, and spill the story.

"Slower," she says, when I say which hospital, the girl's and the social worker's names. The social worker's phone number.

"It's a good thing Carmine is in the shower," she says. "He knew it would come to this."

I lean against the bedroom door. "I'm sorry to bother you."

Tiziana laughs. "No, you're not."

She is right, of course. I say nothing.

She continues. "Not to worry, dear Orla. I will send Malo right away. I hear him in the kitchen. The cappuccino maker is steaming. Let him have his coffee and *cornetto*. He should be at the hospital in two hours. There will be traffic."

I breathe a sigh of relief.

"What's Malo's phone number, so I can be in touch with him if need be?" I run into the bedroom, grab a pen from my night stand, and scribble the number on my left arm, repeating back to Tiziana.

"That's it," she says. "Do not worry, my crazy friend. We will get the girl to safety. But it will take some time."

"Thank you. Thank you, Tiziana."

"Merry Christmas, Orla."

I laugh now. "And to you. Tell Carmine I say hello."

"I certainly will."

I call Signora Rotunno.

"A man named Malo will pick up Adaoma. He is Attorney Tiziana Gargiulo's driver. He will be at the hospital within two hours."

"Good. We are filling out the necessary release papers now. I will wait with Adaoma in the lobby."

"Thank you for your help." I pause, considering. Then I say it. "Don't be afraid of Malo's face. Tell Adaoma that, too."

"Alright. Good bye."

"Good bye."

I go into the bathroom and splash water on my face, then go back to bed. Tino is snoring. I am dreaming of bloodied breasts when he shakes me awake. "*Cara*," he says, "what is the matter?"

I tell him what has happened, and he holds me close.

It is after sunrise. Whatever is happening in Italy, I shall focus on the day ahead of us. Our kiddos have been preparing for this concert for weeks, and I will not disregard them. I will be there for them, the way so many people have been there for me.

*****

We are at the tail end of the school event when my phone vibrates.

The children have presented flowers to their music teacher, Mrs. Blomstrom. They have all taken their bows and posed for a formal portrait. Representatives from the police and fire departments posed with them. Several crates of canned goods are ready to be delivered to needy families at Catholic Charities. The eighth grade students have knitted ten afghans for recently orphaned infants, also designated by Catholic Charities, the babies' late parents all victims of terminal illnesses or random acts of violence. There is sorrow and loss here.

The presence of a hearty Santa dissipates some of it. He greeted the children as they left the stage and led the way to two long tables topped with trays of hot cocoa and ginger cookies. He and Dr. Desjarlais joined hands and called out, "Merry Christmas!"

I recognize Malo's number and hurry out of the gymnasium and into the corridor as I accept the call.

"Yes?" I say

"It is done, Signora Orla. The girl is with Sister Ilaria now, and I am on my way back to Naples."

"God bless you," I say. "Thank you for taking care of her."

"I am glad I was available when you called. I tell you, the girl did not relax her grip on the seatbelt until we arrived at the convent. She had nothing, only a hospital gown, booties, and blanket. She put the blanket over her head. She was very afraid the *maman* would come, see her, and take her back to the street."

"Again, Malo, my sincere thanks. Merry Christmas."

"You, too, Signora Orla. I hope I will see you again."

"Yes, soon."

Parents, grandparents, and children are streaming out of the gymnasium now. Tino and the twins wave at me. I put my phone back in my pocket, hug our children, and give a thumbs up to Tino.

"God bless us every one," he says.

We walk home. We prepare pastina and pork chops with onions and peppers for dinner, and watch one of my favorite Christmas-y films, *Going My Way*. I slip into bed right after kissing the kiddos goodnight. I don't even know when Tino joins me. My sleep is a balm and a solace. A welcome oblivion.

Part Three

It is a serious thing
just to be alive
on this fresh morning
in this broken world.
— Mary Oliver

E quindi uscimmo a riveder le stelle
(And so we came forth once again to see the stars)
—-Dante Alighieri

Chapter Nineteen
March 7th, 2002, Assisi

The Franciscans are hosting a preview of my paintings and a dinner in their massive refectory for the consortium participants and our guests tonight, the evening before International Women's Day. Tad and I arrived in Assisi six days ago. I'm glad he's opted to stay with me in my family's small apartment just up from the main piazza, despite the many stone steps leading to it. It feels like our childhood in St. Suplice where we kept each other company on days off from school and all through summer vacation. The majority of other participants and guests are checked into Hotel Subasio, the tired secular showpiece of the gorgeous medieval town, home of Saint Francis and Saint Clare.

Tomorrow evening's farewell cocktail hour following the consortium will take place on the hotel's terrace overlooking the basilica and its courtyard. It will be a schmooze session for askers, sponsors and donors. Along with Sister Ilaria, I'll be twisting arms on behalf of Casa di Dignità. The convent needs ongoing funds to house rescued girls and their children, as well as seed money to finance a cooperative that will feature sewn and crafted items the girls themselves make. A large white tent hoisted this morning in the courtyard will protect my paintings from the elements. Tad and I will oversee their placement early tomorrow morning, when the event's work crew removes them from the refectory. After a welcome from Friar Martino Otto, Custos of the Sacro Convento, panelists will address the three hundred or so visitors who have registered for the day's program. Sister Ilaria from Casa di Dignità, Naples' Assistant Prosecutor Flavia Esposito, Dottoressa Grazia Fabrizzi from the Brigittine Sisters' ob/gyn clinic in Naples, and myself comprise one panel. Our purpose is to discuss ways in which others can help thwart traffickers. Other panels include members of sectarian government offices that help migrants find homes and legitimate jobs; formerly trafficked women; and philanthropists who have determined their substantial resources should go to health and education services to benefit those abused. Each panel will encourage consortium visitors to commit time and talents and/or financial resources to help mitigate systemic international mistreatment of innocents.

Other than the two weeks I spent researching in Naples last summer when the twins attended Nonna's summer camp, this trip is the first time I've left them during our New York stay. How glad both Tino and I were when Nonna Aurora agreed to visit from the day of my departure until one week after Easter. She arrived in New York a couple of hours before Tad and I were to leave, so Tino and the kiddos had to make only one airport run. Long used to travel from her days as a violin soloist with international orchestras, she managed the trip from Florence to Rome to New York with ease. Evidently, she's going to be a visiting musician at Saints Francis and Clare Academy. Tino also has a whirlwind tour of Manhattan set up for her with a private car and driver so she can visit city highlights without the trek taking a toll on her arthritic feet. What else they will all do while I am gone, who knows? I'm just relieved that Tino will have some help and the kiddos will be distracted enough not to miss me too much. I guess they'll all pay a visit to Mercy and Phoenix, too. My granddaughter entered this troubled world with little fanfare and right on time. A Valentine's Day birthday is hers. Mercy is recovering from the delivery, and I am so glad the baby compels her to focus on the future even as she mourns. Thérèse continues to be a godsend. Though they can never be replaced, the years she spent apart from her daughter have been re-gifted twofold: her daughter and granddaughter all to herself in a new family home in New Jersey. But at such a terrible cost. Mercy without her husband. Phoenix without her father. Sometimes I fantasize that Heaven is a perpetual epiphany, an unending realization that all earthly events, tragic and glorious, singular and mundane, once and for always make sense. That those who love each other will hug in an cosmic embrace.

As she promised she would, way back when she offered us her family's home in Frigento, Amelia and Hal have arrived for the consortium. They'll be off to enjoy a holiday in Sicily right after. Much to my pleasure and surprise, Tiziana, Carmine, and Malo accepted my invitation, as well. ("Consider me a spy from the opposition," Tiziana had teased). I'm eager to see them. I've decided Tiziana's portrait will be my gift to her for saving Adaoma. And a plane ticket to and from New York is Malo's, if he wants it. Flavia's husband isn't joining her. He's chosen to stay home in Naples with their daughter. "'Be careful, he said,'" Flavia confided in me when we spoke by phone earlier today. "'The thugs will be watching. Do not wander the town alone.'"

I hope he's wrong. If he's not, we'll have more than a dead rat to worry about. Again I'm glad Tad didn't opt for the hotel.

Both Adaoma and Hadiza will be at the dinner tonight. "No matter how many times our other residents reassure her, Adaoma is still convinced that her *maman* will come to our sanctuary and take her back to the streets," Sister Ilaria had told me. "She still needs much psychological therapy. And I am skeptical that she can learn to trust again. But you will be happy, I think, to see how much her physical condition has improved."

I realize it's time to get ready. Tad decided to nap while I hiked up to Rocca Maggiore. Serious exercise is how I calm my nerves before every exhibit. After ambling down the mountain, I caught my breath, rehydrated, and relaxed some at Angelina's bar. Now I need to shower and make my best effort to transform myself into Orla the Artist. It's going to take some time.

* * * * *

There is a receiving line in the refectory. All the friars in residence welcome us, each in his own way offering encouragement and support of our goal to free girls and women from the traffickers. A number of the friars have already seen the official consortium pamphlet with Tad's text and photographs of my paintings.

"I must say that I was taken aback by the audacity of several," says Father Caroli. "I hope no children will see them."

Father Martino is particularly touched when he learns that Tad and I have been friends since childhood and have collaborated on projects since our AIDS exhibit in 1989. "There is great solace in a friend with whom one enjoys a shared history," he says. I couldn't agree more. You name it, Tad and I have been through it together.

We head to the bar as soon as we make it through the receiving line. Just as I accept a glass of Prosecco from one of the two bartenders, someone taps my shoulder. I turn and see Hadiza and another girl. Both are dressed in Western style this evening, though Sister Ilaria told me they have decided to present their stories in their native Nigerian dress tomorrow.

"Signora Orla," Hadiza says, "I am so glad to see you again." She looks lovely in a deep raspberry knee-length crepe dress and matching kitten heels. She turns to the other woman, still a teenager, really. This girl wears a sapphire-blue shirtwaist dress and silver flats. "Sister Ilaria tells me you and Adaoma have met before."

I take a step back. I'm awed rather than shocked.

"Adaoma, you are beautiful. I am so happy you are here."

Adaoma bows her head. I hope I haven't embarrassed her. She has some flesh on her bones. Her hair is plaited, with several silver strands running through it.

"I am happy too, Signora. If you had not given me your number, I would not have known where to go." She smiles. The missing tooth has been replaced. No more hissing, a musical lilt instead.

"I'm glad you used it." I put out my hands and she grabs them. "But, tell me, how were you able to keep the paper with you all that time?"

She turns to look first at Hadiza, then looks back at me. "I did not keep it, Signora. I was afraid what would happen to me, and to you, if the *maman* discovered it. Instead, I memorized it, Signora. I repeated it to myself many times a day, just the way the sisters repeat their prayers. I hoped you were not another liar and that someday, if I was brave enough, I would call."

"Good evening, ladies."

It's Tad. Right behind him are Tiziana, Carmine, and Malo.

Adaoma sees Malo and bows her head again.

"I am glad to see you so recovered," he says.

Adaoma smiles.

"Everyone, this is my oldest and dearest friend, Tad. We spent nearly every day of childhood together. I hope he won't tell you everything he knows about me."

Carmine smirks, puts a hand on Tad's shoulder and asks, "Has she always been a great deal of trouble, Tad?"

Tad smiles broadly, then purses his lips and pretends to consider. "Making trouble is her forté, sir. But usually for a good cause, I must say."

Tiziana whispers in my ear. "I understand why you are friends. I like him."

Flavia enters the refectory as soon as the dinner bell rings. I wave her over, then introduce her to Tad, Adaoma, and Hadiza. A friar directs us to our seats, place cards having been set on the long tables that line either side of the refectory. Prosecutor and defense attorney sit either side of the girls. Although I wouldn't have expected it, much laughter rises among them.

Both the food and the conversation are hearty and satisfying. While we are drinking the last of our espresso and eyeing glass bowls of fresh fruit, Friar Otto introduces Sister Ilaria. She takes to the podium with an energetic grace that belies both her years and the taxing nature of her ministry. As always, she is dressed in her signature style—A-line gray skirt, neutral hose, sensible black pumps, and collared long-sleeved blouse. Tonight's is red. Her salt-and-pepper hair is wavy. She wears no veil, and a man's watch surrounds her left wrist. It is her smile that arrests and her directness that disarms.

"Thank you, Father Martino, and your community, for welcoming so many of us this evening and hosting our consortium tomorrow. We at Casa di Dignità, along with all the other religious and civil groups who assist trafficked women, are most grateful for your support. As we have shared many times over the year it has taken to prepare this conference, it would be an affront to our faith if we did not actively protest and thwart this evil treatment of God's own. While many claim, no doubt accurately, that we cannot and will not eliminate trafficking, we assert that we will do whatever we can to impede it.

"As the revered Mother Teresa of Calcutta tells us, 'What we need is to love without getting tired.' Your support and the support of so many others keep us at Casa di Dignità from getting tired. And should all present, and those who will join us tomorrow, need any visual proof of the horrors of trafficking, they need look no further than to gaze at the paintings by Orla Castleberry." She points to me. There is scattered applause. "The thematic presentations Orla has painted over her many years as an artist never fail to wake us up, to compel us to see anew, to face realities we would prefer to ignore." As she goes on, I see two friars slide the draping off each of my paintings at the far end of the refectory. "When you view her paintings this evening, you will certainly be shocked, perhaps even angered. In fact, I hope you are. The artist has painted what she has seen on the Via Domitiana in Castel Volturno. What she witnessed and what once-unsuspecting girls and women live every day and night has made her join our efforts, and I hope tomorrow will garner more people to our cause."

Several people strain their necks looking toward the easels.

"Once again, my sincere thanks to the Franciscan Friars of Assisi for your hospitality and prayers, and to all who have joined us tonight. Most especially I extend my love to the brave women present who have escaped the dehumanizing treatment of their captors and begun new and promising lives at Casa di Dignità." At this she blows a kiss to Hadiza and Adaoma. Hadiza smiles and Adaoma bows her head.

Everyone stands and applauds; then, one by one, or several at a time, people follow Sister Ilaria to the paintings. Tad rises to hand out the pamphlets. "Will you join me?" he asks. I shake my head no. As always, I feel a mix of professional pride and private apprehension. I stay in my seat, not moving toward the display until everyone else has. I watch their faces from afar, preparing myself to handle disapproval and disgust in a gracious manner.

Over the years and many exhibits, critics have called me exploitative. "*Orla Castleberry continues to re-exploit the already exploited,*" the Naples article read (Yes, Tino bought several copies after we tossed the one contaminated with rat's blood.) "*As she targets those who traffick women and girls in her paintings, she once again exposes the victims. Perhaps she is even more cruel than the traffickers, as her paintings freeze the victims in time. Their suffering on Via Domitiana will eventually cease, admittedly in less than acceptable ways, but art endures. Those painted will forever remain exposed. Orla Castleberry fixes their images for all to see and remember."*

That is my job! I want to scream. That is the artist's duty.

"May I take your glass?" one of the bow-tied waiters interrupts my inner apologia.

"Of course, thank you."

He takes the water glass, takes a few steps away, then stops. He turns to me. "You are the artist?"

I nod.

"I am honored to have served you."

"Everything was delicious. Thank you."

He goes. I stand, and my dinner napkin falls from my lap. I bend and pick it up. My lipstick has smeared it in several places. *That's it*, I say to myself, *it's not my paintings I'm afraid people disapprove of. It's me. No matter what I paint, I know the execution is noteworthy, the effect evocative and provocative. My expertise and talent are clear. But it's being dragged over the coals in fundamentalist churches, smeared in the general press, scorned and judged by people who willfully misunderstand what I am trying to do. Ego, ego, ego. "All for art," I like to say, to believe. But that's not true. When I inscribe my name on the paintings, I am writing me. When verbally cut, I bleed paint.*

I walk toward the exhibit while most people are filing out of the room. Tad is placing the extra pamphlets in the cardboard boxes they were delivered in. Sister Ilaria, Hadiza, and Adaoma wave goodnight. Tiziana and Flavia converse, their hands a quartet of energy. Carmine comes towards me.

"Orla," he says, and kisses my hand. His eyes water. He rubs them with a wrinkled white handkerchief he takes from the breast pocket of his blazer. "You have made me remember the night we drove to the Via Domitiana."

I exhale. "I'm sorry, Carmine. I know you regret having taken me there."

He grabs my right arm. Holds it tight. "No," he growls. "I did, but not now. I am not sorry now. Not sorry at all." He twirls his hand in the air as he leaves.

I'm surprised. Pleased, as well. The cynic has softened.

"Ready?" asks Tad.

I smile at him. "Thank you, Tad."

"For what, my friend?"

I stand on tip-toe and kiss his cheek.

"For making me feel as if no time has passed. As if you and I are eleven and twelve years old at the church fair in St. Suplice, my paintings hanging by clothespins on a makeshift clothesline between two magnolia trees."

"Long time ago, Orla. Our lives hadn't happened yet." He takes his blazer from the back of a chair and puts it on, adjusting his collar just so.

I make sure my pocketbook strap is secure on my left shoulder. "Now that they have, we're still together."

"Yes," he says, and rests his chin on top of my head the way he always has.

"It's a good thing, a good thing, Tad."

We separate and head toward the door into a long corridor, sconces either side of us casting long shadows on the walls.

"Yes, Orla. The best thing."

We reach the heavy wooden door that leads out of the Sacred Convent. It squeaks when Tad pushes it open and motions me through.

It's quiet and dark. Tad puts his arm around my shoulder. He is the best friend I have.

"We best get back," he says, as we climb the steep hill to the town center. "Tomorrow will be a long day."

"For sure."

Neither of us says a word until we are inside the apartment.

"Sleep tight, Tad."

"Good night, Orla."

I go into the room where Tino and I first made love, our cocoon ever since, Tad goes to the twins' room with its bunkbed, board games, and toys.

No dreams or nightmares, either. Just deepest sleep, with Tad nearby, in the medieval hill town that promises peace.

Chapter Twenty
Mimosas and Blood

The consortium draws over 400 registered guests, at least 177 of whom pledge financial support during the post-program cocktail hour at the Subasio. Tad keeps count of visitors exiting my exhibit and cajoles me into standing by him to meet and greet them. More than a few ask me to autograph their programs.

An ancient nun from Ghana using two wooden canes to keep herself upright and mobile tells me, "Keep at it. Force the world to see. God bless you." I marvel at her the way Isa does Sister Aloise at school. Her knees creak with wreckage, yet her eyes are sparkling and bore into mine.

A young Italian husband, his teary wife heavy with child, says, "Your paintings were difficult for us to look at, as we are expecting a daughter. But it is right you have made us see."

I take the woman's face in my hands as if I am a native *Napoletana* and wish her good health and happiness with the baby. She smiles.

"I will never let her out of my sight," the father-to-be continues as they leave. "Such evil that could ruin her!"

Right behind them, a leather-clad biker, helmet in hand, a nose-ring piercing one of his nostrils, urges me to "keep kicking ass, Ms. Castleberry. I hope to see the exhibit again when it goes to New York. You rock."

I feel girlish and giggly. "Thanks," I say. "I'll look for you then." As he fist-pumps me and leaves the tent, Tad looks down at my reddened face and rolls his eyes.

By six o'clock, I am keen on heading back to the apartment. I want to get out of my cocktail dress and shower, then slip into a pair of well-worn jeans and one of Tino's fresh-from-the-cleaners pressed button-down shirts. Wiggle toes freed from shoes, and recover from the tempestuous mindset every event like this conjures. I invited the Naples crew over so they could relax afterward, as well. Malo and Flavia demurred and said they needed to get home. Malo offered to drive Flavia back, and they left Assisi as soon as the last panelist exited the stage. On the other hand, Tiziana and Carmine, making a short getaway of their visit, said they'd be glad to come. So it'll be just the four of us. I've invited them for nine o'clock, and just after that Angelina will send up one of her kitchen crew with roasted *porchetta* and rolls for sandwiches, some marinated vegetables, and plenty of wine. I didn't need to order dessert. Unbeknownst to me until the baker's delivery boy rang the doorbell this morning, Tad had ordered a white-frosted cake decorated with sugared mimosa flowers.

Assisi is bursting with them—the actual flowers, that is. Over the years, yellow mimosas have become associated with International Women's Day. It's customary for women to gift other women with a bouquet every 8th of March. Hats off to Assisi's town council for lining the streets leading downhill to the basilica with pots and pots of them. They shine like sunshine against the brown and gray stones of the buildings. So now it's as if Tad and I are marching in a recessional up a steep aisle as we leave the Subasio and make our way back to the apartment. It's not quite dark, and we can hear tourist buses grumbling down and away from Assisi's sacred center and back to the contemporary world. The small shops are closing for the night. Lights are going on in the apartments above us, and the seductive aromas of garlic, baking bread, and roasting meat emanate from kitchen windows opened just a bit. More than a decade ago, Tino taught me that this is the time to enjoy Assisi, between dusk and dawn, when the town owns itself again, when tourists and visitors leave, when quiet descends like the darkness. That is why we consider it our refuge—he from the Emergency Department in Florence, me from critics and callers, commitments and appointments. The children have come to love it here, as well. They can dash down from the apartment to Angelina's bar or run up the too-many stone steps above our hideaway to an open field where they play soccer with local children. Everyone knows them. We feel welcomed and safe. Several times in recent years, Tino and I have considered leaving the apartment and buying a small farmhouse outside of town. Perhaps when the children become teenagers and are no longer willing to bunk in what used to be Tino's office/den. But so far, they consider sharing the second bedroom part of a weekend's novelty.

"By the by, Orla," Tad says between breaths, "a Selena Faci from Feltrinelli Publishers gave me two cards, one for each of us." He pulls the cards from his breast pocket and hands me one. "She wonders if we will collaborate on a book about trafficking. An 'expansion,' she called it, 'with historicity.'"

"Hmm. Are you interested?"

Tad stops walking, looks at me, and says, "Yes. As long as you will allow me to include photos of your paintings."

I stop, too. "Sure." Then, smiling a smarmy smile, I add, "Let's negotiate a deal that will bring in some substantial cash."

"I've already got a proposed contract in mind, my friend."

"Ha! Good. When does Ms. Faci want to negotiate with us?" I scratch my itchy nose.

"I told her we will be leaving from Rome on March 16th." He puts his card back into his breast pocket. "If agreeable to you, she will host us at dinner in Rome the night before our leave-taking."

"Why not?" I say.

"I shall ring her office tomorrow morning, then."

I smile up at Tad. "So you're my agent now. I must say, that's most reassuring."

Tad clears his throat. "Someone must bear the burden, I daresay."

I elbow his waist.

"Watch I do not accuse you of assault," he grins.

We walk again, having only to pass Angelina's bar, bear left, and trudge up the stone stairs. This is why I tell novices to The Boot that it is impossible to gain weight in Italy as long as one walks. In Assisi, steepness is all.

Angelina sees us and comes outside. She wears a net over her graying hair and a cook's apron over her flowered dress. She wipes her hands on a dishcloth.

"Congratulations, Orla. I am told you had a great success."

"Thanks, Angelina. So it seems. Lots of funds were raised to help the sisters' ministry."

She comes out onto the patio where the table umbrellas have been closed and tied for the night.

"And for me, too." She laughs. "Lots of people wanted to eat. Everyone who did not go to the event came here. The drivers, the husbands—many husbands!" She laughs some more. "So thank you."

I demur. "Don't thank me. Thank the friars and the sisters, they put this together. They even snagged a message from the Pope."

Angelina shakes the dishcloth, then folds it into a square. "I will send Antonio up with the food and wine at nine o'clock, yes?"

"Perfect. Thank you, Angelina. Have a restful night."

"You, too. You and your friends."

Because we are not yet beset with summer's press of heat, the walk up the stone steps does not feel too difficult. I take the iron key from my purse and let us in. Tad flips on the lights either side of the black leather couch, and I find a match to light the eucalyptus candle in the center of the island. I also open the shutters and the sliding doors to the balcony just a few inches.

"The view is wonderful," Tad says, and I leave him standing there as I head to the bedroom to disrobe, put on a bathrobe, and gather my clothes for after a shower.

"See you in a few."

As soon as I turn on the overhead light, my eyes bulge and my gorge rises from my stomach to my throat. I see what I can't possibly be seeing. A brown hand, a right hand, hachetted at the wrist, lies on my pillow. Its blood is red, fresh. Shreds of connective tissue hang like waxen threads on the pillowcase. Blood has reddened the white comforter. The hand's long fingernails are iridescent blue. And, then—oh dear God, I know it's for real, on purpose, from them, my enemy—a paintbrush is fixed between the thumb and forefinger. The writing, in blood, on a grocery-list piece of paper on Tino's pillow: *"You've got blood on your hands."* I can't hold myself up. I see my palms meet the comforter at the foot of the bed, my fingers spread like chicken feet. I fall to my knees and vomit onto the comforter. I try to scream, but they have silenced me. They have chopped off a girl's hand because of me. They have put a paintbrush between her thumb and forefinger. She and I are one. At that epiphany the scream tears free, then many screams.

The door bangs open, and there is Tad, breathless.

"Orla!"

Still on my knees, I look up at him. I spit flecks of vomit from my lips.

Tad blanches, is still for a moment. "Stay right there," he says. "Do not touch a thing." I can't move even if I want to. I hear water run in the bathroom sink. "Michael the Archangel, defend us in battle," he says, his voice loud above the running water. "Be our protection against the wickedness and snares of the devil." He comes back with a steaming washcloth and face towel.

"Here, let me help you." His voice is soft and sure. He kneels next to me and wipes my mouth. Bits of undigested canapés and hard-boiled eggs soil the bed. He looks only at my eyes, lifts me up, and leads me to the living room. It's as if we are on an ice rink, I a novice skater, he my coach. He holds both my hands, walking backwards to glide me forward out of the bedroom. He murmurs, "Good, that's right, come now." I follow, my footing unsure, ungainly. When we get to the couch, he lets go my hands and guides me, pressing my shoulders to help me sit down.

"We must get the police here right away."

I point to the refrigerator with the emergency and family numbers on a paper attached by magnets. My whole body is shaking. The door was locked when we arrived. They got in and out with no trouble. *My God, the girl!* I hate them so much.

"Call Marco Pannacci," I squawk. "He lives at the top of the steps. He's a policeman. His son Franco is Lu's friend."

Tino dials the number, then stretches the phone line over the kitchen island. I stand to take the phone in hand, leaning against the island. My body wants to fall.

"You've got to do the talking," Tad says. "I have no command of the language."

I nod. Thank God Marco is home. In less than two minutes he is at the door, uniform shirt not even buttoned, gun in his hand.

We all go into the bedroom together.

"*Gesu,*" he says.

He uses his mobile to call the *questura,* explains what has happened. The police do not use their sirens. Two of them arrive on foot, one holding a camera. While the one with the camera joins Marco in the bedroom, the other one talks with me and Tad, one at a time, separating us from each other, taking notes in the second bedroom. He is an older man with a mustache. We often see him at Mass with his wife at the Basilica di Santa Chiara. That's where Isa likes to go to Mass.

"The girl saint's church" she calls it. The one who interviews Tad and me is boyish and kind. His name badge reads "Arturo Cecchini." He keeps calling me signora. It feels like they are with us a long time. What do I tell Tino? I must protect the children. Oh, my Tino! They have ruined our refuge. Sullied it forever. My fault, my fault.

"Come into the bedroom, please," the officer with the camera says after Tad and I have been questioned. "Tell us exactly what happened, Signora Orla."

I do. Tad puts his arm around my shoulder. I wait for the hand to leap from the pillow and grab my throat. My heart beats too fast and my tongue is thick and foul-smelling.

"Alright," he says when he is satisfied with my narration, "we will take the evidence with us."

The officer with the camera puts it down on Tino's bureau, then reaches into a black rucksack and takes out a plastic bag. The other officer lifts my pillow with the hand from the bed and slides them as if one piece into the bag. He gets another bag for the comforter, as well.

"I'm sorry," I say, pointing to the vomit. "I couldn't help myself."

"Do not worry, Signora," the young officer says. "As long as you were not hurt."

They gather together and head toward the door.

"Are the others looking for the girl?" Marco asks.

The older officer nods. "She either has bled to death or they will have made it quicker."

I close my eyes but cannot block out what I imagine.

"You will stay with her tonight?" Marco asks Tad.

"Yes, sir."

"We grew up together. Tad is my oldest friend." I am crying now.

"Yes," says Marco. I have heard your son speak of him."

"Thank you, all of you," Tad says.

"We will be in touch with you as soon as we learn anything," the officer with the mustache says.

Tad closes and locks the door. I have ceased to see any purpose in locks.

We stand face to face. I am both wracked with guilt and seething with anger.

"I've got to clean this place up. It needs an exorcist."

"I agree," says Tad.

He follows me into the bedroom. We strip the bed and throw what's left of its linens into the trash. Then we re-make it, though I know for sure I cannot sleep in it tonight, or maybe ever again.

"Please, you first," I say, pointing to the shower.

Tad smiles and rests his chin on the top of my head. "Never. You will think me ungallant."

"I'm sorry you had to be here for this."

"I am grateful I was. It is the second time the forces of evil have begrimed your exhibits. First the Klan back in St. Suplice when we were not yet teenagers. Now the Camorristi when we are older, if not wiser."

"But now I have a husband and children in danger because of me."

I am crying. Tad holds me for awhile, then says, "Go, now. The others will be here soon."

Hot water streaming over me, soaping, soaping every inch of my flesh and hair, even brushing my teeth under the cleansing rush, I yearn for Tino. But I mustn't phone him until after the children are asleep. I mustn't be hysterical. I must remember what he told me after the dead rat episode: "They want to scare you. They want to stop you. If they wanted to kill you, you would already be dead." I am crying again. *Stop it*, I tell myself. It's the girl I should be crying for. All the girls. They think they can own me by putting my brush in her hand. Fuck them. Cut off their balls. Knock their teeth out. And God help her. Please, God, help her.

As promised, there is a knock at the door as the piazza's clock strikes nine. It is Angelina with Antonio, one of her kitchen boys. I motion them to come in.

As Tad helps Antonio with the trays, bags, and wine bottles, Angelina asks, "Are you alright, Orla?" She takes my hands in hers. "My God, you look like a ghost. What happened? The police told us there had been a break in up here and asked if we had seen any suspicious people around."

"Did you?" I ask.

"Yes," Angelina says, then puts her forefinger to her lips. "Wait."

Antonio comes out from the kitchen.

"Go, Antonio," Angelina says. "There are still customers downstairs."

Tad hands the boy a tip, closes the door behind him, and offers Angelina a seat.

"Please, you tell her," I say, and sit on the couch, tucking one leg under me, while the other swings back and forth, back and forth.

Tad joins me. Speaking in his reassuring modulating tone, he relates what happened as he might to a jury. Angelina crosses herself three times as he speaks.

"But what did you see, Angelina? You said you saw something suspicious," Tad says.

"There were many people today. We were very busy." She crosses her right leg over her left and rests both hands on her knee. "When the police came in, I told them that a man with a physician's bag had sat down at a table with a nun. They each ordered an espresso and some pastries, paid me, wished me a good evening, and left. But what struck me as odd was that the doctor called the nun 'Doll.' He said, 'Let's go, Doll, we have a long ride home.'" Angelina uncrosses her legs. "Nobody calls a nun 'Doll.' Nobody."

"What did the police tell you?" I ask.

"That there had been a break-in at your apartment and they were searching for the culprit."

"They didn't say anything about the hand?" asks Tad.

Angelina stands up. "Not a word."

"Can you not say anything, either, please?" I ask.

Angelina zips her lips with her right thumb and forefinger.

"Thank you."

"And I pray for the girl, whoever she is," Angelina says, and crosses herself once more. She turns to go. "Does Tino know yet?"

I shake my head no. "I'll have to tell him soon," I say. "I don't want him hearing about it in the news."

"God bless you," Angelina replies, and kisses me on both cheeks.

Once she's gone, Tad doesn't ask, but just pours two glasses of scotch straight up.

"I know this is not a traditional Italian cocktail," he says.

"Who cares?" I answer.

We down two each before Tiziana and Carmine knock. It's almost nine forty-five.

They sweep in, Tiziana smelling of perfume and smiling through ruby-red lips, Carmine twirling his right hand in the air at the sight of the bottle of Laphroaig on the kitchen island.

"I hope you've both had some time to unwind," Tiziana says. Then she looks at me.

"*JGesu*, did somebody die?"

*****

Evening News, March 9, 2002

Mutilated Woman Discovered in Haystack Linked to Gruesome Assisi Break-in

By Clarissa DiStefano: Reuters

A mutilated corpse was discovered by a farmer this afternoon in Assisi, Italy. The victim was a young woman whose right hand had been chopped off. She had also been sexually assaulted, according to the medical examiner. Police officers found an empty syringe several feet away from the corpse. An injection site on her left arm "points to death by a fatal substance," according to Officer Marco Faci of the Assisi questura.

Last evening, a residence identified as the holiday home of the American artist Orla Castleberry and her husband, Doctor Celestino Bacci, of Fiesole, was broken into. According to a government official in Assisi speaking on the condition of anonymity, the murder victim's severed hand was discovered in the artist's bedroom. The official believes both the murder and the break-in are the work of the Camorra, the criminal organization well known for human trafficking in the Naples area. A consortium highlighting its illegal trafficking enterprise was the focus of International Women's Day in Assisi. Ms. Castleberry's paintings on display there provided a visual affront to the System, as the Camorra is commonly called.

Police have yet to make an arrest. Ms. Castleberry was unavailable for comment.

Chapter Twenty-one
Lift High the Cross

Very few people believe in the devil these days, which suits the devil very well. He is always helping to circulate the news of his own death. The essence of God is existence, and He defines Himself as: "I am Who am." The essence of the devil is the lie, and he defines himself as: "I am who am not." Satan has very little trouble with those who do not believe in him; they are already on his side.

—Fulton J. Sheen

A navy-rimmed notecard Isa handed me yesterday was from Sister Aloise. It was an invitation to take tea with her at four on Holy Thursday, an hour after school lets out for the Easter weekend. Written in gorgeous Palmer-Method longhand was the priest's quotation above.

"Come in, come in," Sister Aloise says, having instructed me to arrive at the convent rather than the school door. "Thank you for joining me."

I hand her a potted lily. "My pleasure. Thank you for the invitation."

A table is set for two in a nook right off the kitchen. It might as well be in London. There are cucumber sandwiches and scones on a tiered tray. Butter and jam in silver servers. And two tea cups in a pink rose pattern. The tea is already steeping.

"Please," says Sister Aloise, motioning, and I sit as she rolls her chair to the window ledge adjacent to the table. She places the lily there and smiles at it. Then she wheels herself opposite me, reaches over to the tea pot, and pours.

"Isa tells me you are sad."

I am mortified. Hot. Speechless. No preamble or soft prelude during which to prepare.

The nun continues. "At daily intentions, since you have returned from Italy, Isa prays that the evil doers you painted will leave you alone."

I take a breath. Blow it out my mouth. Repeat. I lean forward, across the table.

"Sister, I had no idea she could read me like that! I thought I was a better actress."

Sister Aloise smiles with her lips closed, spreads some butter on a scone, and hands it to me. I accept it and place it on the rose plate.

"She told me she hears your praying in your bedroom."

"Of course she does. I pray the rosary in my bedroom every evening after dinner. Both children know that. Sometimes they join me. Otherwise they take a walk with their father."

Sister Aloise smiles again. This time I see her teeth. She takes a bite of a cucumber sandwich, then presses an ironed napkin to her lips.

"Do the children know all that happened in Assisi?"

I inhale again.

"I don't think so. At least I hope not. Tino and I have kept our comments general."

"Understandable."

She finishes her sandwich, pats her mouth again with the napkin. "Would you like a sandwich, too?"

I have not yet touched the scone on my plate.

"Thank you, no."

I am in no mood for food.

"You know, Orla, the mobsters are not your real enemy."

I raise my eyebrows. *What is she, nuts?* I aim for pleasantness.

"You don't think so?"

Sister Aloise spins her chair around as if it is a Disney amusement park ride.

"No. The Devil is. They are merely his instruments on earth."

"Merely" is hardly a word I'd associate with them. Tell *merely* to the girls they ruin.

"You're serious."

This time the nun cannot possibly miss the sarcasm in my tone. She spins her chair again, then cranes her neck over her tea cup and plate.

"Deadly." Her eyes flash.

I don't know whether to be angry, to laugh, or to agree.
"You see, Lucifer wants you to despair. And judging from your daughter's upset, he has almost succeeded. He is working to destroy Isa's confidence in you next."

If Isa didn't love this woman so much, I would already be on my feet and out the door. At least that is what my mind is telling me.

"Orla,"—the nun's voice is one of mother love now—"don't let him. Fight the bastard the way you fight the mobsters. Your life, your art, your marriage, your children depend on it!"

The nun wheels herself from the table mid-room so I can see all of her. She lifts the bottom half of her habit and I cover my mouth with both hands. The black oxfords resting on the wheelchair's footrest are a ruse.

"They are nailed to the footrest per Mother Superior's orders," she says. "So as not to frighten the children."

I examine the shoes, then look up at her.

"You don't have prosthetic legs?"

Sister Aloise shakes her head.

"No. My body ends just south of my posterior."

For the second time since arriving, I am at a loss for words. The nun lets her skirt fall.

"The man who hit me was driving south in the northbound lane of Route 684. It was ten in the evening and raining. I had just dropped Sister Eleanor Marie, may God rest her soul, here, and was returning to the motherhouse in Poughkeepsie. His car hit ours at seventy-five miles per hour. My legs were crushed, my ribs broken, and my forehead"—here, she lifts her wimple to reveal several scars on her forehead—"cut from the windshield's glass. I am lucky to be alive."

"Sister, I am so sorry. I hadn't known."

She wheels herself closer to me.

"Why would you? But here is what I want you to realize. I did not initially consider myself lucky. 'Blessed' is actually the term to use. I thought my life was over. I certainly could not take my science students on nature walks, I needed help to bathe, and my days of yoga poses were over."

I drink all of my tea at once. "I can't imagine the loss you felt."

She folds her wrinkled hands on top of her lap.

"I planned to kill myself."

"You did?"

"Yes. May God forgive me." She points to the tea pot. "Have some more."

I do.

"I was out of the hospital just a month, convalescing at the motherhouse. It had snowed, perhaps two or three inches. I excused myself from table at lunch, and wheeled myself outdoors. I did not put on a coat or even one of the stoles we often wore during the winter recreation hours. After all, what would have been the point?"

I am mesmerized by her telling.

"I wheeled myself to the edge of the long rock staircase leading from the motherhouse grounds down to the river. It was exactly 217 steps. We had a dock there, where we kept two war canoes and three kayaks. All I had to do was roll my chair over the top step. All the steps were nice and icy. It was a good option."

I sip my tea. "But you didn't do it. Why not?"

She adjusts her veil.

"Just as I was about to, I heard someone call my name. 'Aloise.' It was a woman's voice. I turned to my right and looked at someone I did not know. She wore a dark gray, rough-hewn dress cinched at the waist with a brown leather tie. Like mine, her head was covered in a wimple and a veil, only hers were rough, parchment-colored. Her feet were wrapped with cloth and tied around her ankles with twine. One could hardly call the coverings shoes. Her feet must have been freezing. 'Who are you?' I asked. 'Julian,' she answered."

"Julian who?"

Sister holds up her hands. "Wait, please."

The clock chimes the half hour. She continues.

"This Julian walked back and forth in front of my wheelchair. 'If you do it,' she said, 'Mother Superior will probably decide it was an accident due to the snow and ice. You, of course, will know otherwise, and your eternal damnation will be the regret you will feel in the falling. You will die a coward. Living requires courage. I believe you can live.' She walked behind the wheelchair. I spun it around so I could see her, but she was gone."

I sigh. "Were you on any medication?"

Sister Aloise grins.

"Morning vitamins. Caffeine."

I look at my tea cup, then back at her. "How do you know she was real?"

"I could do with another sandwich," Sister says, and she returns to the table.

We both sit in our original positions once more.

"She was most real, Orla," she replies between bites. "As I learned later that evening, when I looked in the card catalog under 'J' in the motherhouse library. I soon found her. She is Julian. Julian of Norwich. An English anchoress of the Middle Ages. Here is what she said."

Sister Aloise takes from under her plate a folded paper. The words are again written in her flowing script. She hands it to me to read.

En Plein Air

He said not, "Thou shalt not be tempested, thou shalt not be travailed, thou shalt not be dis-eased"; but he said, "Thou shalt not be overcome."

My throat aches and my eyes well up. My heart does not beat too fast like it does when I'm afraid. No, no. It is steady, its rhythm telling me I am alive and must be well. Of a sudden I feel better than I have since the night of March 8th. This nun has done something to me. Something fast, unexpected, unasked for, and REAL. And I know—dear readers, if you have been listening to me since I was eleven years old, you understand—that she has given me grace, graced me, made a miracle. I believe in miracles because I have known them personally. The realization of my true paternity when I was eleven, for instance, and its life-altering gifts. Mercy coming into my life and saving Luke's when he first intended to end it. Our Lady directing my brush to achieve my best ever painting, a contemporary Madonna and Child. The Contessa granting me Tino from the wreckage of a war. Tino saving Tad from once-certain death. Mercy challenging Brody's mortality with the birth of his daughter. In the guise of a tea party this broken-bodied nun, this Sister Aloise, has infused me with a potion that feels like medicine. Something that is firing me up inside and out. Making me believe the unbelievable: that good can come, not from evil, but in spite of evil. That evil doers can be thwarted, smitten, gulled, ground up, cut down. I know, I know, dear readers, that evil cannot be defeated or permanently done in. I'm not an innocent, that's for sure. But not to fight evil, to allow it to burgeon without a battle, to despair from it, that's a sin.

"Despair is narcissistic," pops out of my mouth. I didn't think to say it. I didn't think at all. The utterance was as spontaneous as a sneeze or a burp. I stand up. I wish I had a trumpet to blow.

"Exactly," Sister Aloise says, spinning her chair around twice.

I cross to her side of the table and plant a loud kiss on her cheek.

"Thank you, Sister."

She lets me push her wheelchair to the door.

"Let your Good Friday end tomorrow, like the Lord's, Orla. Easter is coming. Don't you forget it, Orla. Easter always comes."

"Go to hell, Lucifer," I say, as the nun closes the door behind me.

Chapter Twenty-Two
Unexpected News at Easter

Easter Sunday isn't turning out as expected. Mercy has the flu, so she's been relegated to the guest room in her new house while Thérèse bottle-feeds Phoenix and sees to her other needs at a distance from her mother. They won't be joining us for dinner as initially planned. The kiddos are most disappointed, having filled a giant basket of infant goodies for their niece.

"Why don't we go to St. Patrick's for Mass?" Tino suggests. "And then watch the Easter Parade on Fifth Avenue. We will all be tourists."

Everyone likes his idea, so we're in a cab heading to midtown by nine-fifteen.

St. Patrick's is as close as Manhattan Roman Catholic churches get to the storied cathedrals and basilicas in Italy. The music is glorious (violinist Nonna approves), the banks of lilies fragrant enough for those with allergies to sneeze periodically, and the celebrant's homily full of hope.

"May we walk in the parade?" Isa asks, as we exit the cathedral down its front steps.

"Good grief," Lu says, and rolls his eyes.

"Lu, won't you escort me?" Nonna asks.

Tino's eyes hone in on our son's.

"Of course, Nonna."

And so we walk. Four of us do, at least. Isa skips. Our Sunday best clothes pale in comparison to the costumes on display. Full-bodied white bunny outfits complete with whiskers, a three-piece pink suit tailor made to perfectly fit the dandy wearing it and twirling a walking stick; matching violet shirtwaists for two women sporting silver kitten heels, purple ribbons trailing down their shoulders from broad-brimmed straw hats. Tino's and Lu's standard Sunday uniform of blue blazers, khaki slacks, rep ties, buttoned-down cotton shirts, and loafers are a kind of sartorial white noise along the parade route. Nonna's, Isa's, and my lady-wear fares slightly better. As always for special events, Nonna appears in a floral midi-dress, today's number featuring blue and white hydrangeas. Her shoes are soft sky-blue leather numbers with one-inch squared heels. She wears a white shrug and crocheted wrist-length gloves, as well. Isa is skipping sunshine in a yellow dress with smocking from the Peter Pan collar to her waist. White tights and shiny Mary Janes mimic the color of the headband holding her wavy hair in place. I'm in a coral pants suit with taupe leather wedges, dangling gold earrings, an oversize ceramic bangle on my right wrist, and the turquoise ring Tino gave me when he proposed. When several fellows, all three wearing feather boas around their necks, begin singing "Easter Parade," the kiddos link arms with Nonna; and Tino and I join hands to sway with the rest of the crowd. We still miss Mercy, Phoenix, and Thérèse, but the made-in-Manhattan celebration, part religious, part gay pride, part Mardi Gras meets New Year's Eve, distracts and pleases us.

Later, around the dinner table, we mix traditions. Fettucine with asparagus, Virginia baked ham with clove and mustard, deviled eggs, and ricotta cake. Pinot grigio. Espresso, fruit, and, of course, chocolate rabbits for all.

"What shall we do tomorrow?" Nonna asks. "Perhaps visit the seaport?"

Lu goes to her and puts his arm around her shoulder. "We have school, Nonna."

My mother-in-law looks surprised. "You do? No Pasquetta here?"

"Unfortunately not, Mamma," Tino says. "No 'little Easter' in the U. S."

Nonna stands to help me clear the table. "Unfortunate." She pauses. "But how about I meet you and Isa after school and we go to the seaport then?"

We all are standing now.

"Yes, yes," Isa says.

"I'll buy you a souvenir for you to take back," says Lu. "I saved some of my allowance, so it will be just from me." He sticks his tongue out at his sister. She pretends to punch him.

And so it goes until their bedtime.

I must say I'm glad Aurora agreed to stay through Easter. She has been a fixture in my life from the first week I arrived in Fiesole in 1989. Initially as an information source for my paintings, then as a friend, and finally as my mother-in-law. I love her, love that our children love her. She seems to feel at ease in our temporary New York home. And it's been wonderful watching her and Tino together again. How she pats his cheek every night before she heads upstairs. How he delivers a cappuccino to her bedroom every morning. I'll be sad to see her go. We won't catch up with her again until we leave the States from New Orleans July 10th, after visiting my parents and brother. The year will have been one for the books, that's for sure. But I'm probably unwise to get ahead of myself. We have April, May, and June to contend with yet.

"Good night, good night," the kiddos say, interrupting my thoughts.

Tino and I kiss them. Nonna says, "Remember, we have a date after school."

They clatter up the stairs, grumble about taking turns in the bathroom, slam a door or two, then, as if rendered speechless, succumb to silence.

"Shall we have some brandy?" I ask.

"Why not?" Aurora says.

Tino gets three snifters from the kitchen and sets them on the coffee table near the fireplace. I retrieve the brandy from the caddy we have made a bar. Aurora relaxes into a wing chair while Tino pours, then joins me on the couch. I kick off my shoes and get comfortable, my left leg under me, my right foot resting on the floor.

"Thank you," Aurora says, "for inviting me to stay the month."

"The thanks is ours, Mamma. I could not have manage-ed without you. And I know that Orla felt less guilty about leaving the children as long as you were with them."

"True." I offer a toast, "To you, Aurora," and we sip.

All of a sudden, Aurora sits up straight, crosses her legs at her knees, and folds her hands under her chin. She looks serious and clears her throat.

"What, Mamma?" Tino asks.

She clears her throat again. "I am going to tell you something that may upset you."

Tino sits up straight now, too.

"Are you ill, Mamma?"

"No, quite the opposite, my son. I am very well. Almost completely content with life."

Tino remains poised for the worst.

Almost.

"What would make '*almost*' disappear, Aurora?" I ask.

My mother-in-law unfolds her hands and places them one on each knee.

"Orla, I think you can guess."

I know I can. Shall I?

"Dieter," I whisper.

Now she leans forward in her chair. I put my arm around Tino's shoulder and hold him close. He waits.

"Yes. Dieter and I have been corresponding by mail. I initiated," she says. "I wrote first." She drinks one, two sips from her snifter.

Tino leans back. "I am glad you are not ill, Mamma. When," —he pauses—"when did you write?"

"Several weeks after you left for New York," Aurora says. "I missed you all, you see. And I realized that as long as you two and the children were with me in Fiesole, I could keep Dieter in the past, in the back of my mind. I could be distracted by the love at hand. I've done so since you married, and even more so since the twins came into the world."

Her right hand shakes as she puts down the empty snifter. I let Tino go, stand, and offer her more brandy. She nods yes and I fill her glass. Tino swallows his drink in two gulps and motions for me to pour him another.

"But, Tino, I do not want to die without seeing him again. I am seventy-four years old, but he is eighty-four. And since his sister with whom he lived in Germany died last October, he is free. I have invited him to Fiesole and he has agreed to come. He will arrive the first of June."

Tino's hands turn to fists, but his voice is modulated.

"I understand, Mamma."

Aurora takes a deep breath. "I want you to know him and he to know you, your wife, and his grandchildren."

Tino stands and paces behind the couch.

"Time is running out, you see." She puts her hand to her mouth and waits.

"I understand, Mamma. I do."

I envelop myself in silence. This is not my story to decide. I watch and wait. Tino walks back and forth behind the couch as he speaks.

"But I find it difficult to forgive what he did to you, what he was party to. He was a Nazi, for heaven's sake, Mamma. He killed our people."

Aurora looks up and across the couch at her son. "He did nothing to me, dearest Tino, except to love me and to give me you. It was the war that forced our hands."

Tino paces faster. "He murdered the three resisters. Three Fiesolani."

Aurora stands now.

"Just as I stood by outside the door of Room 109 at the Hotel Aurora while one of his officers raped my friend Constantina, another maid at the hotel. I am just as guilty, if not more so. I had matches in my apron pocket. I could have—I should have—started a fire and screamed. I might have saved her. But I did not even try. I listened. Can you imagine, Tino? I listened!"

Tino stops pacing. "You never told me that."

Aurora walks to her son, faces him. I don't turn to look.

"Because I am ashamed."

They both stand still, remain so silent that I hear the ice-maker grinding in the kitchen, the grandfather clock ticking by the stairs. Aurora moves first, circling around the couch and coffee table back to her chair. She sits. Tino follows suit and joins me on the couch once more.

"Think, Tino. The Contessa and the Professoressa, both resisters themselves, could not bring themselves to kill Dieter when they each had the chance. No, instead they saw to it that I would have a husband and my child a father. They forged the documents to make it so. They knew that were it discovered I was carrying a Nazi's child, I would be tarred and feathered, shorn of my hair, and, worst of all—unspeakable, my son— knifed and slashed until you, the infant I carried from love, were dismembered and killed."

She stops her mouth with her hands. Tino goes to her, kneels, and takes her in his arms. "Mamma."

She weeps now, as do I. Then she gathers herself and raises her hands, resting them on Tino's shoulders.

"Dieter, the Contessa, the Professoressa," she whispers, "each of them gave me you. The war, only the war, took, took, and took. Those three, my Tino, gave me my life and yours."

"Mamma," Tino says.

The two of them clasp one another. I leave the couch and tiptoe up the stairs.

I don't know when I fell asleep or when Tino and Aurora came upstairs. When I wake, though, it is still dark, and Tino is sitting on the edge of our bed beside me. He is dressed in his pajamas, but his hair is mussed and his reading glasses are perched on his nose.

"Here," he says, and puts a piece of paper into my hands. I sit up and turn on the reading lamp. The clock on the night table shows four o'clock. I say nothing, just read.

> *Dear Father,*
>
> *I address you so because that is who you are. It has taken me the twelve years since I learned of you, along with my mother's recent Easter confession that she can no longer abide living without your active presence, that I write.*
>
> *Mamma tells me you will come to Fiesole in early June and perhaps reside with her in her home. I understand you visited that home, then owned by Professoressa Antonella Ghiraschi, to ensure Mamma's safety the night you German soldiers were fleeing Fiesole. You knew my mother was with child, your child, and trusted that the professoressa would keep her and the child safe to full term when the late Contessa*

took over our care. Mamma has told me numerous other facts about you that have tempered my original horror and anger at your Nazi affiliation.

My wife Orla and I invite you to join us at our home in Fiesole with Mamma. My most fervent wish is that Mamma lives out her days in happiness. She has made me realize that you are the key to such happiness.

My family and I shall arrive from the States the morning of July 11. Although with some trepidation, I want to meet you and come to understand you. I want my children to know each of their four grandparents. Until now, they know and love only three.

Please do not hesitate to be in touch in the meanwhile.

Until July, then, I wish you good health and a safe journey to my mother.

Sincerely,
Your son, Tino

Chapter Twenty-Three
Heartbeats

When I called Amelia to wish her a Happy Easter, she told me, "It will be all denouement starting now. Before you know it, you'll be back in Fiesole." She was correct. From Pasquetta to today, Saturday, June 8th, we've been preparing to leave New York. Our visits to the zoo, the seaport, Broadway, another Saturday afternoon cruise around Manhattan on the Circle Line, have felt like a farewell tour. Our final two commitments will be Phoenix's baptism and the children's good-bye to Saints Francis and Clare Academy. Tino and two of the others in his research group are drafting a paper about the positive and negative side-effects of the latest AIDS treatments. Once it's vetted, they hope to present it at a conference in Rome next autumn. Tuesday, he and I will attend a parting lunch his research group has planned at the hospital. At NYU I've lectured incoming art majors and cleaned my studio, and shipped Tiziana's massive painting to her Naples apartment. I also painted a portrait of wonderful Keys, which I gave to him my last day at the studio. His eyes had filled and he took a wrinkled handkerchief from his back pants pocket to wipe them.

"Thank you, Orla. I hope to see you again."

We hugged and I gave him our phone number in Fiesole, "should you ever want to visit."

The kiddos are writing thank-you notes to their teachers, and Tino and I plan to make a significant donation to the school that so lovingly welcomed our children and cared for them well throughout a tumultuous year. Without a doubt, Saints Francis and Clare has been a stabilizing force for our family, and many others.

This morning Tino has taken Isa and Lu to the Bronx Zoo. They wanted to ride the subway to and from, pay special attention to the apes and the snakes, then return home by way of F. A. O. Schwarz. Their being gone has made it much easier to turn this place into the kind of bed and breakfast my parents and brother will enjoy. Their flight from New Orleans is due at six-ten this evening. I've arranged for a car to meet them at JFK. "Chinese take-out" was the unanimous decision regarding supper. So now that the guest room beds are made, the bathroom spotless, towels at the ready, I'm free to head to the beauty salon for a haircut, color, and pedicure. I ought to be home early enough to catch a nap.

My mobile rings just as I'm walking out the door. Fumbling through my purse, I pull it out and see my dad's number.

"Hi, Dad. Are you at the airport?"

Pause.

"No, Orla. I'm afraid we won't be coming. Your mamma collapsed on the tennis court at The Links early this morning. She had a seven o'clock reservation for a doubles. And a good thing she did. The other three ladies phoned for an ambulance right away and did everything right while they waited."

I lean against the entry hall closet door.

"Oh, no! Is she okay? Are you with her?" My top teeth bite into my bottom lip.

"We don't know yet. The ambulance crew took her down to the little hospital in Convent. She has a fractured ankle and a concussion for sure. Her blood pressure is running high. She needs a better-equipped hospital, so I've got her in an ambulance now, heading to Tulane Medical Center in NOLA. I want a brain scan done. Your brother should be here soon. He'll drive us both there to meet her. I wanted to tell you before I phone Mercy."

I walk into the kitchen and take a seat at the table. Cross myself. Wait.

"You there, honey?"

I wipe some tears off my cheeks. "Yes, I'm here."

"Okay. I see Arthur pulling up. I'll phone you again the minute I have some news."

"Please do, Daddy."

"Alright, then."

"Oh, Daddy, one more thing. Do you want me to call Mercy?"

"No, I want her to hear the news from me. I'll phone her when I have some answers."

"Alright."

"Sit tight, Orla. I promise I'll phone as soon as I have more to tell you."

I look at the wall clock. Almost one.

"Daddy, tell her I love her, will you?"

"Count on it."

"Love you, too. Tell Arthur not to get a ticket on the way."

Laughter. "I will."

Click.

Mamma! Her name repeats in my head throughout the afternoon. Walking to Tesora Salon. Stopping at Duane Reade for deodorant. Through the empty house when I return. It's almost four-thirty when Tino and the children find me sitting in the wing chair, knees under my chin, staring into space.

"Your hair looks so pretty, Mamma," Isa says.

"It's the color of honey," Lu decides. "One of the lions had a mane that color." He heads toward the kitchen and opens the freezer door for a popsicle.

"Did you have a nice time?" I ask.

Tino looks at me. He can tell something's wrong. His face is a question mark. He stands still.

"When will Mamerva, Pappa Prout, and Arthur get here, Mamma?" asks Isa.

Tino waits. I lower my legs to the floor and lean forward in the chair. "I'm sorry to tell you they won't be coming, Isa."

"Why not?" Lu asks. He sucks on the red popsicle and kneels down right in front of me.

I repeat the tale my father told me. Isa elbows her way by her brother to sit on my lap. She rubs my cheek.

"I'm so sorry," Tino says.

Lu takes the popsicle out of his mouth. His face turns red. "Is she going to die, too?" He flings the popsicle into the air. It falls on the planked floor. Tino wraps our son in his arms.

My phone rings. I stand so we make a tight circle. Everyone hovers close to hear.

"Orla, Dad here. The brain scan shows no damage. But your mother has an irregular heartbeat. The cardiologist is trying to regulate it medically now. She's decided to admit her. I'll stay with her overnight. Arthur will drive home."

None of us moves.

"She'll be alright, then?"

Isa folds her hands as if in prayer. Lu watches my face. Tino rubs my shoulders.

"We'll see, Orla. Time will tell. I'll be staying right with her."

I hand the phone to Tino. He and Daddy talk doctor lingo. Lu picks up what's left of the popsicle and throws it into the kitchen trash. Isa follows him, wets a paper towel, then returns to clean the sugary spot on the floor. When Tino ends the call and hands my phone back to me, he pulls me to him. He kisses me on both cheeks as if we are back in Italy and I have just arrived home from a soccer match with the kiddos. He takes my right hand in his left.

"Your mother and I are going to take a little nap," he says. "Then we will order the supper you ask-ed for."

Lu nods, and Isa walks up the stairs ahead of us.

"I'm going to rest, too, Mamma," she says, "and say a prayer for Mamerva, like Sister Aloise would."

"That is a good idea," Tino says.

"Thank you, Isa."

"I might as well play solitaire, if nobody else is sticking around," Lu says. He takes a deck of cards from the game box on the coffee table. We leave him leaning over the columns of cards.

Tino closes our bedroom door behind us. We lie down facing each other. He wraps one arm around my waist. I close my eyes and listen to my heart. I think how hard Mamma and I have loved one another from the very start, no matter how angry we made each other. I want to love her harder still.

Chapter Twenty-Four
Baptism and Leave-takings

Brody's parents have flown in from Prague, his brother from Paris. Martin Bercik insisted on reserving hotel rooms for the three of them at a nearby Marriott until he leaves next Friday. He is a litigator and has to return to Paris to prepare for a trial. "Then you may enjoy my parents 24-7 for a month," he told Mercy. "God help you."

We all laughed. But, truth be told, it will be interesting to see how Thérèse, Mercy, Miloslova and Franto manage. Phoenix will certainly be attended to, coveted, cosseted, and well-loved. But will they fight over her? Squabble in the kitchen? Drive Mercy mad? I'm glad the house is large enough that everyone can find privacy when it's wanted. I'm gladder still that I'll be an hour's drive away, at least until mid-June, when the distances will grow even greater: all the way south to St. Suplice through July 10th, then across the Atlantic to home in Fiesole. By Christmas, when Mercy, Thérèse, and Phoenix intend to visit, I'll be yearning for them.

Brody was keen on buying an older home in a neighborhood with mature trees, a family place within walking distance to a school, a church, and village shops. I must say, he and Mercy found what they sought. Their place is the fourth house on a cul-de-sac of twelve homes. It has a deep front porch, and a back deck that runs the length of the place, with sliding doors leading to it from the kitchen, the dining room, and the den. There are five bedrooms and four baths, four of the bedrooms and baths upstairs, and one down. The downstairs one is Thérèse's. The kitchen is spacious, with detailed oak cabinets and fine marble countertops and backsplash. Mercy purchased some of the former owners' furniture so that she moved in with a fully-decorated dining and living room already in place. The house looks as if she has lived in it for years. Only Phoenix's nursery is brand new. Her father's portrait hangs facing her crib, and several photographs of Mercy and Brody are scattered on the open shelves behind a rocking chair that belonged to my Grandmother Castleberry. Mercy selected a circus theme, so I painted a big top and a merry-go-round on one wall, with a juggler and a Dalmatian dog between them. A tall bookcase houses all of Mercy's childhood favorite reads along with a selection of picture books that Isa and Lu bought at Barnes & Noble: *Goodnight Moon, The Cat in the Hat, Where the Wild Things Are.*

Just after ten o'clock we gather at the house for coffee, bagels, babka, and croissants. Phoenix's baptism will take place during noon Mass. Brody's parents are gregarious and modern. I expected the first, but not the second. Can't tell you why. Perhaps I've watched too many post-WWII films. I'm embarrassed by my facile bias. Miloslova is sleek in a fitted navy dress and higher heels than I can manage these days. Her hair is a soft brown, styled in a low bun. She wears a fascinator with a white carnation and a mesh veil. Franto sports a pin-striped suit. Its gray-blue color matches his eyes. Martin looks the Parisian he has become in pointy black shoes, a fitted linen blazer, open-necked starched shirt, and tan slacks that have been pressed.

When Franto speaks, it sounds as if Brody has come back to life. This is both thrilling and sad. Mercy tears up from time to time during our coffee hour. Miloslova does, too.

After breakfast, the men go outside, as do Isa and Lu. There is a swing set in the back yard. From the kitchen window I see them kicking themselves high up. I head upstairs to freshen up. At the top of the stairs I see Mercy in the nursery, dressing Phoenix in her father's baptismal robe that Miloslova has brought from Prague. She is singing "You Are My Sunshine." I smile. My mother sang it to me all the time. I knock on the open door. Mercy turns and smiles.

"Come in, Mamma. Doesn't she look the little princess?"

Phoenix coos. Mercy hands her to me. We smile at each other.

"Her hair is black silk, just like yours."

Mercy nods. Then a sob she can't suppress escapes from her gut.

"Mercy," I say, stroking her hair even as I hold her daughter.

She moves away from me and sits in the rocking chair. Back and forth, back and forth. My body keeps time with her rocking and Phoenix is closing her eyes. We are quiet. I hear dishes and silverware being collected downstairs.

"Sometimes it's okay, Mamma. Every now and again even an entire day is okay."

She stops rocking and places her hands underneath her body.

"Then, all of a sudden, I think I cannot go on. I feel as if I'm at sea and a life raft has been taken out from under me."

She lifts her hands and grabs the arms of the rocking chair.

"I want to scream. I hate God. I love Phoenix. She deserves to have a father."

Her shoulders droop and she sighs. I don't have wise words, or even soothing ones. How can she be soothed? How can I return the missing part of her existence?

Phoenix gurgles. Her mouth is a heart. Her cheeks are rosy and plump like her father's were.

"Are you and my granddaughter ready?" It is Thérèse calling from down the staircase.

Mercy stands up.

"Yes, Mother. We're coming."

I hand her the baby.

"I'll be right down."

In the bathroom I look in the mirror, floss my teeth, and fluff my hair. Huh. Mercy has never met her father. I had two. Phoenix is left only with Brody's DNA, some photographs, and a closet full of clothes she'll never see worn. Traces of a man. Why is all this? What does it mean? What if it just is? Jesus.

We all walk two blocks to church, several of the neighbors joining us as we go. This feels European, a procession in the village, right for the occasion.

Amelia and Hal meet us there. They had been delayed from Long Island by not-unusual traffic. Hal is holding a camera and

Amelia has nosegays for Mercy, Miloslova, and me. Phoenix doesn't cry when Monsignor Coffey pours holy water on her forehead. Wiggling instead, she raises her little hands in the air.

"A hallelujah from the girl," the monsignor says, and the congregation laughs. He speaks with an Irish brogue. When he announces, "Child of God and member of our parish, Phoenix Brooklyn Bercik," Amelia holds my granddaughter up to face the congregation. Everyone applauds and, one by one, stands.

After Mass ends, Monsignor Coffey invites everyone downstairs to the church hall for a reception. "You are all invited. The New Mothers' Group awaits you. And now, one of Brody's special friends, the man who suggested he and Mercy might like to join our parish and neighborhood, will lead us all."

Mercy looks to me, sitting in the pew behind her, with a deer-in-the-headlights expression. I scrunch my shoulders and shake my head; I am not in the know. On the monsignor's cue, the sound of bagpipes from the vestry. Mercy raises her hands to her mouth. Tim O'Shea, the bagpiper who led Mayor Giuliani into Windows on the World every January 2nd when the mayor celebrated NYC's first responders, bows before the altar. He nods to Mercy and her entourage, and leads the monsignor down from the altar. Row by row, we follow, Mercy with Phoenix in her arms flanked by godparents Martin and Amelia. Overused as the expression is, dear readers, there really isn't a dry eye in God's house.

Downstairs, young mothers and fathers and babies form two lines either side of us. Several babies wail at the sound of the bagpipes, while others wave and clap their hands. Lu is delighted. "Just like in Scotland!" Isa hold her hands over her ears.

After Tim's last note, informality ensues. Introductions are made, hugs exchanged, platters of ham and eggs Benedict, fruit salads. Coffee cakes are placed on a buffet. A bartender is concocting Bloody Marys and mimosas. Coffee is percolating. Specialty teas are arranged by type. When most are seated, Monsignor Coffey takes to the stage, stands next to Tim, and speaks into the microphone an altar boy hands him.

"Thank you all, especially the New Mothers' Group and Tim, for welcoming Phoenix and her extended family to St. Patrick's Parish today."

I brace myself for a boring lecture, but am instead surprised.

"Everyone here is keenly aware of the great joy at Phoenix's birth and the tremendous sorrow at her da's absence."

Mercy is leaning into Thérèse's bosom. Miloslova pats her eyes with her napkin. Franto is tight-lipped. Tino grips my hand. Sitting across from us, Isa and Lu look to Tino and me.

I mouth the words "It's okay." Tino nods at the twins and puts his forefinger to his mouth.

"We hope Mercy, Thérèse, and Phoenix will be long, if not lifetime, members of the parish."

"Here, here!" Several parishioners hold their glasses upward.

"And we want to ensure that Phoenix will have the opportunity to join the pre-school, our elementary school, and eventually, a Catholic high school of her family's choice."

I think I know where this is heading. Amelia's husband walks from their table and kneels in front of the stage with his camera.

"So,"—Father motions to Cathy Strilickis, the founder of the New Mothers' Group I met just moments ago—"I give you Cathy."

Cathy hands her baby Natalie to Steven, her husband, and bounds up the stairs to the stage. Though she has been practicing medicine for five years, she doesn't look at day over sixteen in a sky blue sundress and white shrug. She stands between the bagpiper and the priest holding an envelope and smiles all the while she speaks.

"On behalf of our group, and with the extremely generous donation from Tim O'Shea," —she raises her hand toward Tim —"we would like to present Mercy with a fifty-thousand-dollar scholarship that will cover Phoenix's schooling through high school and even a bit further."

I am dumbfounded. Thunderstruck. Overjoyed.

"Won't you join us, Mercy?"

Mercy hands Phoenix to Miloslova and climbs the steps to the stage. The top of her head just reaches Tim's shoulders. He holds her in a bear hug until Cathy nudges him, puts the microphone on the floor, and whispers into Mercy's ear. Monsignor Coffey rests his broad hands on Mercy's shoulders for a moment, then gestures a blessing on her forehead. Cathy hands her the envelope. Mercy's hands are shaking. Applause fills the auditorium.

"How wonderful," Tino says.

"Yes. Wonderful."

Isa jumps up and down. Lu stands and claps his hands.

All of a sudden, Mercy takes two steps forward on the stage. The auditorium goes silent. Tim, Cathy, and Monsignor Coffey move stage right. Will Mercy speak? I watch her compose herself. Gather up her reserves. Focus like a competitive swimmer braced for the firing shot. Facing us all, dear readers, my daughter is silent. Radiant. A vision in her pink silk shift. Her ivory ballet slippers. She takes a deep, long breath. Fingers her wedding band. Looks out at us all. Then she folds her hands. And, just as Thérèse did in New Orleans in 1989 when she re-united with this beautiful daughter we share, she bows from the waist. A slow, deep bow. This beautiful, injured, disciplined girl turned mother.

What the world gives us, dear readers, is beyond my understanding. Such horrors and losses, such splendidness and generosity. Phoenix is crying for her mother now. She wants to be fed as we have been. Waits to be sated, as we are. Emotion unites us, then separates. Each of us trying to make sense of it. To shape it. When we leave St. Patrick's and walk back to the house, it is not in a group procession, as it was only three hours earlier. No, we are solitary walkers now, contemplative and silent as we follow the route home to the future.

Chapter Twenty-Five
St. Suplice

We are forty-five minutes from landing in New Orleans. My brother Arthur plans to meet us outside Arrivals and drive us home to St. Suplice, the tiny, sultry, beloved place of my birth. Lu is dozing beside me with *Treehouses: How to Build Them* open across his lap. The book was a gift from his Navy-Seal math teacher who tricked his students into loving mathematics by having them design and construct things. All year long they dreamed, postulated, measured, multiplied, divided, cut, fit, hammered, and so on. After they built the deck for the school, they constructed a toddler-sized swing set, several bedside tables for the sisters, a coffee table that converts to a chess board, and a sideboard for the convent dining room. On the last day of school, Seal presented Lu with the book and told him, "I'll expect to see a finished product when I visit Fiesole next summer."

Meanwhile, Sister Aloise sent Isa off with a holy goodies bag: wooden rosary, a missalette with Italian text on the left pages and English on the right, and a Saints Francis and Clare banner. "I will keep you in my prayers, Miss Isa," Sister Aloise said, "and please keep me in yours." Both my daughter and I sniffled a little as Sister made the sign of the cross over us as we leaned down to her in her wheel chair. Now, across the aisle, Isa is also asleep, her head nestled just below Tino's shoulder. Her fingernails are bright coral. She asked me to paint them last evening "so Mamerva will notice." As you might guess, my mother enjoys a vibrant manicure.

Tino and I exchange glances. "Bittersweet," he said, when I asked him last night in bed how he felt about leaving New York. "I have always like-ed Manhattan. The energy, the mix of cultures, enlivens, don't you think? And my colleagues were the best in the business. So open to new ideas."

I will miss Manhattan some, too. What continues to amaze me is how determined New Yorkers were to resume "normal" life after 9/11. Doing so was their middle finger to the enemies who attacked them. That's why Mercy said she plans to stay. "I was driven out of Saigon. I won't be driven out of the home we chose."

We'll all miss seeing Phoenix regularly. I never expected to be a distant granny, but so I will be. She'll know our voices if we phone often. And hopefully we'll be together again in Fiesole for Christmas.

"Please place your seats in their upright positions and prepare for landing."

Tino and I each nudge the children awake.

"Are we there?" Isa says, her voice a squeak as she rubs her eyes.

Lu closes his book and reaches under the seat for his duffle bag. He unzips the bag, slides the book in, then returns the bag to its takeoff and landing position.

We're off-boarded down roll-up steps. The moment I step out of the cabin, I know I'm home. The humid heat falls upon me like a damp blanket. Since we've already shipped the majority of our clothing back to Fiesole and are lugging carry-ons only, we breeze through Arrivals and find Arthur awaiting us. He's standing beside his school's van dressed in Jesuit High School soccer shorts, ready to coach a summer camp match soon after he deposits us.

Isa was correct. The first thing Mamerva says to her after she drops her bag on the veranda is, "Why, aren't *you* ready for a bright summer. Those nails match my bathing suit." There is much hugging and bustling on the veranda, then more inside. Daddy bounds down the stairs, kisses us all, then, on Mamerva's insistence, leads us all up to our respective rooms.

"Freshen up some," Mamerva says as we head upstairs, "then we'll have an early supper. I'm sure you're all tired."

The children are fond of the bedrooms they've come to consider theirs. Lu is in Daddy's boyhood room, still painted Wedgewood blue and still sporting Prout's high-school sports trophies. He likes the rocking chair for reading. Isa's in what used to be Arthur's spot until he got his own place — a condo in NOLA not far from his school. On the way home he told us he now heads the Computer Science Department. Mamerva has feminized the room for Isa. Imagine violet-painted walls, white trim, and eyelet bed wear and curtains. Miniature paintings I gave my Mamma during my adolescent years grace the walls, and I am touched that she has arranged them so artfully. Isa flops on the bed, then hops up to arrange her clothes in the dresser and closet.

Tino and I get Grandmother Castleberry's former enclave. It has been a sanctuary to me since the day Mamma and I moved into the house, less than a month after grandmother's death, when we were unexpectedly and suddenly rich, the beneficiaries of Grandmother's steely, insistent love. The en suite bathroom sports a guest's dream of a tub/shower big enough for two, and the down comforter resembles a cumulous cloud.

We all stay up way too late, most of us until well after midnight, just catching up with one another on the veranda. Potted citronella candles decorate the veranda railings and keep the bugs at bay. The kids play Monopoly and then poker with Daddy while Mamma, Tino, and I talk, the three of us stretched out on the teak lounge chairs. Town gossip, mostly. Mamma waves off any and all questions about her health.

"It's Mrs. Charbonneau who's been dealt a horrible blow. Can't speak anymore, can't walk, doesn't recognize her husband or son. She just lies in her bed with her nurse sitting next to her watching a used-to-be brilliant woman vanish moment by moment."

I sit up in the lounge chair. "I plan to visit her tomorrow, Mamma. Then ask Mr. Charbonneau and Tad to supper, if that's alright with you. I'll see to the groceries and cooking."

"How nice, honey. That's fine with me."

Daddy pauses from his poker playing, lights a cigar, and turns to me. "Okay by me, as well. About six-thirty, Orla, so I can get a swim in after office hours."

Daddy looks the same as he did when I saw him last Christmas. Still enjoys his scotch on the rocks with a twist of lemon. Still wears bright striped cotton button-downs and bow ties under his doctor's coat to the office. Mamma is bit worn from her recent scare, but primped and primed nonetheless. She might model for a ladies-of-a-certain-age Talbot's. Tonight she pretty much matches Isa's bedroom. She also outdid herself in the kitchen, sating us with fried fish, pulled pork, mac and cheese, coleslaw, and ice-box cake. She's the first to go to bed, just after eleven. When the rest of us finally say our goodnights and settle in upstairs, the deep night dark envelops me in as perfect a rest as possible. Even with Tino beside me, I find a respite I can only describe as my childhood nights. My body relaxes completely. I listen for crickets. Feel the cool air circulate. Curl up under the lightweight down comforter. "Now I lay me down to sleep." Then, forgetfulness.

I must have been unusually tired, for I don't wake up until well after ten. Tino stirs when I leave the bed, but lingers while I throw on a robe and go peek into each child's room. Much to my surprise, both are still sound asleep. Downstairs, Mamma has already protected us from the sun and heat. The curtains are drawn, the Roman shades lowered, the air-conditioning turned up, and the ceiling fans whir on the veranda. The house is quiet. I don't hear Mamma on the phone (Her morning "check-in calls," as she terms them, can take her from eight all the way to eleven some days), and Daddy no doubt walked down to his office several hours ago. He sees patients between nine and one o'clock most days, but likes to prepare for the day alone before he unlocks the front door and his secretary, Hallie LaFlamme, arrives. Hallie has been with Daddy since I was thirteen. Like him, she shows no sign of calling it quits.

"Got to have a reason to spiffy up every morning," she tells anyone who asks. "One gets old if one does not spiffy up."

Having no one to tend to, I decide to go upstairs and shower. No sooner have I stepped into Grandmother's cavernous tub with movable shower heads than Tino joins me. "Be right there!" he calls out to Lu, when our son bellows, "Where is everyone, anyway?"

I emerge from the bedroom in my standard hot-day outfit, a linen shift and strappy flat sandals. Today I've chosen a pink palette. After visiting Mrs. Charbonneau, I want to take Mamma to The Links Spa for a massage and whatever else she likes, then stop at the grocery store to pick up fixings for dinner. My menu is a simple one: shrimp cocktail, grilled salmon, asparagus, "dirty" beans and rice, and ice cream sundaes. Daddy's bar has everything else the adults will want. The children will relish making the sundaes.

A handwritten note greets me from the kitchen table where Saran Wrap covers a plate of coffee cake, a spinach quiche, and homemade sourdough bread:

> *Coffee set to be plugged in. Daddy should be back just after one. I have an appointment in the salon at eight, if you can believe that! Big wedding, the Courtmanche's youngest daughter, with six bridesmaids, two flower girls, and the couple's mammas who couldn't be more different. Hers tall and*

stately, the groom's petite and perky as a new puppy.
Hope they will pick the dresses before noon!

I look at the clock. It's almost eleven now. I peek out the back door over to the salon and see four cars in the drive. I hope at least one of Mamma's two seamstresses is helping. Both of them, Tawnysha Evans and Vondela Spicer, now in their seventies, joined Mamma right after Grandmother Castleberry left Mamma money to start a bridal wear business and Mamma invited women from Reverend Makepeace's black church to work with her. Eleven clients at once is a "potential triumph or a possible disaster," as Mamma is prone to say anytime a wedding party includes more than the bride, one attendant, and two mothers. "Bring the grandmothers in and you'll often find some generational differences of opinion as to what's proper." But Mamma's the consummate diplomat, if you ask me. God knows, she must be. Her business has been booming since 1963.

"I'm hungry," Isa says. She bounces into the kitchen, hair already braided, and wearing a one-piece halter/shorts combination we bought in New York. White Keds, too, like I wear whenever I paint. The only difference is, hers remain white. She's a stickler for cleaning them.

Soon Lu and Tino follow, once again keen to enjoy Mamerva's bounty.

"What shall we do today?" Tino asks, as we make short work of the buffet.

"Go fishing," Lu suggests. "Off the dock at Uncle Tad's cottage."

"Yes, yes," Isa says. "I like it there."

"Alright, then, right after we eat, we will go."

I smile at Tino. He knows I want to spend time with my mother.

We wipe our plates clean.

"Go, go," I say, and have fun. I'll tidy up here."

In minutes, the kiddos are in their swim suits and floppy hats. Tino wears Bermuda shorts, Italian sandals, and a New York Yankees hat. He takes Mamerva's keys from the key holder on the wall by the kitchen door. "My car is your car," she always tells him.

"Let us go," he says. "We must gather the fishing rods in the shed. Then we will stop for water at the grocery store."

I wave them off, then go upstairs to brush, floss, and pretty my face some. I'll join Mamma next door and see if she has any energy left to head to The Links after I come back from the Charbonneau place.

Good. The cars are gone. I walk the hundred or so feet to the shop.

"Hi, Mamma, how did it go?"

She's not in the main salon. She's probably in the office writing orders. Debussy is the background music playing today, and white peonies fill the vase on the table by the entry. An ivory silk column of a gown with spaghetti straps (Think body-skimming and elegant at the same time) hangs from one dressing room door. A lengthy lace veil rounded at its hem hangs beside it. On the next door, an ice-blue number, also with spaghetti straps, runs straight until the very bottom, where the front rises in a half-moon. *The bridesmaids will have to wear lovely sandals*, I say to myself. And, finally, on the doors of Rooms 3 and 4, the two mothers' picks, I'm guessing. The first, midnight blue, all lace, with a boat neck, fitted waist, and elbow-length sleeves. The second, silver-gray silk, a full-length shirtwaist with a significant bow at the waist. And, laid on an armchair, a sleeveless little girl's dress in ice-blue with navy cummerbund.

"Mamma!" I call out again as I walk into the kitchenette on my way to the office. Several champagne bottles are empty, as are all the glasses. Two Coke bottles remain open, both with some soda remaining. Several macaroons are left on the cookie tray.

I head into the office. Mamma is not here, either, though I see she has indeed been writing orders for the dresses. Might she have gone back to the house?

As I'm about to leave, I hear water. *Ah, she's in the bathroom.*

"Mamma, I'm here. How did the appointment go? Would you like to get massages at The Links?"

Nothing. I knock on the bathroom door. Again.

"Mamma?"

I turn the knob and go in.

"Mamma!"

She's on the floor, not completely sideways, a little pool of blood under her right ear. Her eyes are wide open. I kneel, touch her face, her hands. She is cold. I slap her cheeks. "Wake up, Mamma, come on now, wake up." She doesn't. I stand and turn the hot water handle so the water stops running. I kneel again to make sure. I am sure. I phone Hallie.

"Hallie, tell Daddy to come right away. It's Mamma. She's fallen again. I'm calling the ambulance. Please tell him to hurry." 911. "This is Orla Castleberry. I'm at my parents' house and my mother has fallen. No, she is not responding."

I wait outside. The ambulance arrives just as Daddy does. He's driven Hallie's car. He leaps out carrying his doctor's bag, sees me shake my head no, and runs inside. The EMTs follow, go in fast, but come out slow. "So sorry," they say. "Very sorry, Orla. Big loss to us all. A good woman, Minerva. Very sorry, Doctor Prout."

Mamma's body is gone before the bells from St. Marguerite's chime two. I clean the bathroom floor with wet paper towels. Dump the remaining Coke down the drain. Fill the Coke and champagne bottles with soapy water. Put the glasses in the dishwasher. Daddy stands and watches me. He loosens his bow tie, then rips it off.

"Come on," he whispers. He takes my hand and we walk back to the house. The kitchen is empty, but she is everywhere. Her green-checkered apron drapes over the chair by the wall phone. Her spare horn-rimmed eyeglasses rest on top of a cookbook page that reads "Dutch Coffeecake." The latest edition of *Good Housekeeping* in the mail tray is opened to the article "Laura Bush, First Lady and First Reader."

I reach for my cell phone and sit at the table. My eyes are wet. My heart is beating too fast.

"I've got to let Tino know. We have to tell the children."

Daddy is already dialing Arthur.

"Call me back as soon as you can, son, there's been an emergency."

Daddy sits across from me. He is crying now, and reaches into his pocket for his handkerchief. I walk around the table and wrap my arms around his shoulders. He wipes his eyes, motions for me to sit next to him. Then he listens while I speak into my phone.

"Tino, don't let the children see you react, please, not yet."

"I am listening. I am here."

I take a deep breath.

"Mamma is dead."

Pause. Throat clearing. Pause. "I see. When would you like us to arrive?"

I try to think.

"Anytime. The ambulance has already taken her."

"Okay. Are you alone?"

"No. Daddy is here, too."

"Good. We will come soon and tell them together. Is that how you want to do it?"

"Yes, good. I think together is best."

Daddy and I look at one another.

"We have to call Mercy," he says.

"Dear God." I stand up. "How much more can she take?"

Daddy stands, too. I punch the numbers. Mercy's phone rings and rings. The mailbox is full.

"Later, then."

"Yes," Daddy says.

The two of us go into the den and sit on the couch next to each other. Daddy asks what happened, step by step. I feel as if I'm watching a film for the second time. We are still sitting, holding hands and saying nothing when Tino pulls into the drive with the children.

Chapter Twenty-Six
Farewell and Fireworks

It is the Fourth of July. We leave for Fiesole in six days. Mamma's sequestered in the Castleberry mausoleum, her permanent home on earth. I feel like a lump of un-kneaded dough. Don't want to talk or go through her clothing or write thank-you notes to Father House, who celebrated the funeral Mass, or those who came to it: my childhood friend Katie Cowles and her mother, using a cane now; Tad and his father; Reverend Makepeace's son Spencer, all the way from Atlanta where he has a dental practice; Mamma's tennis ladies from The Links; Daddy's doctor friends and his can't-do-without Hallie; Mamma's seamstresses.

I need to stop by the grocery to thank Mr. and Mrs. Macron for the veritable banquet they sent here without our even placing an order. I've got only a few days to do all that. Daddy's counting on me. He's trying to tend to his patients even though he feels as if "half my soul is gone."

Tino has been great, driving the children to the New Orleans' zoo, to several NOLA museums where my paintings are featured, to see *Star Wars: Episode II—Attack of the Clones*, while I allegedly "take care of Mamma's unfinished business." I can't thank him enough. He is careful with me when we are alone at night. And I make sure that I pray with the children before they go to sleep "like Sister Aloise would." They seem okay. They trust us.

Both of them took the news as best they could, Tino and I sitting them down at the kitchen table while their catches of the day lay in an ice-packed cooler by the sink. They nodded their heads in unison when Tino told them their Mamerva's injured heart gave out. "I promise you, she did not suffer," he said, as Isa sniffled and Lu wiped his eyes.

"True," their Grandfather Prout concurred. "I'm very glad she did not suffer."

They let me lean down and hold my arms around their shoulders as long as it took Tino to get the fish into the sink, cleaned, and wrapped in plastic for the freezer.

Telling Mercy didn't go as well. After ensuring she wasn't alone, Daddy and I spoke to her together. She screamed and hung up on us. In a moment Thérèse called back. Phoenix was crying in the background as Miloslova sang to her. Thérèse repeated everything we told her, I guess for Mercy's benefit. When Mercy eventually took the phone in hand, she said, "Mamma, Grandfather, please don't make me come. I don't want to leave Phoenix and I don't want to take her with me. I'm afraid to fly. I'm sorry. I just cannot fly."

Daddy paced, and I tried for composure.

"No worries, Mercy. Maybe the nice priest who baptized Phoenix can say a Mass for Mamerva up there."

Phoenix had stopped crying.

"You won't hate me, will you, Mamma, Grandfather? You won't hate me if I don't come?"

Daddy and I had looked at each other first.

"Of course not," we spoke into the phone together. A duet of assurance.

How can we not understand? It was a plane, after all, that had distanced her from her birth mother until Mercy was twenty-two. And it was a plane that had obliterated her husband. Flying is a risk she's not ready to take yet, if she ever will again.

At any rate, Mercy did not come. We've spoken every day, taking turns initiating the calls. *"Oh, my maimed darling, my skittery pigeon,"* I want to say to her, even though she is not dead, like the poet Roethke's student thrown by a horse. But parts of her have perished. And this mother's love cannot revive them. *"If only I could nudge you from this sleep...."* But I can't. No miracles from me.

Arthur has taken it the worst. Unable to believe such a fate should befall the woman he loved to torment, barely in jest, he expresses surprised outrage. Since he arrived in St. Suplice only hours after he returned Daddy's call, he has not left. He's upped his usual six-mile run to ten, mowed the lawn with a push-mower twice in three days, and falls asleep every night on the leather couch in Daddy's office after drinking too much scotch. He hasn't shaved since the funeral.

I force myself to shower and dress, drink two cups of chicory coffee black, then walk over to the salon. I see the shocking pink cardigan Mamma put on when the air conditioning made her cold. It is hanging on a clear plastic hanger at one end of the veils rack. I take it off the hanger and hold it to my face, inhaling Mamma's scent. Partly her, partly Dove cleanser, a whiff of Arpège. I'm going to take it, wear it on the plane when we leave. I drape it over my shoulders now.

Mamma's seamstresses have assured her brides that they will be taken care of. They've finished placing the Courtmanche orders, and Mamma's desk is neat, her files alphabetized. I look at Mamma's cane swivel chair. Sitting on its chair pad with pink flamingos is where I'd find her every day after high school. She'd be calculating, reading the latest bridal magazines, calming soon-to-be brides and their mothers by phone. I'd come in, she'd wave up at me, then point to the kitchenette where there was always fruit or sweets for an after-school snack. We'd talk or argue or down some food together. "I'll be up to get supper going," she'd always say. I never expected her to be gone. She'll always be gone.

I walk around the salon from room to room. It will be different the next time I am here. I study, memorize the spaces, watch how light and shadow fall right now, in this moment. My throat catches. I'm afraid to blink.

Mamma, know that I have loved you, craved you, even when, *especially* when, I did not understand the life you were demanding for me. When I could not comprehend your intention. When you dared Grandmother Castleberry not to love me. When you gifted me to her no matter the cost to yourself. Thank you, Mamma. Thank you.

I look at the beautiful gowns, especially the lace ones. So intricate. So particular. Snowflakes come to mind, each one unique, yet of a type. God, the women who have loved me! Mamma. Grandmother Castleberry. The Contessa Beatrice d'Annunzio. Aurora Bacci, Tino's mother, the only one left alive. Each of them wise. All of them liars. They lied as if their children's lives depended on it. And their children's lives did. Have.

I have lied for love, too. I told Mercy her godfather Tad and I could not find her father. A lie, and one that Tad did not dispute. I did not tell her that her father wanted no part of her, as he put in writing to Tad. And Thérèse would not reveal his name to her birth daughter, either. God help us should she ever find the letters between Attorney Tad Charbonneau and Mr. Hoyt Demirs. Yet another part of her will perish, abandoned and betrayed.

Tino and I have told Lu and Isa that their paternal grandfather was "lost" in the war. Another lie. What will we tell them when we return to Fiesole? What will Aurora and Dieter Ahl say?

Must we lie? Is doing so as much a part of parenting as teaching them to brush and floss, mind their manners, do their homework, say their prayers? A trail of precedents seems to suggest so. I need some wisdom, but the wise I knew have gone to their reward or doom.

I open the door, leave the salon, and walk into the sun. I squint and make my way to the house. Pausing at the steps to the kitchen door, I ask myself, what would Sister Aloise say? I imagine her spinning in her wheel chair, quoting the medieval mystic who dared her not to go off the cliff:

"Be a gardener. Dig a ditch. Toil and sweat. And turn the earth upside down. And seek the deepness. And water plants in time. Continue this labor. And make sweet floods to run, and noble and abundant fruits to spring. Take this food and drink, and carry it to God as your true worship."

*****

Tad has invited us to his cottage on the Chartres River for fried catfish, coleslaw, corn on the cob, pulled pork. Daddy has asked Arthur to bring an array of beers, sodas, and bottled water. I'm to see to dessert.

"Brownies," declares Isa.

"With vanilla ice cream," her brother adds.

"It will be just my father and your family," Tad tells me by phone. "Bring your bathing suits if you like. I will provide tubing, and rope in a swimming area for the children. It appears the weather will allow us to dine on the dock. I suggest insect repellant or cigars, whatever your preference."

Tad knows Daddy will bring a box of stogies. I may join the men myself. Make smoke signals to Mamma.

We arrive by five o'clock. Having this commitment has forced me to accomplish what had to be done. I've written, stamped, and mailed the thank-you notes, sent flowers to Mamma's assistants, and laundered the last clothes that Mamma wore the day she left us. We park in the driveway and unload two cars. We are dressed for the festivities, the children in red, white, and blue, Tino in a button-down shirt with an American flag sewn on the breast pocket. I've tied a stars-and-stripes scarf around my straw boater. And Arthur has put on clean shorts and a tee shirt imprinted with an outline of the Twin Towers. I guess that grim reminder suits the scene, or at least contextualizes our time in the States.

Arthur still hasn't shaved, nor has he returned calls from his Jesuit colleague, Tom Ingerstadt, the psychologist at his school. Daddy and I are worried about him. Daddy tells me he plans to phone Tom himself and invite him to the house for drinks and supper. An intervention of sorts. "Arthur will be furious," I say. "Too bad," Daddy told me. "I'm in no state to help him. Tom's our man."

"Hello!" Tad waves, bringing me back to the moment.

He and his father greet us in Bermuda shorts, Tad's colorful madras, his dad's standard khaki. They've set up a 12-foot folding table on the dock with matching folding chairs for all of us. Tad's arranged plastic dishes decorated with whimsical sea creatures on them. Red, white, and blue plastic tableware. Sparklers for after dark in jelly jars.

"I'm glad you all decided to join Tad and me." Mr. Charbonneau has always carried himself as graciously as Cary Grant did in his films. An overlay of sadness accompanies his graciousness these days. The salt-and-pepper hair I remember from a past visit has turned white.

"Minerva always enjoyed Independence Day," Daddy says.

"Well, then, let us toast Minerva," Mr. Charbonneau replies.

Arthur opens the cooler and gives all the adults a bottle of Abita Amber.

"Ah, Louisiana's favorite beer, as I have been reminded many times," says Tino.

"Coke?" Arthur asks the children.

They look to me. Soda is not one of their choices at home.

"Sure. It's a special occasion."

Daddy motions for Lu and Isa to stand by him. Then he looks to Arthur, Tino, Tad, Mr. Charbonneau, and me in turn. He raises his bottle. We raise ours.

"To Minerva," Mr. Charbonneau says.

"To Mamerva," Isa and Lu say.

"Hear, hear," the rest of us chant.

Daddy smiles at us all. He has granted us permission to enjoy ourselves.

"Who's up for a swim?" Tad asks.

I'm the first to dive off the dock. I've decided to spend a traditional St. Suplice Fourth here and now. Just the way Mamma would want. Boom, boom, splash, boom. Arthur, Tad, Isa (she jumps feet first), then Lu. We're pounding the water as if we can push it down, make it still. Tino films us. A motorboat zooms by, causing waves that buoy us up, let us down, make us laugh. Mr. Charbonneau takes the water toys out of the shed by the cottage and brings them to the edge of the dock. He and Daddy fling them into the water. One is a rubber raft in the shape of a swan, another a slab of Swiss cheese. Water wings, malleable twisty cylinders, and four swim-through rings. We are playing, all of us like children now. Feeling the warm water loosening our muscles, looking up at a mostly blue sky, watching the water droplets bubble on each other's faces and hair.

I swim towards Tad.

"Thank you."

He comes close, kisses me on my forehead. My very best friend. First, still, always.

After an hour or so, he asks, "Would anyone appreciate some dinner?"

A yes by resounding acclamation, and we clamber up the ladder onto the dock, dry ourselves off, and settle into the feast.

"Let me help," I say to Tad.

"Thank you."

We eat well and linger at the table, sated and damp. Then it's time for insect repellent when dessert and dusk meet.

The children help Tad and me clear. Daddy, Mr. Charbonneau, and Arthur close the long folding table and carry it into the shed. Tino arranges the chairs facing the river. The men return, Daddy hands out cigars, and the men light up. Human fireflies. Tad brings out pots of citronella and lines them up either side of the dock. When he takes a deck of cards out of his pocket, the children and he sit cross-legged.

"Setback, this time," he says.

I smile and walk towards the cottage, stop just short of it, turn to look long and hard at everyone and everything. This night will become a painting. A meager homage to the past and the future. St. Suplice, old friends, the father I didn't know until puberty, a menopause baby brother, my dear, dear husband, and two of three children I never expected to mother. Together here. Remnant and hope. Reason enough to go on. But oh, I am missing the gone. Always missing the gone, the slipped away, running like the Chartres River through my consciousness.

"Look!" Lu shouts and stands up from his cards. "Over there!"

He points over the tree line on the other side of the river to a herald of sparkles in the night sky.

"It's time," Mr. Charbonneau says. "Fireworks are starting on Hester's Ridge."

We gather close together at the edge of the dock. Tino douses his cigar, gets his camera recording again. I find Daddy's cigar case beneath his chair.

"Mind if I have one?"

"Certainly not." He takes a lighter out of his breast pocket and lights the cigar for me.

"Mamma, you look silly," Isa says.

I shrug my shoulders.

"Here." Daddy pats his knees, and both children take a seat as if he is an easy chair.

"We have a nice clear night," says Mr. Charbonneau.

"Yes sir," says Tad.

Tad comes and stands by me. Tino photographs us one, two, many more times. Arms at our sides. Arms around each other's waists. Serious. Smiling. Then he snaps several of Daddy holding the children.

A *crack!* that sounds like lightning striking a tree makes me jump. The sky lights up, sizzles, crashes. Green, red, purple, white. Circles, zig-zags, color bursts, streams of color falling like rain. The river is illuminated. I am enchanted. This never gets old.

"I love tonight," Isa says. She leans back on her grandfather's chest and watches.

Lu turns around to me and says, "Mamma, was it like this when you were a kid?"

"Yes, it was. When both Uncle Tad and I were kids."

"You were lucky. It's nice."

Out of the mouths of babes, just when I need some wisdom. I was lucky, am blessed. It's no small thing to be standing here alive with folks who love each other watching the exploding lights in the sky.

Part Four

To live in this world, you must be able to do three things: to love what is mortal; to hold it against your bones knowing your own life depends on it; and, when the time comes to let it go, to let it go.
—Mary Oliver

A man to be greatly good, must imagine intensely and comprehensively; he must put himself in the place of another and many others; the pains and pleasures of his species must become his own. The great instrument of moral good is the imagination.
— Percy Bysshe Shelley

Chapter Twenty-Seven
Homecoming

It is difficult to leave. It is a relief to leave.

As I have every time I've left St. Suplice to travel by air, I've taken several books from my mamma's extensive library for the flight. "You can bring them back next time you visit," she always said. Some of the books were hand-me-downs from folks whose laundry she took in when I was a young child. Others were offered her by Mrs. Charbonneau, who, as some of you will remember, was the head librarian in town for over thirty years. Every July the library removed some books from its shelves and replaced them with new tomes. Then it sold the well-used volumes during a two-day tent sale. I know in my heart that Mrs. Charbonneau spent her own money on the books she gave Mamma. But she never let on. I'm sure the weekly dinners Mamma sent over to the Charbonneau house once Mrs. Charbonneau took ill were reciprocation. After Grandmother Castleberry died and made us rich, Mamma bought her own books. She treasured them more than any other objects besides the paintings I made for her. Every time I hold a book in my hands I remember Mamma.

For our route back to Italy — New Orleans to New York, New York to Rome, Rome to Florence, then by car up into the hills of our home in Fiesole — I've selected three volumes. Beryl Markham's *West with the Night*, *The Complete Poetical Works of Robert Browning*, and Dante's *The Divine Comedy*. Once I've calmed myself down from knowing Mamma won't be at home in St. Suplice when I visit next summer, I decide to read Markham's book first. Next to me, Lu's deep into Seal's book about building tree houses, and, across the aisle, Tino is reading the latest issue of the *Journal of the American Medical Association* while Isa alternates between gazing out the window and writing a letter to Sister Aloise. All is subdued on the plane for the moment. We're lucky enough to be in first class where the atmosphere is one of a private club. Boundaries are respected and voices modulated. We've been advised that a meal will be served when we're somewhere over Nova Scotia during our overnight flight. For now, peace.

Markham stops me mid-read with this:

I have learned that if you must leave a place that you have lived in and loved and where all your yesteryears are buried deep, leave it any way except a slow way, leave it the fastest way you can. Never turn back and never believe that an hour you remember is a better hour because it is dead. Passed years seem safe ones, vanquished ones, while the future lives in a cloud, formidable from a distance.

I want to share this with Tino, but now is not the time. He is apprehensive about meeting his father, concerned about what and how much we should tell the children, not wanting to hurt his mother.

"Much as I enjoy-ed the past nine months' opportunity," he confided to me last night in bed, "I am more than ready to return home." He threw his arm across my waist. "I plan to work a seventy-two-hour shift in the Emergency Department to see how things are running and to catch up with my team. I want also to check on the remaining two guests in our AIDS Hospice and see if they are well enough to be release-ed permanently."

I turned to face him. "I understand. You have much to do."

He caressed my hair then. "Beside-es, it is my home. Our home."

I touched his cheek. Closed my eyes. Remembered the tiny house Mamma rented for us when she was only Grandmother Castleberry's maid and not yet her daughter–in-law. How I had loved my bedroom, narrow as a convent cell, with aluminum containers of water colors and plenty of parchment stacked on a scratched used bookshelf, all courtesy of my teachers who knew I was an artist before I did. Then, after Grandmother Castleberry died and we moved into her house, how my bedroom felt like heaven—sun-bleached comforters that looked like cumulous clouds, a bed big enough for four, down-filled pillows to sink my head into, and a ceiling fan that purred all night long. And since 1989, the Contessa's villa, her gift to her godson Tino and me, his bride, whose Grandfather Castleberry had been her wartime lover. For all their substantive man-made and natural beauty, the villa and its grounds are not what make this place my present home. No, dear readers, it is that throughout its history this venue has offered safe refuge to anyone needing it. My husband and his mother would not be alive were it not for the Contessa and this blessed property. I would not have met Tino and enjoyed the kind of marriage I sought but never expected. And, then, the children. A double gift. Who could want more?

Whether or not it is the same for fathers, for mothers, I think, the place where we've adopted or given birth to our children becomes the most compelling home. I know it is so for me. When a judge declared me Mercy's mother in 1975, New Orleans became the locus and focus of my love for her. Likewise, as soon as Tino laid Isa and Lu on my chest in the delivery room at Ospedale Santa Maria Nuova, Florence/ Fiesole felt as primal and urgent as the milk that gorged my breasts to nourish them. Dear readers, were I to paint a self-portrait, you'd see my torso hovering over the mid-Atlantic facing you, my right leg stretching all the way to New Orleans, and my left leg all the way to Fiesole. My arms, likewise, and open palms would reach in opposite directions. I'd not look graceful or genteel or even pretty. No, think of me instead as a wild-eyed goddess, naked and boldly female. My breasts full. My hips broad enough to contain and sustain life. That's what motherhood has done to me. Made me live on and crave two continents, given me a singular child and twins a generation apart, realize that all three of my children belong to a world more expansive and complicated than the places where I first called them my own.

And just as Mamma's passing will have taken a palpable chunk out of St. Suplice when I visit again, changing my relationship to the town, so too will Dieter Ahl's presence in Fiesole alter my dear Tino and his sense of home. My goodness, just learning that his father is here and may well stay until the end of his days has already affected his mindset. He and his mother no longer two, but three. Himself a father, but, suddenly, also a son. Lu and Isa grandchildren of a man who they thought barely existed as a cypher.

It is morning in Italy when we de-plane. Roberto, our handyman and groundskeeper, awaits us. "Mina is so glad you have returned. The villa has been too empty all year, she says. And our daughters cannot wait to see you."

We're all eager to see Alessandra and Anastasia again. Ala, five, and Ana, seven, have been constant playmates with our two. The girls have always had free rein in the villa, sometimes helping Mina as she works in the kitchen, sometimes frustrating her efforts. Isa is looking forward to camping out with the duo as soon as possible. Roberto sometimes sets up a tent between the groundskeeper's house and the equipment shed for them.

Lu has persuaded Tino to let him construct a tree house by next spring.

"We will survey the property," I hear Tino tell him just before landing, "and find a suitable place."

The ride up the mountain never disappoints. One leaves Florence proper, then travels through the leafy suburbs, then higher and higher up to the ancient town with its piazza fountain, the Hotel Aurora, the basilica, a gelato shop, two ceramic stores, and several *trattorie*, the amphitheater nearby. The children become animated, pointing out of the car windows.

Isa says, "Look, the four cats are still sitting on the stone wall by the taxi stand."

Lu sees the sign for his nonna's music camp. "I want to go again, Mamma. May I go?"

Farther and farther up we ride, zipping through the main piazza, heading to the top of the town. The views are many, each worthy of its own landscape painting, all begging to be photographed. Finally, we arrive at the iron gates. They are open, and Roberto pulls into the demi-lune drive.

"At last!" Mina runs outside. She is still, always, lanky and kinetic, her hair in its gamine cut, now with several strands of gray. The girls are behind her. They hold up a sign they painted: "*Benvenuti!*" There are balloons in primary colors floating around the text. Alessandra is jumping up and down. She and Anastasia put the poster down on the ground and skip around the car. Tino gets out and kisses Mina on both cheeks. She and I hug. The children run off to the swing set Roberto built eight years ago.

Tino and I walk into the house. "Home," he says.

"I'm going to shower, first thing," I say.

"I want to stop by the hospice first," counters Tino. He pecks me on the cheek and sprints away.

I start toward our suite off the main foyer. But an image on the front page of the morning's newspaper resting on the phone table stops me cold. It is of Filumena Curti. The headline above it reads, "Lady Camorra Released from Prison."

I shudder, grab the paper, bring it with me into our bedroom, and fling it onto the bed. I tear off my clothes, curse, and, once in the bathroom, turn the shower handle to as hot as I dare.

The clock strikes noon as the water streams over me. I scrub and scrub. I'll never be as clean as I once was. I have sullied myself by association.

Across the Atlantic in St. Suplice, Daddy will be waking to his six a.m. alarm. In New Jersey, Phoenix will want to be nursed. A mile and a half down the mountain, Aurora Bacci and Dieter Ahl are together again. And here, at home, Tino and I and our children begin anew. But there are evil eyes trained on us now. I pray to God I have the courage to stare them down.

By July 12th, I feel as if we'd never left. The children are attending their *nonna*'s music camp from nine until two every weekday through mid-August. Lu plays soccer Tuesday and Thursday evenings. Isa is learning to throw pots in the gallery next to the *carabinieri* station during pretty much the same times. Tino and I drive them to and from, and find some time to chat alone sitting in the very top row of the bleachers.

"Mamma met me for lunch at the hospital today," Tino tells me. Lu's team is down by two points. We face the field as we speak. "I told her you and I will attend her concert Saturday evening in the amphitheater. She will reserve center seats. And I promised we would talk with the children about their grandfather."

I applaud as Enzo from Lu's team scores. Lu looks up at us and we wave. "I'm glad, Tino. It's time."

My husband turns to me. "She wants to bring him to Sunday lunch." I nod. "He has move-ed from the hotel to her house. He is going to stay." His voice wavers. I take his hand in mine. Enzo scores again. We focus on the field. The game ends in a a tie. Lu and the other boys are jumping up and down. Their team will not be mocked.

We drive from the field to the main piazza, find a parking place, pick up Isa, then get some gelato. We sit on a stone wall watching Florence light up from below.

"It's good to be back home," Isa says. "But it's not as exciting here as it is in New York." She has sprinkles on the tip of her nose.

Lu wipes hazelnut chocolate off his lips. "Anything can happen, Isa. Anything. Even here."

I finish my raspberry and lemon combo. "You are a philosopher tonight, Lu."

Tino laughs. "Perhaps a prognosticator."

"What's a prognosticator?" asks Isa.

Our ride home sounds like a vocabulary class.

Much later, in bed, Tino and I decide we'll tell the children Sunday morning, announcing Dieter's coming as a welcome, long-awaited surprise. Make a party of his joining us. Give them the basic facts: Nonna and Dieter fell in love but had to separate because, once Mussolini was gone, their countries were enemies. They were married in secret — my mother-in-law's mentor, la Dottoressa Ghiraschi, arranged for the forged marriage document. Dieter came by stealth to la Dottoressa's home to sign it, thereby ensuring that Aurora and her unborn child would not be shamed. We'll tell the children Dieter dared not return to Fiesole during the post-war years as doing so would have endangered his wife and son. The Fiesolani would have labeled her a traitor and taunted, perhaps assaulted, her son as the enemy's child.

"They'll buy it. They trust us," I say.

Tino sighs. "I don't yet trust myself, *Cara*. I will myself to love Dieter because my mother does. I do it for her."

I nod.

"I do not know if I can ever *feel* the love, however. He murdered the three *carabinieri* and abandoned the two of us. That knowledge plays in my consciousness like a mantra."

I watch him sleep, remember meeting my father, Prout, for the first time when I was twelve. It was scary. I was nervous. My whole former life had turned out to be a sham. I had to come to terms with why my mamma had lied. Why Mrs. Castleberry had done the same. Over time and numerous sleepless nights, I came to understand. But it wasn't until Prout introduced me to Mrs. Sharp as his daughter, when we paid a post-partum visit to her in The Hollow, that I believed everything would be alright. I hope Tino will have a moment like that.

It's Saturday night. Isa will camp out with Ala and Ana on our property. Enzo's parents have offered to take the boys to their older son's game in Florence. Mina will await Lu's return at the main house while Tino and I are out.

The concert, "An Evening with Violinist Aurora Bacci," is sold out. Even after her touring days ended a decade ago, Aurora still draws a crowd. I like to think it's for two reasons: the first, she is a world-class violinist; the second, she is not a diva. She establishes rapport with her audiences, greets them with a smile, offers a word of gratitude for their interest, invites them to forget their worries and burdens and let the music infuse, relax, and revive their souls. Audiences love her as much as her music. So much so that she has lately become a monthly guest on one of Florence's morning radio programs.

Tino and I sit midway between the stage and the rim of the amphitheater in the seats Aurora reserved for us. I wonder where Dieter is. Both Tino and I scan the crowd to no avail. Miniature white lights have been strung along the aisles. Squat fat candles run a ribbon of light around the stage's edge. It is a warm night, but a breezy one. Most of us women have wrapped ourselves in filmy shawls. The men wear linen jackets. Tino's is robin's egg blue. When Aurora walks onto the stage, she is greeted with enthusiastic applause. The spotlight follows her, and she moves with her usual grace. But, tonight, dear readers, there is something else about her. Her smile is not only welcoming; it is electric. Hair and makeup aside, she glows. Her long lace dress is silver, shot through with clear crystals that glitter. When she nestles the violin under her chin, the crowd goes silent. There is only music.

She plays for over an hour without an intermission. After Beethoven's *Violin Sonata No. 9 in A Major*, she pauses, holds her instrument at her left side, and walks close to the edge of the stage. She is careful to avoid the candles.

"You have been a wonderful audience," she says. She sweeps her arm across the amphitheater. "And I want to thank you with a special piece tonight. Some of you will recognize it, Bériot's *Grand Duo Concertante No. 1 for Two Violins*." There is scattered applause. "I invite Dieter Ahl to join me on stage so we may play it for you." She smiles and says, "The last time Dieter and I performed this piece in Fiesole we were both very young."

Tino tenses and sits up straight. I place my hand on his knee. Dieter, in a black tuxedo, his hair a white wave, climbs from below stage right to walk across the stage to Aurora. He is slim and tall, still walks like a young man, and holds his violin with ease. A stage hand brings a second music stand and sheet music for him. Then he and Aurora nod to one another and, in an instant, begin.

They play as if they are making love. Two, but two together. In synchrony. Deliberate. Alternately impassioned and delicate. Assured. Attending to the notes, forgetting the spotlights, the audience, even themselves. They surrender to the music. Their bodies are making the music.

Their artistry is transporting, transcendent. I wish they could go on forever, carry us with them over the heat, beyond the breeze. Make us forget the biting spider, the scurrying mouse, the person whose knee keeps jarring our back.

Then they are done, each drawing out the final note until there is only silence.

Tino is the first to stand. Tears stream down his face. Aurora looks up. She sees him and waves her bow. Looks to Dieter. He waves his, as well.

"*Brava! Bravo!*" someone calls out. More voices join in until the words become a chant. The crowd claps in unison. People leave their seats to fling red and pink roses over the candles onto the stage.

Aurora Bacci and Dieter Ahl place their instruments on the stage floor, join hands, and bow. The crowd roars. I am so happy for Tino.

La Dottoressa Ghiraschi, Aurora's mentor and protector, often spoke Robert Browning's words to her students: "*Who hears music, feels his solitude /Peopled at once.*" She voiced the words like a command. But here, they resonate as an accord, a communion. Tino is not alone.

Chapter Twenty-Eight
Need to Know Basis

"Seriously, Babbo, you never ever saw him in person until last night?"

"Seriously, Isa. I saw my father only in a photograph the Contessa had from the war days, then later in the painting your mother made from it."

We are in the kitchen, just home from seven o'clock Mass, and eating *cornetti* and fruit. I have placed all the ingredients for lunch on the counter by the sink. *Cavatelli* fresca, broccoli *di rape*, a porchetta seasoned and tied with string, peppers and onions for grilling. I am chopping the peppers. My fingernails are flecked red and green.

I wash my hands, leave the counter, walk across the main foyer to the library, and pull Tad's book, *The Orphans of Fiesole: A World War II Physician's Photographs and Letters.* When I return, Isa and Lu close in on either side of me as I sit next to their father. Tino finds the page. We stare at the photograph while Isa reads the text aloud.

"**The Nazi Violinist:** A high-cheek-boned young officer, in full German uniform, with impeccably groomed hair and nails, his side part as straight as a ruler, his nails rounded and smooth. His eyes are closed and his violin is tucked under his chin. His calm demeanor leads one to believe he has left the war and successfully escaped into a completely musical realm. Beside him is **The Girl Violinist with the Rapunzel-like Braid.** She sits next to the Nazi violinist. Their knees—his left, her right—touch. Her thick braid, which reaches all the way to her waist, is tied with a wide ribbon that has been starched and pressed. She wears a peasant's coarse apron over her simple smock. Her eyes tend toward his lidded ones even as she balances her instrument under her chin. Her lips are slightly open and voluptuous, through her breasts might as well be flatbreads. Her nails are bitten to the quick.

"Ha, ha, Uncle Tad wrote that Nonna has no boobs," Lu says.

Tino laughs and pulls our son's head to his chest. Isa rolls her eyes at her brother.

"She's just not voluptuous like Mamma," counters Isa.

Tino winks at me over the children's heads. "Voluptuous, yes. Did Mamma teach you that word, Isa?"

"Of course, Babbo. She told me it is a more classy word than what the American boys used to say about her breasts in St. Suplice." She turns to me. "Is it 'built,' Mamma? I forget."

"That's right, Isa."

Tino ogles my breasts. "Built," he murmurs.

"About the photograph..." I try to refocus them, though I find it amusing that our children's comments have initiated foreplay between their father and me.

"Nonna looks so young!" says Lu. "The soldier, I mean our grandfather, looks older."

"Well, she was," Tino says. "Mamma told me she was a teenager when she got married. And that Dieter was ten years older than she."

"That means he is eighty-four," Lu says, after a moment.

"Yes, but he looks younger and walks with ease. He managed the stage last evening with no trouble at all." I keep talking, but also stand up and return to my chopping. Onions are next. "Nonna was a girl from a poor family. She worked as a maid at Hotel Aurora. It was *la Dottoressa* who noticed her natural musical talent. Without her help and that of the Contessa, Nonna would never have been able to afford music lessons. Nonna and Dieter played together at Mass every Sunday during the German occupation."

Tino stands now, as well. He circles the table as he speaks. "And after I was born, the Contessa had us move into where the AIDS hospice is now. She called it the 'La Casa dei Bambini.' It housed orphans and others who had lost their families or homes during the war."

Lu asks, "Were you an orphan?"

"Not exactly," Tino goes on. He stops by the fruit bowl and takes a banana. Peeling it, he continues, "My father was withdrawn from Fiesole with the rest of the Germans. No one knew where he ended up." He throws the peel into the trash receptor. "By war's end, Mamma was a good enough violinist to go on tours. The Contessa, my godmother, saw to it that I was care-ed for here while Nonna was away once or twice a month. Although I did live with many orphans.”

“Oh,” Isa says. “What shall I wear for the party, Mamma?”

Good. Isa is satisfied with our explanations. She is on to other topics.

Lu says, “What shall we call him, Babbo? Does he speak only German?”

Tino finishes his banana, washes his hands at the sink, then looks to the children.

“‘Nonno’. He is your *nonno*. And he has moved to Italy now. If he does not already speak Italian, he must certainly learn how.”

I turn and smile at Tino.

“Do you think my white eyelet dress is a good choice, Mamma?”

“Perfect.” I am placing the onions and peppers in two small plastic bags.

“I’ll go change, then.”

She heads out the kitchen door into the hallway and the stairs to her bedroom. Just outside the door she stops. “I’ll make him a welcome poster, too, like Ana and Ala did for us.”

“Very nice,” says Tino. “I am sure he will like that.”

Lu, meanwhile, looks again at the photograph in Tad’s book. Then he looks at Tino. Back and forth, back and forth.

“I need to see him in color, Babbo, with his eyes open. Then I’ll know if you match.”

Tino smiles. He runs his hands over Lu’s wavy brown hair. “What I need *you* to do, Lu, is teach me how to be as good a son as you are. Isn’t it strange? I’ve learned how to be your father before I know how to be Dieter Ahl’s son.”

Lu taps the table with both hands as if he is drumming at a jazz fest.

"Don't worry. I'll help you." He play-punches Tino's shoulder. "May I be excused?"

"Certainly," Tino says.

The kiddos gone, Tino comes to the counter and wraps his arms around my waist.

"And what shall *I* wear, dear wife?" He kisses the back of my neck.

I could go to bed with him right now. Instead, I pat some perspiration off my brow with a paper towel and turn to face him.

"Come as you are, Tino. Just the way you are."

He fondles my breasts, and whispers, "Voluptuous."

"Lech."

"No, just an admirer of my 'built' wife."

I laugh.

"May I request a date with you tonight after whatever is to happen does?"

"Count on it."

"Good," he says, and kisses my forehead.

Then he turns to leave. "I think I'll go for a run, then shower again."

I nod.

"Nerves, you understand, *Cara*."

I take off my apron and decide to use the Contessa's blue hydrangea plates and monogrammed silver service. I caress my husband's cheek as I head to the dining room.

"Yes, Tino, I understand. I truly do."

Chapter Twenty Nine
En Plein Air

"They're here, they're here!" Isa calls, as the Fiat's tires crunch the stones in the drive.

We hurry outside together. Isa holds up her sign. She has written in black marker and placed primary-color stars around the words. "*Benvenuto, Willkommen,* Welcome, Nonno!" She is adorable in her white eyelet dress, red leather sandals, and pigtails with red ribbons.

Aurora steps out of the driver's seat. She smiles at Isa. Lu hugs her as she comes around the trunk of the car. Dieter swings his long legs out the passenger side, then stands. Their star-struck aura is gone, replaced by a comfortable geniality. Aurora wears a floral tea-length dress and wedges, as is her summer Sunday habit. Dieter sports a turquoise cotton button-down shirt and white linen slacks. Brown leather sandals and a matching belt. Tino is decked out in a turquoise rugby shirt, parchment-colored linen Bermuda's, and calfskin driving mocs. I'm in the pinkest shift I own and slim black sandals. The pearl earrings and necklace I've selected were Aurora's gift to me when Tino and I married.

"I'm so glad to meet you," I say, and take Dieter's hands in mine.

He is handsome, brown from a month of Tuscan sun. One can tell Tino shares his DNA.

Isa puts her sign down beside her and walks toward her grandfather.

"Hello, Nonno, welcome home," she says and curtsies.

I have never known our daughter to curtsy.

"I am glad to be here," Dieter says. "*Grazie, Danke,* Thanks," he says, pointing to the sign and counting on his fingers.

Aurora giggles like a girl and puts a hand to her mouth. Then, recovering, "How lovely you are, Isa."

"Thank you, Nonna."

Lu steps in front of his sister. "Pleased to meet you, Nonno," he says, and puts out his hand.

He's put on a clean yellow shirt, navy Bermuda shorts, and the Sperry Docksiders that Tad gave him on the Fourth of July.

Dieter takes Lu's hand and grips it as if they are sealing a deal.

Lu turns to Tino, then, and winks as if to say, *"That's how you do it, Babbo. Easy as pie."*

There is a pregnant pause. Tino and Dieter stand facing one another. They are the same height. Both lock eyes and take stock. Tino makes the first move, taking two steps forward.

"Father," he says, "welcome."

He imitates Lu, puts out his hand. Then, in a flash, changes course. He spreads out his arms instead and pulls his father to him. Each wraps the other in his arms. We are all quiet. The hall clock strikes one-fifteen. Ana and Ala squeal from the swings. Then Dieter looks straight into his son's blue eyes. He might as well be looking in a mirror. "I'm sorry," he says. His voice sounds like toasted bread crusts. "So sorry."

Tino lets go, takes a step back, and says, "I, as well, Father. But now we are all together and I am glad of it."

Aurora has been standing motionless, her eyes fixed on her lover and her son. Now she sways as if she is about to faint. Both Tino and Dieter catch her, Tino grabbing her left arm, Dieter her right.

"Let's get you out of the sun, Mamma," Tino says. He is all doctor now. "I'll get some water."

Isa and Lu stare, then scurry after me into the kitchen. By the time we get Aurora settled under the fans on the shaded porch near the pool, she has recovered.

"I didn't mean to make a fuss. I'm so sorry."

Tino kneels before her. "Don't worry, Mamma. It is hot."

"It's just that I am so happy. I was overcome by happiness."

"Mamma," Tino says. He takes her pulse, examines her eyes, insists she drink a full glass of water while Dieter stands behind him and looks on.

"You are fine now, Mamma. Your pulse is good and the roses bloom on your cheeks."

Dieter smiles.

"Just rest awhile. It is cool here, and you can lie back and rest."

Catastrophe averted, the children go ahead with the plan they proposed earlier.

"Nonno," Lu says, "Isa and I would like to give you a tour of the place. Would you like to come with us?"

Dieter looks to Aurora.

"Go, go," she says. "I'm fine." She sits up straight in the cushioned lounge chair. I take a pillow from the rocker couch and place it behind her head. She leans back on it. Folds her hands as if in prayer. "It's just that I've dreamed of this for so long. And now my dream is realized."

Dieter kisses the top of her head. Mina arrives, moving like a filly.

"Hello, Mina," Aurora says. "Will you sit with me while my family gets some exercise? Have you met Dieter?"

Tino nods to Mina.

"Hello, Dieter," she says. "Welcome."

He bows.

"Of course, Signora Aurora, it will be my pleasure to sit with you. I want to hear all about your concert last night."

I take my straw hat from the hook at the far end of the porch and grab the camera I inadvertently left on a side table nearby after the concert last night. Tino and I enjoyed several Aperol Spritzes out here well after midnight and I forgot to take it in.

"The *porchetta* will be done by two o'clock, Mina, and I've already set the table."

Mina takes a seat next to Aurora. "Alright, thank you, Orla. Don't worry about a thing. Signora Aurora and I will enjoy each other's company."

The children, Dieter, and Tino are already many steps ahead of me. They are just coming out of the d'Annunzio Chapel. "Mamma and Pappa got married here," Isa tells him. "And here is where our saviors are both buried," Tino says. He leads them round to the cemetery in back of the chapel and points to the graves of la Contessa and la Dottoressa. Dieter kneels before each headstone and crosses himself both times. I catch up with them all while they stand before the entryway of the former Casa dei Bambini, now the AIDS hospice, and what I hope will soon become the Bacci Arts Center and Retreat. (I haven't yet broached the subject with Tino and his parents.) I say nothing, just listen to the children speak with pride of place about their home. Watch their grandfather revel in their attention and energy. Look at Dieter and Tino practice being father and son.

Every now and then, I snap photos from behind. When we near the gardens and the cliff where Luke was lost, where resisters leapt with messages about their occupiers' plans, where AIDS-ridden Father Dona and I sat and contemplated the fraudulent Catholics we were, I run ahead and shoot them walking toward me. I capture the children's energy, Dieter's obvious pleasure, Tino's love gaining ascendance over anger and pain.

When the photos are developed, I'll hang them in my studio and turn them into paintings, create a subjective historical record of who we are now in this place at this time. I'll sit outdoors *en plein air* as long as the clement weather holds. Get cozy in the studio when rain and snow come. Just me and the Contessa's easel which, save for one narrow crack down its left leg, has survived a world war and a circuitous journey from Fiesole to Naples to Manhattan and home to Fiesole again.

I'll paint pictures that narrate the little lives we lead in a universe full of little lives. That remind us that history is context, tableau, canvas on which we imprint ourselves, two feet, one mind, one heart at a time. That through invasions and occupations, airstrikes and destruction, abandonment and loss, kidnapping and abuse, what we each seek is love, the abatement of pain, our longings fulfilled, and simple joys that bring tears to our eyes, allowing us to forget and compelling us to remember at the same time.

For months now I have been listening to poetry on my morning walks. Doing so opens my mind and prepares me to paint. The North American poet Mary Oliver spoke to me this morning as the sun was rising and I strode around the property. Dew dampened my sneakers, several butterflies flitted among the peonies, and a garden snake slithered near the cliff's edge. Here is what Oliver said:

> *If you suddenly and unexpectedly feel joy, don't hesitate.*
> *Give in to it.*
> *There are plenty of lives and whole towns destroyed or about to be.*
> *We are not wise, and not very often kind.*
> *And much can never be redeemed.*
> *Still, life has some possibility left.*
> *Perhaps this is its way of fighting back,*
> *that sometimes something happens better than all the riches or power in the world.*
> *It could be anything, but very likely you notice it in the instant when love begins.*
> *Anyway, that's often the case.*
> *Anyway, whatever it is, don't be afraid of its plenty.*
> *Joy is not made to be a crumb.*
> Amen.

Epilogue
December 19, 2002

My father, Prout Castleberry, arrives in Fiesole this afternoon for Christmas and the New Year. He is joined by Tad and Mr. Charbonneau. Mrs. Charbonneau passed away on October 20th after five years of suffering. May she rest in peace. Baby brother Arthur is ditching the family and traveling instead to Red Lodge, Montana, to meet his girlfriend's parents. Her name is Layla Dillon. "She's the one," he told Tino and me by phone when he called to decline our invitation.

He and Layla met at Brennan's in NOLA when she was on holiday just before Halloween. Arthur is a goner. Full of enthusiasm and absolutely ebullient on the phone. No sarcasm whatsoever. "A changed man," Daddy says. I'm eager to meet his lady. Layla trains horses, so I imagine she can handle "King Arthur" with aplomb. I certainly hope so.

Mercy, Phoenix, and Thérèse cancelled their flight just two days ago, as Mercy has been hospitalized for suicidal thoughts and clinical depression. I am bereft. She is in Bellevue Hospital's psychiatric ward in Manhattan at the urging of both her medical doctor and the psychiatrist he referred her to. The only person Mercy will speak with or see is Cathy Strilickis, the founder of the New Mothers' Club from St. Patrick's, who is also a physician. Thank goodness for Thérèse, who is caring for Phoenix full time. My father and I will go to them January 3rd while Tino tends to Isa and Lu. May God bless Thérèse and help our beautiful, maimed Mercy and her innocent baby girl.

Aurora and Dieter will renew their marriage vows (i.e., actually marry in the eyes of the Church) in the d'Annunzio Chapel on Christmas Eve. Tino and I will be their attendants. They join us regularly for Sunday lunch and attend all the children's school activities.

Tiziana Gargiulo has invited Tino, myself, and the children to Conca dei Marini for a week's stay next August. I wonder how Carmine Famiglietti feels about that! I hope Malo will be there still so the children can experience his gentle kindness.

Tino surprised me with a *piccolo casale*, a small farmhouse, in Assisi, after having sold the apartment in town where the Camorristi did its dirty work. The house has rooms enough for the six of us. God willing, we will spend Easter there, "down-size-ed from the villa," Tino says, "for the ease of our bodies and souls."

Tad and I have signed a contract with Feltrinelli. Our book about Italian nuns working against the Camorra's human trafficking enterprise is slated for release in March, 2004.

The Bacci-Castleberry Arts Center and Retreat will open March 8th, 2003. It offers individual guests and groups one- and two-week respites from daily life to revel in the arts. Art and music workshops will be offered by local artists and musicians. Aurora Bacci, Dieter Ahl, and myself will host guests at welcome and farewell dinners that include art exhibits and musical entertainment. Our first guests will be the sisters and clients from La Casa di Dignità of Caserta, who have already accepted our invitation.

Sister Aloise and I correspond monthly. She is my miracle, a lifeline to hope in this messy, broken, heart-wrenching world.

The End

Acknowledgements

With ongoing and sincere gratitude to Michael James, Lauren McElroy, Chris Wozney, Emily at Emily's World of Design, and Danielle Boschert. You work magic.

To Ben Catanzaro and Nancy Bradley for their technical and design expertise, patience, and friendship.

Grazie mille to Carol and David Ross of *Sophisticated Italy* for connecting the dots throughout The Boot. Your attention to detail, fleet of knowledgeable and personable drivers and guides, and most of all your friendship, have been nothing short of a boon. We look forward to our next visit with you. *A presto!*

To the Comune di Frigento, you have my heart.

Sindaco Carmine Ciullo

Guide and scholar Nicola Sasso

Luigi Collela, dear friend and mentor in Naples and Campania, sincere thanks. To many more excursions and dinners together. See you soon in the U. S.

Lydia Ganz of Largay Travel, thanks for ensuring we take flight.

Profound thanks to mentors Rachel Basch and Lou Bayard.

Fellow writers, thank you for the community we form: Chantel Acevedo, Christopher Castellani, James Benn, Sari Rosenblatt, Midori Snyder, Jeanne Archambault, Francine Knight, Nan Parson Rossiter, Marly Youmans, Steve Parlato,

Lisa Acerbo, Carol Snyder, Jackie Bickley Mayes, Susan Cossette, Lucia DeFillips Dressel, Sean Crose, Jocelyn Ulevicus, Lizzie Thorpe, Lou Aguilar, Helen Hollick, Cosimo Vannini, Jane G. Harlond, Joanna Clapps Herman, Raeleen Mautner, Joan Keyes Lownds, Kerry Sloan, Tracey O'Shaughnessy, Edith Reynolds, Tom Santopietro, Amity Gaige, Tim Watt, Tracie Mauriello, Terence Hawkins, Sandra Lambert, Umberto Mucci, Thomas McDade, Gabe Pietrorazio, Matt Lannon, Liora Wilkins, Kathleen Green, Christian Lewis, Ryan Aghamohammadi, Faith Christian-Ferri, KC Chiucarello.

To friends Antonella Rocchini, Giampaolo and Tiziana Girardi, Pierpaolo Pezzuti, Francesco Donnarumma, Andrea Famiglietti, Matt Santucci, Federico Manetti, Anita Graveson, Kyle, Pam, Maura, and Kaden Kahuda, Joe and Leslie Hadam, Lisa Carlson, Molly Emmer, Lindsay Slattum Johnson, Colleen Altenburger, Bob and Liz Cutrofello, Cole Cutrofello, Gus Haracopos, Nedra and Rich Gusenburg, Doreen Kiefer-Kopecky and Tomas Kopecky and family, Ann Gygax, Diana Smith, Martha Kellogg, Gerard and Mary Chiusano and family. Susan, Brendan, and Sue Hemingway, Yasemin Keles, Maria Pecoraro, Sara McConnell, Estibaliz Garris, Lisa Altarescu, Dan Greene, Jesse Lloyd, Andrea Cordovez, Nyasha Chiundiza, Steve Bergin, Bob Dorr, Joan Ruggiero, Barbara Ruggiero, David Whitehouse, Phil Benevento, Frank and Ruth Steponaitis, Elaine Muldowney and Robert Morgan, Linda Sloan, Rena Shove, John Shove, Peggy and Doug Columb, Maria and Don Michaud, Marion and Robert Bradley, Vic and Kathleen Lembo, Denise Ryan, the Vance, Alves, and Perrone families, the Bernetsky family, Ann and Don Lengyel, Sue and Bill Mis, Jan Schuck, Karen and Chip Longo, Wendy and Mark Hopkinson, Sandy and Rich Solomita, Joann Smith Overby, Cirie Smith Dorosh, Sally Smith, Nancy and John King, Amy Davis, Brian

Humpal, Jackson Davis, Sheryl and Tom Feducia, Gail and Bill Fredericks, Carmine and Paula Paolino, Becca Paolino and Chris Holshouser, Dante Paolino and Isabella Gonzalez. Janet Parlato and Rich Peronace, Rev. Martin Breski, OFM Conv., Rev. Ricky Manalo, CSP, Rev. Aloysius P. Kelley, SJ, Rev. Leonard Kvedas, Rev. Mathai Vellappallil, SDB, Rev. Joy Jacob, SDB, Rev. Ronald A. Ferraro, Sister Kathleen Dorney, CND, Janet Canepa, Carolyn Garibaldi, Colleen McGinn, Frank and Jennifer Ficko, Stephen Haessler, Theresa Fratamico, Pam Hull and Mark Eastridge, Patricia and John Philip, Suzanne Noel and Jim Wigren, Sharon and Dan Wilson, Daniel and Joyce D'Alessio, Rick and Joanne Waldron, Connie and Tony Bonacorsi, Ivy Bennett, Cathy Buxton Holmquist and Russell Holmquist, Lila Lee Coddington, Peggy Healey, Kathy LaPorta DiCocco, Marilyn LaPorta Baker, Greta Solomon, Sam and Linda Lazinger, Ken and Carla Burgess, Pam Burros, Dennis and Michelle Lapadula, Robin Masciewicz-Morehouse, Nina and Gorgen Gostas, Wim Caers and Charlotte Smekens, John Tkacik, Jim Dansereau, Jeanne Dansereau, Karl Mallick, Laura DeFrancesco, the Ritrivi family, the McCavitt family, Robyn Moran, Kelly and Sam Hahn, Susan LaJoie and family. Renee Donnarumma, Sun Mee Steiskel Ryan, Lisa and Joe South and family, Lyn and Ron Ryan and family, Susan Bogart, Michael O'Rourke, Tom and Bev Pratt, Linda and Mark Narowski and family, Tom and Tina Mulinski, Kathy and Tom Niezelski, Don and Alice Baldwin, Diane Betkoski, Barbara Betkoski, Jack Betkoski, Sue Cable, Alice Smith, John and Kate Smith, the Lombardo family, Michael Peloquin, Sam Bacco, Tom, Lori, and Olivia Alosco, Lenny, Kelly, and Samantha Crone, Steve, Karen, and Rosemary Minkler, the Harte, Butler, Johnson, Feldman, and Brayton Families. Taleesha Christian. Tim Grace, Larry Halloran, Kevin and Phyllis Braun. Phil Sherwood, John

Twomey, Karen and Clyde Armstrong, Jeff McHugh and Carly Matasavage, Andrew and Julia Svitlik, Stephen Sopko, Karen Sopko, Andrew Catropa, Christine and Gene Shugrue, Mary Anne Creto, Audrey Harrell, Jeffery Wacker and Julia Metcalf, Claudia Csuka, Mary Kress Lemley, Diane Warzoha, Mary D'Aquila, Kevin Marques and Jessica Bilyard, Catherine Ciullo.

To past and present colleagues for your collegiality, encouragement, support.

To my beloved students.

To the late Ruth Kipp, seventh-grade teacher, who suggested I use my own words to tell stories. To Daniel D'Alessio, eighth-grade teacher, who revealed the power and possibility of twenty-six letters and to this day encourages and inspires.

To Jeanne Basile and Dave Dostaler, David Dostaler and Giavanna Brunelle, Scott Basile, Kory Basile, Rosie Alexander, Gino Basile.

Reverend Raimondo Leone and Reverend Alessandro Brandi in Rome. We look forward to hosting you.

Lucia in Tolve, Italy. Thank you for confirming our paternal *nonna*'s birthplace and birthdate.

To the Pelosi, Ciampi, and D'Avino families of Frigento, Italy; the Gubitoso family, the Becce, Crupi, Pesino, Mitchell, Chiucarello, Ferraro, and Giordano families.

To the Fabry, Cohen, and Plasko families; the Horny, Petlock, Kane, Ohrin, Janoski, Swatkoski, and Hurn families, the Lychock, Johnson, and Sudy families, Martin Sarnik and the Sarnik family of Prague; family and friends from Plavec and Hromos, Slovakia.

Grin and Gron, Jenny and James in Belfast.

To Fran and Maureen Donnarumma, Ed and Teresa Wasil, Mike and Ellen Donnarumma; Alessandra Donnarumma and Chris Ryan; Egon Donnarumma and Sara Slayton O'Rourke; Matthew and Caroline South; Colin Donnarumma; Emily Wasil, Ethan Wasil, George Donnarumma, Erin Donnarumma.

To Cashen, Connor, Joseph, and Tanner South; Clara and Henry Donnarumma; Linnea, Huxton, and Otis Ryan.

To my late loving parents, Louise and Carmen Donnarumma, and the inspiring aunts and uncles and godparents and cousins who enjoy eternal life with them. I miss you more and more. To my loving mother-in-law, Veronica Sharnick, and my late father-in-law, Robert Sharnick, who never missed a book talk. Intrepid and generous supporters all.

With unending thanks, palpable joy, and deepest love to my husband, Wayne Sharnick.

"You have not chosen one another, but I have chosen you for one another."
—C. S. Lewis

Mary Sharnick

Mary Donnarumma Sharnick is the author of six novels, the first of which, **Thirst**, is being adapted for the operatic stage by composer Gerard Chiusano and librettists Robert Cutrofello and Mary Noonan-Chiusano.

Mary was a recipient of a Wesleyan Writers' Conference Fellowship in 2008, as well as a fellowship from the Hartford Council for the Arts Beatrice Fox Auerbach Foundation in 2010.

Orla's Canvas and **Painting Mercy**, the first two novels in **The Orla Paints Quartet**, were awarded prizes from the Connecticut Press Club and the National Federation of Press Women in 2016 and 2018. **The Contessa's Easel**, the third novel in the quartet, garnered a Connecticut Press Club Honorable Mention in 2021, as well. **Orla's Canvas** was also a finalist for a Kindle Award in 2017, and is now available in audio format at Audible.com. It was the September 2023 book club selection at the Newport Art Museum, Newport, Rhode Island.

Mary teaches writing at Post University, Waterbury, Connecticut, and mentors aspiring writers. She writes from her home in Beacon Falls, Connecticut. Research for her books takes her to New Orleans and to Italy, the country she considers her second home.

Orla's Canvas

By

Mary Sharnick

Narrated by eleven-year-old Orla Gwen Gleason, Orla's Canvas opens on Easter Sunday, in St. Suplice, Louisiana, a "misspelled town" north of New Orleans, and traces Orla's dawning realization that all is not as it seems in her personal life or in the life of her community. The death of St. Suplice's doyenne, Mrs. Bellefleur Dubois Castleberry, for whom Orla's mother keeps house, reveals Orla's true paternity, shatters her trust in her beloved mother, and exposes her to the harsh realities of class and race in the Civil Rights-era South. When the Klan learns of Mrs. Castleberry's collaboration with the local Negro minister and Archbishop Rummel to integrate the parochial school, violence fractures St. Suplice's vulnerable stability. The brutality Orla witnesses at summer's end awakens her to life's tenuous fragility. Like the South in which she lives, she suffers the turbulence of changing times. Smart, resilient, and fiercely determined to make sense of her pain, Orla paints chaos into beauty, documenting both horror and grace, discovering herself at last through her art.

PENMORE PRESS
www.penmorepress.com

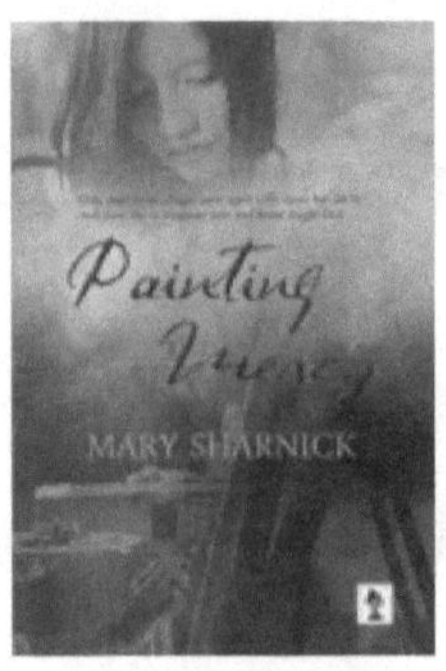

Painting Mercy

By

Mary Sharnick

In Painting Mercy, the sequel to prize-winning Orla's Canvas, Orla, now twenty-four, has been studying and painting in New York City. It is 1975. Saigon has fallen to the Communists, and Vietnamese refugees have been invited to settle in New Orleans by Archbishop Hannan, a former paratrooper and military chaplain in WW II.   Orla's childhood friend and forever confidant, Tad Charbonneau, is practicing immigration law in New Orleans, where he mitigates challenging adoption cases involving children, many of them bi-racial, recently airlifted from Saigon and in need of new families. On her way back home for Katie Cowles' wedding and a summer painting in misspelled St. Suplice, Orla reconnects with Tad and contemplates her future. While she anticipates marriage and family with her undisputed soul mate, she discovers upsetting news about Tad's sexuality and learns that her forty-three-year-old mother is pregnant. Adding to her troubling personal revelations, Orla becomes involved in the devastating costs of war for former GI and Katie's brother Denny Cowles and Mercy Cleveland, a Vietnamese orphan who eventually becomes as essential to Orla as her art. Orla once again calls upon her art to make sense of loss and gain. Through her craft she reimagines how Love and Home might look, finally charting a future for herself she had not previously considered possible.

PENMORE PRESS
www.penmorepress.com

The Contessa's Easel

By

Mary Sharnick

"I know you never knew your grandfather, but now you can touch what his hands touched and create beauty.... Be like him, dearest Orla; recognize, make, and be beauty in an often ugly world." These words were to have a profound effect upon Orla. The acclaimed Orla Paints Quartet continues! Orla Castleberry returns to her New Orleans home after a year as artist-in-residence at Manhattan's New York University. Her topical exhibit "Portraits of AIDS" has earned world-wide praise and notoriety for its realistic representations. Orla prepares for her next exhibit, to be held in Fiesole, Italy, in celebration of the forty-fifth anniversary of the town's liberation from Nazi occupiers. The portraits she paints will also be featured at a premier book launch for The Orphans of Fiesole, written by her friend, immigration attorney and historian Tad Charbonneau. The book is based on letters and photographs composed by Orla's own grandfather, so the project becomes intensely personal. Orla takes to heart the words of William Faulker: "The past is never dead. It's not even past," as tragedy, loss, and surprises transform the lives of her friends and family, even before she boards the plane for Italy. It isn't only Orla's understanding of the past that changes, however. Her future, too, will change remarkably. For years, Orla has sidelined her longings in order to be and do what others needed from her. Now, her love for the truth of art is leading her to discoveries of love.

PENMORE PRESS
www.penmorepress.com

The Measure of Ella
by
Toni Bird Jones

The islands frightened her with their uncivilized rawness. They looked like a place where anything could happen, a godforsaken outcrop at the end of the world.

Sea-faring chef Ella Morgan is an honest woman — until her life falls apart. When her dream of owning a restaurant is shattered by the death of her father and loss of her inheritance, she is suddenly alone in the world. Desperate for money, she signs on as crew for a Caribbean drug run, only to find herself fighting for her life in an underworld ruled by violent men.

Set in the Caribbean, The Measure of Ella is a dramatic story of love, murder, high-seas action, and the consequences of pursuing a dream at all costs. Like Patrick O'Brien's novels, including Master and Commander, The Measure of Ella captures the breathtaking and perilous world of blue-water sailing. Like Girl on the Train, it unwinds with gripping suspense from a woman's point of view. With its brave, strong, complex female protagonist at the helm of a high seas adventure, the novel is entirely unique.

PENMORE PRESS
www.penmorepress.com

Rembrandt's
Angel
by
Steven Moore

A Neo-Nazi conspiracy threatens Europe . . .

Esther Brookstone's life is at a crossroads. A Scotland Yard inspector who specializes in stolen art, she's reluctantly considering retirement. A three-time widow, she can't quite decide whether paramour and colleague Interpol Agent Bastiann van Coevorden should be husband number four. Decisions are put on hold while she and Bastiann set out to thwart a neo-Nazi conspiracy financed in part by artworks stolen during World War II. Among the stolen art is the masterpiece "An Angel with Titus' Features," a work Esther obsesses about recovering.

The case sends the intrepid pair on an international hunt spanning several European countries and the Amazon jungle. Evading capture and thwarting death, Esther and Bastiann prove time and again that adrenaline-spiked adventures aren't just for the young.

PENMORE PRESS
www.penmorepress.com

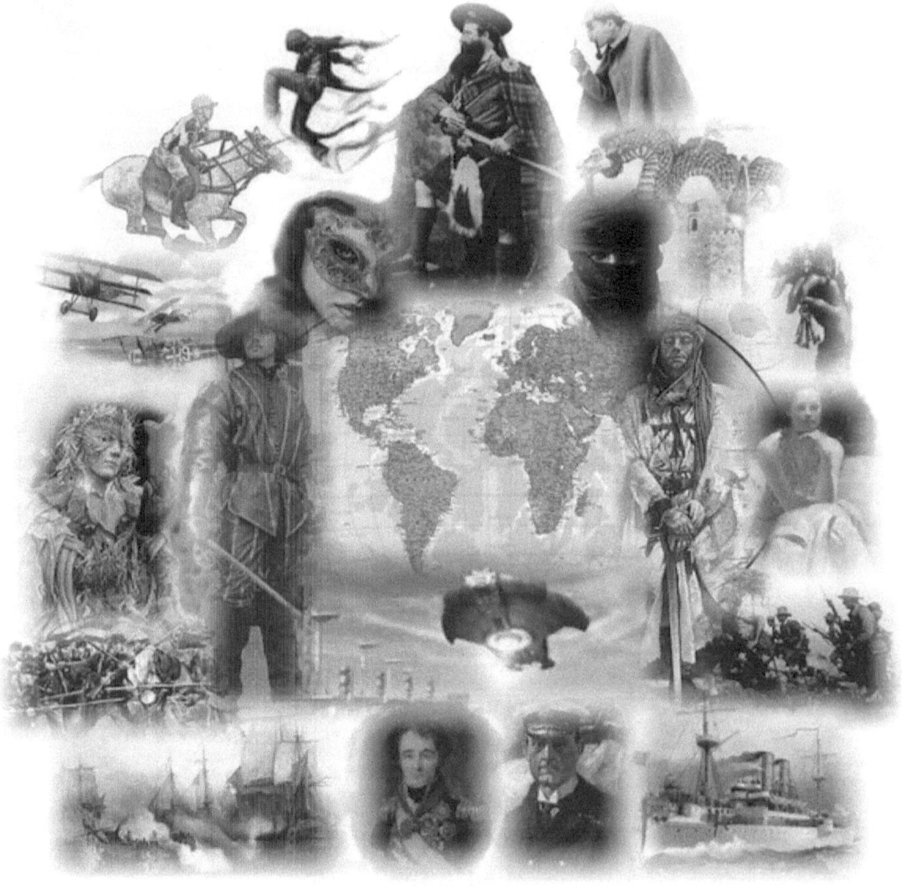

Penmore Press

Challenging, Intriguing, Adventurous, Historical and Imaginative

www.penmorepress.com